Saturn's Favorite Music

Laura Lee

*"Can you hear me?" -- First successful radio
transmission, Guglielmo Marconi, 1897*

Saturn's Favorite Music

Elsewhere Press
Rochester Hills, MI

ISBN 10: 0-9657345-5-2
ISBN 13: 978-0-9657345-5-4 (paperback)

ISBN 10: 0-9657345-8-7
ISBN 13: 978-0-9657345-8-5 (ebook)

Acknowledgments

Kimery Campbell, Jennifer Hunter, Mary Lanphier and Carol Lee, your assistance and feedback helped make this book what it is.

Thank you to supporters Joanne Copeland, Kristin Hertz, Maryl Huntington, Victoria Kesler, Naomi Rogers, Roger and Melinda Shaner and Tracy Utech.

2012

As Is

Listing

Saturn Real Estate

100 Radio Drive
Saturn, MI

Building in need of work, asking price does not include
any value for the structure. Former WRTV
Radio Station, sold "AS IS."

1992
Saturn's Favorite Music

As she passed an old gas station, with two rusty pumps and propane tanks for rent, Clara popped the cassette out of the dashboard of her Chevy Chevette, cutting off Pearl Jam's Eddie Vedder mid-moan. She had left the interstate behind some time ago, and was now heading north on a pine tree-lined two-lane highway, marked occasionally with the bloodstains left by unfortunate deer. Ed Gildenstern, the manager of WRTV had told Clara that she should be able to pick up the frequency of the 100,000-watt FM station at this point in her journey. Its transmitter was located on one of the highest points in northern Lower Michigan, just outside the small town of Saturn. She turned the radio dial, rolling it back and forth until it landed on 92.9. Even though she was still almost two hours out from her destination, she could hear the last strains of "Peg" by Steely Dan emerge from light static. As it faded, she heard a stinger and a deep voice, "Your light rock, more music station, Saturn's favorite music RTV." The outro of the liner faded into a track by Michael Bolton. "Your light rock, more music station," Clara repeated. "Your light rock..." What was it? "Saturn's favorite music."

Michael Bolton was far from Clara's "favorite music," but that hardly mattered. "I'm Clara Jane on your light music... Shit. Good morning,

I'm Clara Jean on Saturn's favorite... bringing you Saturn's favorite music."

She reached up with her right hand and checked that her black hair was still in a tight bun. It had seemed like a professional look when she pinned it up in the morning, but now she was wondering if it read more "grandma." She glanced over at the open map on the passenger seat. Saturn was barely a dot. When Clara had called to get directions and asked how she'd find the station when she got into town, the woman on the phone laughed. "When you come down the hill to the stoplight, it's on your right. Look for the Incredible Broadcast Machine."

Michael Bolton faded into Kenny G and then an announcer's voice, "Good morning, 10:37 on RTV, your light rock, more music station."

"Light rock, more music," Clara repeated.

"I'm Rad Farr, it's a sunny 72 degrees. Beautiful day. I've got another Superstar Seven in a Row coming up with music from Joshua Kadison, Mariah Carey, and Barry Manilow, plus a song written by Lennon and McCartney, but not performed by the Beatles. It is all coming up in the next hour. Stay tuned."

"Barry Manilow," Clara thought. "Sheesh."

When she had enrolled in the Harrison School of Broadcasting, Clara had not imagined that she would be desperate for a job playing "some of the lighter hits by Phil Collins and Whitney Houston." The road to radio fame begins in the small market. It's called "paying your dues." They call it that, Clara mused, because if they called it "having the worst job on earth in some godforsaken place for barely enough to make rent just so that one day you might be able to show up the kids who teased you in high school" no one would put up with it- probably.

Clara was imagining herself back in the studio of the trendy modern rock station where she had completed her internship. As one song faded into another on the car radio, she mentally pushed up the sliders on one channel and lowered them on the next, watching the meters to be sure the new track was at the right audio level. Clara was not sure if she should emphasize being a Harrison grad. Many famous broadcasters had gotten their start at the school, but the professional DJs she met in Detroit sometimes made fun of Harrison's enthusiastic "lowly interns."

If she played her cards right, after a year or so of dues-paying in the middle of nowhere, she'd have a good enough tape to get a gig on a station where she'd have a big audience of regular listeners and would rub elbows with rock stars. (The DJ she interned with was fond of telling the story of the time Bono from U2 got him high. "That was before he was God.") But first she had to get the job.

Clara was interrupted in her musings when she passed Gill's Guns and Ammo. Under the image of two rifles, it had a sign reading "Jesus Saves." A few miles later she passed billboards advertising cabin rentals and Vacation Bible School. Finally, Clara came down the hill to Saturn's single stop light. Saturn was one long road of two-story brick facades. There was a drug store, a sporting goods store, a town museum, a post office and the aforementioned stoplight, which is where the more modern structures, probably built in the late 1960s, stood. To the left was a police station, and next to it a gas station with modern pumps and a run-down convenience shop. Across the street was a bank with a sign that flashed the time and temperature, and on the right was a small, brown, single-story building, unremarkable except for a large antenna in the back and a painted Winnebago in the parking lot emblazoned with the words "Incredible Broadcast Machine." To Clara, the bus was decidedly credible. Comical was, in fact, a better description.

Clara parked next to the Broadcast Machine, took a deep breath and checked her appearance in the side view mirror. She decided her eyeliner was little too thick, and she tried to tone it down with her forefinger, which made it smudge and made her look even more like an alternative rocker playing dress up, or perhaps a crying raccoon. She just had to hope that the grey power suit would counteract the effect. She rummaged under the map to find the folder with her resume and the cassette with her Harrison School-approved demo.

Getting the tape approved had been a frustrating process, recording and re-recording, editing and re-editing. Harrison's airchecks were initially recorded on reel-to-reel tapes. By advancing and rewinding the tape over the machine's playback head, Clara could find a flubbed word, mark the beginning of the sound with yellow grease pencil, then advance, and mark the end the same way. Next, she would lay the magnetic tape flat on a metal surface, and slice it at each of the marks with a razor blade. She always found it gratifying to transform a mistake into a physical form that she could literally throw in the trash. That done, the two splices were taped together, and it played as if nothing had ever been there. After several days in an editing suite, she had taken out every awkward pause, "um" or stutter. If only you could edit the rest of life like that.

What if someone in the interview process actually put her in a studio and asked her to be the announcer that she was on her doctored tape?

Clara felt a sudden urge to run away. Deep breath. "Fake it till you make it." She straightened her jacket and walked inside.

Sitting at a desk behind a grey Formica counter was a woman with short hair, the color of nutmeg, styled in a feathered shag that reminded Clara of Princess Diana. She looked like she was about 35. Her compact, pleasant face was complemented by light, natural makeup. She was wearing a green short-sleeved blouse with bedazzling around the collar.

"Hi," Clara said. "I'm here to see Ed Gildenstern."

"You must be Clara," the woman said standing and reaching out her hand. "I'm Leslie. Have a seat. Ed will be out in a few minutes." She gestured towards what appeared to be an abandoned orange and yellow love seat. In some other context, the furnishings might have been hip and retro. Here they were just outdated. The love seat backed up against the most distinctive feature of the small waiting area, a large window where you could see into the broadcast booth, like watching fish in an aquarium. A large speaker mounted above the window played the broadcast signal. A young, slightly heavyset man with spiky blond hair was standing behind the microphone. He was looking down, and appeared to be making notes of some kind. Clara took a seat and glanced at the outdated magazines on a scratched coffee table. The worn *Sports Illustrated* and *Newsweek* had address labels with Ed Gildenstern's home address blacked out. The setting reminded her more of waiting for an oil change than a business meeting. Clara's leg bounced as she glanced at a stack of fliers showing a map with a series of circles representing the WRTV signal's impressive reach and prices to run ads in various dayparts. Between the AM and FM signals, if Clara got the job, her voice would be broadcast over most of lower Michigan, almost everywhere except Ann Arbor and Detroit.

"Don't worry." Leslie looked to the left and the right, and then in a stage whisper said, "You're the lead candidate." She put a finger over her lips in a "Shhh" motion and then turned away, rolled some sort of form into an IBM Selectric typewriter, and started typing. Her move to the typewriter revealed a line of framed family photos on the filing cabinet behind her, Leslie, a man, presumably her husband, and a chubby little boy. The sign on Leslie's desk said "Leslie Ash, Office Manager, Traffic Director." A traffic director does not go into the street and wave at cars. In radio parlance, it is the person who schedules the commercial slots on the programming grid and then makes sure that they run correctly.

The song faded out and the announcer began to speak. "That was Vanessa Williams with 'Save the Best for Last.' Rad Farr on your light rock, more music station. It's 12:48 and time for the obituaries brought to you by the Alexander Funeral Home, honoring your loved ones with compassion and dignity. Mrs. Edith J. Morris of Maple Hill passed away Friday at the age of 88. She is survived by her son Martin Morris of Maple Hill, daughter Dorrie Fitzpatrick of Flint, three grandchildren and one great-grand daughter. Services will be held at noon on Sunday at the Anderson Memorial Chapel. Edith J. Morris of Maple Hill..."

This is when a short man with curly light brown hair, dressed in khakis and a faded RTV t-shirt came around the corner. "Clara? Hi, I'm Ed." Clara was overdressed. Ed led Clara past Leslie's desk to a large open room behind the audio booth. This is when Clara discovered that the waiting room love seat was part of a matched set. The worn, orange couch was against the back wall of the audio booth. Next to it was a sturdy dot matrix printer humming as it printed out news copy. There were metal desks around the back wall, and across the room, an open door revealed a small editing studio and beyond it another door. Through the darkness Clara could just make out racks of LPs. Ed directed her to an office on the right.

"Did you have a hard time finding us?" Ed asked as he opened the door.

"No, it was just like Leslie described it," Clara said. Ed took his seat behind a large wooden desk and gestured for Clara to sit down. She tried to sit in a way that projected confidence and professionalism, which instead made her self-conscious and awkward. She crossed her legs, then uncrossed them and battled with herself over whether to use the armrest.

The wall behind Ed was decorated with radio memorabilia. Along the various radio event posters, there was a photograph of Ed shaking hands with Sonny Bono and beside it a photo of Ed on stage with someone who appeared to be a member of a '70s band. She also noticed that Ed displayed his framed Harrison School diploma. The resume and demo tape Clara had previously mailed in were already on the desk, so she kept the copies she'd brought on her lap.

"Clara Jane..." He paused before pronouncing the last name Andrzejewski. "Is it An-dre-jew-ski?"

"That's good," she said. "Yeah, but I just go by Clara Jane on the air. Too many..."

"Syllables?"

"Right."

"A fellow Harrison grad," Ed said, gesturing towards his diploma. "Did you like working with Josh Osmond?"

"Get on the clue bus," Clara said. She had started speaking alone, but Ed joined her and they finished in unison.

"What a great mentor," Ed said.

The familiarity put Clara at ease. "Is that the clue bus outside?"

"What?"

"The clue bus. In the parking lot."

"In the parking lot?"

"The Incredible Broadcast Machine."

The smile fell from Ed's face. "We use it for remote broadcasts," he said. Ed clearly did not find the name of the bus humorous, in fact, Clara now realized, he had probably named it himself. She flashed back to the interview training at the Harrison School. "Don't make jokes." Where did she think she was? The Comedy Castle? She shuffled in her seat.

Ed picked up Clara's resume and squinted at it. "So, Clara Jane, what are your career goals?"

Clara decided against telling Ed about her fantasies of radio fame, free concert tickets and parties with rock stars. "I've always wanted to be a radio announcer," she said, "My goal is to eventually work my way up to a major market station. I'd like to do a morning show maybe. One day, I might like to be the program director of a station, but I will always want to be on the air."

Ed cleared his throat and sat back in his chair and began what seemed to be a practiced speech. "RTV is a unique station," he said. "You've seen the reach of our signal. There aren't a lot of stations in the country that have that kind of reach. So we want to create a station that's worthy of that. A lot of our area is rural and we are the voice that connects people. We want to have people's trust and be part of the community, and to feel like they know the people on air."

"Of course," Clara nodded.

"Everyone wants to be a radio star," Ed continued. "This isn't the place to do that. It's a conservative station for a conservative town. Saturn only has a weekly paper. So if you want a daily update of what is happening in the community, this is where you turn. We do lost pet reports. We do obituaries. We cover county commission meetings and high school sports. We play songs for listeners' birthdays and anniversaries. We play a lot of 70s and 80s, some oldies and a current mix of light AC." AC was the abbreviation for Adult Contemporary, a radio format that was designed to be poppy, but inoffensive enough to be played as background music at offices. "I'm looking for someone who can be the voice of this community. I need someone to BE Saturn. Do you think you can do that?"

To Clara it sounded dreadful. "Absolutely," she said. "Obviously, I don't have a lot of experience, but I have a lot of enthusiasm and I am willing to learn."

Ed nodded. After a few more basic interview questions, he asked, "Would you describe yourself as someone who has a problem with authority?"

Clara was sure there had to be a story behind that question, but she didn't ask. Instead she tried to quickly triangulate what type of person Ed hoped she would be.

"I would say," she answered slowly, "that I have a healthy relationship with authority."

"Okay. Well, it's a salaried position, $10,000 a year."

Clara nodded. It was just a bit above minimum wage, enough to starve on, but that was to be expected when "paying your dues."

"You'll be doing middays," Ed continued, "10-2 just after the morning team. It's our third most popular daypart after mornings and afternoon drive. There isn't a lot of special programming then."

"I'll be doing middays? Are you saying I've got the job?"

"Oh yeah. Can you start Monday?"

It was Wednesday.

Go!

Clara was the first among the friends in her class to land a real radio job. It seemed to confirm everything they dreamed. It would not be long before they would all be all over the airwaves. In three to five years, they would be TV and radio stars. To celebrate the beginning of this adventure, Clara invited the group to a place she was going to miss, City Club.

If you were into alternative music in Detroit, there were only a few places to go. Her old radio station hosted a weekly "Club X" at the State Theater, and there were a couple of suburban spots, Jagger's on a Tuesday night, and an odd night or two at 3Ds in Royal Oak. Downtown there was St. Andrews and then there was City Club. It was the real deal. Hidden in an old hotel, it did not advertise and had no sign. You just had to know it was there. You entered through the lobby of a building that must have been grand when it was built in the 1920s for a different Detroit. The hotel still operated, and yet seemed abandoned. The club occupied what had once been a grand ballroom.

Up a dark staircase through black concrete, the students were transported to a different world. They were greeted by a woman in a black corset, her head shaved except for a thick, asymmetric blond fringe. She checked IDs and collected the cover charge. From inside "Everyday is Halloween" by Ministry was blending into the industrial aggression of Nine Inch Nails. Once their eyes adjusted to the darkness, the dream-like paintings on the walls started to emerge, illuminated by green lights. The bulbs and the colors flashing from the dance floor did little to counteract the overall black impression: black brick, black furnishings, black clothing, much of it purchased at Noir Leather, famous for its fetish fashion shows.

Dressed in a Siouxie and the Banshees t-shirt under a flannel shirt, paired with a short black skirt, black tights and Doc Martens, Clara was in her element, but not out of step with the rest of her classmates who had mostly dressed as they did in class, in casual shirts and jeans. Her face lit up as Ministry's "N.W.O." started to play. Julie, who hoped she'd soon be reading news at a TV station, was wearing wide-legged white slacks with a pastel satin blouse. Her permed hair was held back with a white scrunchie. She looked around with wide eyes.

"Are you sure it's safe here?" she shouted into Clara's ear.

"Oh yeah," Clara shouted back. "Everyone's cool. It's a friendly place." A suggestion of danger always animated the spaces occupied by the cultural underground, but Clara found it welcoming. It was a place for people who felt out of sync with the polished world outside. It seemed to beckon, "Not everyone gets it, but if you do, come in, you're one of us."

Julie did not look convinced, and she stayed nervously by Clara's elbow as though she was seeking her protection. Until she had discovered alternative music in high school, Clara had always felt like an outsider and a loser in the endless competition to be the most pretty and popular. Julie seemed to Clara to be the type who would have been popular in school. Clara enjoyed having the tables turned.

13

There was nothing unique, of course, in being teased and bullied in school. It was an unpleasant rite of passage, but the barbs that Clara's tormentors had thrown had burrowed deeper into Clara's psyche than she cared to admit. Somewhere in her secret heart, there was a part of her that believed a radio career would be her revenge. She liked to imagine those grown-up bullies listening to her on the radio and boasting that they knew her back when. Who's popular now?

Clara raised a hand over her head and pointed to the bar. "I've got this," called Joe. Joe's Def Leppard shirt didn't identify him as a City Club regular, but if he was uncomfortable it didn't show. He started handing back pint glasses until everyone had one. The Harrison School group crowded onto a sofa near the door, sitting on the arms as well as the seats. Joe lifted his glass. The first time his fellow students had heard him speak there was an audible gasp. He had *that* voice, the voice that sells Ford Trucks or intones "In a world" in the movie trailers. They all assumed that he would be hired before the class had finished its first lesson. Now his deep baritone was toasting Clara's new life. "To Clara, the voice of Saturn, Michigan." "To Saturn," Julie said.

Clara took a sip of her drink and then gestured towards the dance floor. As she swayed to Tones on Tail doing the "Ya yas" in "Go!" she let her fears fall away. She forgot all about her packing, the lease on her new apartment, and how much her life was about to change.

On Air

Clara found an apartment on the opposite edge of town from the radio station. The porch had a bench with a view of the highway and the parking lot of the grocery store across the street. Even so, there was vacation cabin vibe to the place. Maybe it was the pine-scented air that created the impression. Funny, Clara thought, she never noticed that the air she breathed in Detroit was dirty. Saturn had vacation air. The sounds were different as well, especially on the side of the apartment facing away from the highway. There was a small orchestra of nature, insects that sounded like castanets and police whistles, birds or frogs (she wasn't sure which) that sounded like kazoos and the jingle of car keys. In the distance, she could hear a rooster announcing the crack of 3 PM. The property was a mid-century ranch house that had been divided into two apartments. Next to her door was a big letter "S" for South. The other half of the house was labeled with an "N." Her apartment consisted of one long room with a small kitchenette in the back corner and a bedroom and attached bath through a door at the end.

Clara had been nervous signing the one-year lease. She had a strange relationship with her own talent. On the one hand, she believed that she was destined to be one of the lucky ones who would make it to a major market and a life of radio stardom. On the other hand, she was afraid that she wasn't good enough and that she would be fired before her lease ran out. Somehow, she was always able to hold those contradictory beliefs. She was an embarrassing failure and an unappreciated star. "Did other people feel like that?" she wondered.

In any case, she was excited to have her own place for the first time. With no roommates, she could make this space a pure expression of herself, to the extent that she could afford to. Clara had grown up Grosse Pointe Park, one of the more affordable of the Grosse Pointe suburbs. Grosse Pointe had a connotation of luxury and old money. But the Andrezejewskis were far from the auto barons whose mansions lined Lake Shore Drive. The family had bought a small, red-brick bungalow not far from Alter Drive, the dividing line between Grosse Pointe and Detroit. Living there had always been a stretch to the budget, but Clara's parents wanted Clara and her older sister to be able to list a Grosse Pointe school on their college applications.

Clara grew up with a sense that the other side of Alter was a dangerous and forbidden place. When she was in high school in the 1980s, Grosse Pointe made a series of moves to firm up the border, creating one-way streets and blocking off roads. This only made the city seem more exciting to Clara. In the suburbs, life's highest virtue seemed to be security. It was different in Detroit. The city was Motown. The city was Greektown. The city was live music and festivals. The city was for people who wanted to be near the action. It was life.

Clara's parents were never entirely comfortable with her punk fashions or her desire to attend late night alternative music concerts downtown. They tolerated it, but expected her to grow out of it. Clara hoped her deep attraction to music, counterculture and night life was something she would never outgrow.

Clara's parents had paid her sister's college tuition and were now supporting her as she earned her master's. But when Clara announced she wanted to go to the Harrison School instead of college they balked. They held a "family meeting" and explained that radio was a fine hobby, but not a stable career choice. If she wanted to study broadcasting, they would support her, but only if she did it at a four year college. She needed a degree to "fall back on."

Clara did not want to wait four years for her life to start. She certainly did not plan to "fall back" to a safe and boring job. A couple of weeks after the meeting, Clara packed her things, took the money from her savings account, and moved into a shared apartment in the city. She was determined not to ask her family for anything until she could come back as a radio star and prove that she knew what was right for her own life. She paid her way through the Harrison School by waiting tables. She was proud that she had done it on her own, but she also had the debt to prove it.

At the moment, her interior décor did not stretch to furniture. Everything that Clara owned fit in the back of her Chevy Chevette. She'd managed to acquire a used air mattress, a folding table with a green vinyl top and two metal folding chairs, a mushy bean bag chair which she plopped in front of the 15" color TV and VCR, balanced on a plastic stand. The only items of any value that she owned were her stereo with a record player, cassette and CD decks, and her large, and very heavy, collection of records. She could do without furniture as long as she had her alternate pressings, white labels and imports with gatefold sleeves.

When she had unloaded all of her boxes and bags from the car, hooked up the VCR to the TV and plugged in the stereo, she unpacked her posters from their cardboard tube and positioned them around the walls: Kraftwerk, Primal Scream, Sugarcubes, Bauhaus, Nirvana, The Cure. With that, it felt like her place.

She started to think about dinner. The refrigerator and cupboards were bare, which was fine, really, as she had no plates or cutlery anyway. She thought about ordering a pizza and flipped through the thin phone book that the landlady had left on the counter. It looked like there were only two pizza places in town. Then she remembered that the phone was not hooked up yet. The only way to get a meal was to get into her car and go to a drive-through. On the way back, she stopped at the grocery store and picked up a six-pack of beer. In order to create some ambiance, Clara lit an incense cone.

Normally, Clara liked to watch TV while she ate. She turned on the television, waited a moment for it to warm up, and then started turning the dial for the stations. With no cable, she only managed to find one station. She played with the antenna, moving it to the left and to the right. By standing and extending her arm she could make the channel come in clearly, but it was not a comfortable position, and hardly worth it just to see a talk show about parents who don't like how their teenagers dressed.

Clara turned off the TV, put Stone Roses on the stereo, and then gave a solitary toast to her new adventure. When she was halfway through her burger she noticed a strange smell. Somehow she had forgotten that the incense cone would burn all the way to the bottom, and she had not put anything between it and the table. It had burned a circular hole in the vinyl tabletop, leaving the apartment smelling like a record album that had been left out in the sun. At least she had managed to avoid burning the place down on her first night in town.

Clara finished her dinner. She got up and turned the record over. With no more unpacking to do for the moment, she was left alone with her thoughts. At the Harrison School, one of her instructors had started class by asking, "Does anyone here have an inferiority complex?" No one raised a hand. Clara had been struck with the strong urge to raise hers and say, "Well, I sort of have one, but it's not very good." But because there was a lot of truth to this, she said nothing.

Clara was attracted to alternative music and culture because the artists seemed like they were not afraid of the dark. Clara felt like she was afraid of everything. She had no idea what her debut at WRTV would bring. Would she know what to do? Would she humiliate herself on the air? If she was fired from a job in little Saturn, would that be the end? What would she do with the rest of her life? Then she would imagine her nightmare scenario, a desk job in a soulless office, responsible for maintaining the bureaucracy of a company that does something no one cares about anyway. "Fake it 'til you make it," she repeated to herself. She went to her suitcase and pulled out a dog-eared copy of *Feel the Fear and Do It Anyway*, and read some of her favorite passages until she thought she had settled her nerves enough to sleep.

Clara went into the bedroom, put on her pajamas and inflated the air mattress. She was not used to having a house to herself. With the lack of furniture and amenities, it felt as though she was spending the night alone in a campground. That is to say, it was how she imagined camping might be if she had ever done it. People from small towns liked to talk about the dangers of the city, but Clara was more afraid of finding herself alone in the middle of nowhere. The quiet of her apartment reminded her of a scene in a thriller just before the killer materializes in the middle of the room. When the freezer started to hum, Clara sat up with a start.

She lay staring at the ceiling, taking deep breaths. She finally got close to sleep, but then her mind drifted to the clock radio that was set to wake her in the morning. What if it didn't go off and she showed up late for her first day? As she imagined arriving at work, she remembered the sales brochures in the lobby with the diagram of the station's signal. If she was a terrible DJ, almost the entire state was about to find out. "I am prepared," she told herself. "Harrison signed off on my tape. They said I was ready." Idiots.

She turned to the left and to the right, and the air mattress seemed to be getting thinner and closer to the ground with each turn. At around 2 AM she was lying on a plastic sheet on the hard floor. Clara took her pillow and blanket, and the clock radio into the front room. She plugged the radio in near the beanbag chair. She reset the clock to one minute after the time it had been on when she unplugged it. Then she tried to find a comfortable position to sleep on a beanbag chair. She was not successful. Clara did not think she had slept at all, but she must have, because the sound of The Beatles on the clock radio woke her up.

"Yes, it's the nearly infinite 'Hey Jude' on your light rock, more music station," said a male voice over the fade out. "Good morning. It's 7:31. I hope you were singing along to that one."

"How can you help it?" asked another male voice.

"I was just looking through the calendar of events to see if there was anything interesting for today."

"Is there?"

"Well, it's Fungal Infection Awareness Week."

"I see. Are you aware?"

"I am now."

"So how do you observe Fungal Infection Awareness Week, Seth?"

"I thought I might throw a Fungal Infection Awareness Week party. Maybe have a barbecue."

"Nice."

"If you're having your own Fungal Infection Awareness shindig, you'll have good weather for it. You can expect another beautiful, sunny day here in Saturn, isn't that right, Bill?"

"Indeed, it is."

"But that is just the local weather. What if you're on your way to somewhere exotic like Paris or Honolulu or Cedar Rapids, Iowa? You're in luck; the travel weather forecast is coming up along with the local weather and traffic. We have to pay some bills and then we'll be back with that and music from Mariah Carey, Rod Stewart and Christopher Cross. Eye opener trivia is coming up in the next hour. Lots of reasons to stick around."

A commercial started to play. "Are you paying too much for long distance calls?"

Clara sat up and swiveled her stiff neck. Then she got up, and turned the radio off. There was nothing in the kitchen for breakfast, but she didn't mind because her stomach was in knots anyway. Ed Gildenstern had told Clara that she didn't need to dress in a suit; she could just wear her everyday clothes. "No one sees you, but us."

Clara put on a Nine Inch Nails t-shirt with a red plaid skirt that hit just below the knee and just above her Doc Martens boots. She made up her face with a pale foundation and thick black eyeliner. She let her long black hair hang freely.

When she arrived at the station, Leslie looked up and said, "May I help you?"

"It's me, Clara Andrzejewski. I'm here to train for the midday shift."

"Oh, Clara," Leslie said, blushing a little. "I'm sorry, I didn't recognize you without the suit. You look... younger."

"Thank you?"

"Oh, yeah, it's good. Young is good."

"Mr. Gildenstern said that I should just wear my normal clothes. I hope this is OK."

"You don't need to call him Mr. Gildenstern," Leslie said. "Everyone calls him Ed. I don't think it matters what the jocks wear in the studio. No one sees you."

Leslie led Clara to the back room. As they approached the studio the "On Air" light started glowing, so they stood outside the door.

"The morning show is a little different than what you'll be doing," Leslie said. "It's the only time you have more than one announcer working in the studio. They've already been running around for hours by the time I come in."

A speaker in the back room let them monitor what was going out over the air. "8:19 on your light rock, more music station, Saturn's favorite music, RTV. It's 67 degrees. The RTV traffic report is coming up, but first it's the RTV news with Al Lear."

Through a window Clara could see into the room marked "Studio B" which appeared to be a glorified closet. A man with thinning white hair and a pair of large, out-of-date glasses was reading the local news report from a sheet of paper on a stand in front of him.

"We call him Al "Overworked" Lear, Leslie said. "You'll see why. He's been here longer than anyone. I used to listen to Al when I was growing up."

When the news report wrapped up, the "On Air" light over the door of Studio B went off. Clara could see Al take off his headphones and rustle through some papers as Seth Jones' voice played over the speakers. As this was happening, Al came out of studio B. "Al," Leslie said, "this is Clara Jane; she's going to be doing middays."

"Nice to meet you," Al said, reaching out for a firm handshake. "Looking forward to working with you. I have to go record a feed." He disappeared into a door marked Studio C.

"So Bill," Seth's voice said, "What does the weather have in store for us today?"

"Glad you asked, Seth."

Then there was the sound of women's voices singing in close harmony, "RTV Weather!" followed by an instrumental smooth jazz bed, which sounded as though it had not been updated since 1962. Bill spoke over the music, "Time now for the RTV Weather Center Forecast brought to you by Gill's Guns and Ammo, reminding you that hunting season is just around the corner. Sunny today, but it won't be a whoop-dee-doo warm up yet, so you won't have to synchronize your bikinis. Highs today around 74 with clear skies. Currently in Saturn it's 67 degrees. That's your RTV Weather Center forecast, I'm Bill Katz."

"Bill is a real meteorologist," Leslie said, "Don't ask him about the weather unless you really want to know."

As Phil Collins' "One More Night" started to play, the On Air light went off.

Leslie led Clara into the main studio. Along the entire back wall was a shelf filled with vinyl records, LPs on the bottom, and 45s on the top with cardboard dividers indicating the letter of the alphabet of the artists. Above them was a rack with CDs. To the right were two turntables. The DJ was looking down with his headphones on, focusing on cuing up a 45. Coming out from a small passage behind a large bank of electrical equipment with meters and patch cords was a tall man with close cropped red hair and a neat beard. He was dressed in khakis and a button-down shirt.

"Bill," Leslie said, pointing to Clara, this is the new midday girl, Clara Jane."

Bill shook Clara's hand. "Bill Katz," he said. "Do you go by Clara Jane or just Clara?"

"Just Clara is fine," she said.

The DJ finished cuing his record, and removed his headphones, setting them on the console in front of him.

"This is Seth Jones," Leslie said.

Seth stood up to shake Clara's hand. Seth appeared to be in his mid-thirties. He was slim and barely taller than Clara, with medium brown hair that didn't quite qualify as either short or long. He was dressed in jeans and faded t-shirt for an RTV event promoting the grand opening of Stephen's Grocery Store. He was holding a worn-looking RTV coffee cup, which he set down to shake Clara's hand. His hand was warm.

"I have a voice for broadcasting and a face for radio," Seth said.

This was an exaggeration. Seth had a long, prominent nose that seemed to elongate his entire face. His thin lips exaggerated the effect. His dark eyebrows were tilted in such a way as to make his dark brown eyes appear sad, almost haunted. The overall effect was soft and appealing in an odd way, mildly and touchingly comical.

"Nine Inch Nails," Seth said, looking at Clara's shirt. "You're going to hate it here."

"He's kidding," Bill said.

"Oh, really?" Seth said, he raised his eyebrows and leaned into the board to crossfade from Phil Collins into Kenny G. The board didn't have sliders like the modern rock station where Clara had interned. It had

25

pots, short for potentiometer. Basically, pots were oversized volume knobs. Above them on the console were a series of mysterious toggles and switches.

"Don't let him scare you," Bill said. "We have a lot of fun here."

"Seth will show you the ropes," Leslie said, "And then you'll go on at 10."

Today?! Clara's face stretched into a smile that she hoped could be read as confidence and not what it really was, sheer panic. Right now they were treating her as one of them, but in one hour the clock would run out on "fake it 'til you make it." Would she be revealed as a fraud?

"Did you bring your license with you?" Seth said, pointing to a bulletin board on the wall in a corner by the LP shelf. He was referring to the FCC license that DJs were required to have in order to sign off on meter readings and operate the board. There had been no test to get it. Clara just filled out a form and sent in a check, but when the license had arrived in the mail, she felt like a professional. Clara took the yellow card out of her purse and pinned it on the board next to Seth's.

"Oh, Bill," Leslie said, "I almost forgot. Someone called to say the weather phone has yesterday's weather."

Bill sighed. "I forgot. Thanks." He walked out of the studio.

Clara looked left and right, unsure of what had just happened.

"You know how you can call a phone number to get the weather forecast?"

"Yeah," Clara said.

"In Saturn, that's us. We record the RTV Weather phone. Well, Bill records it."

"There's a chair behind the guest mic," Seth said, "Why don't you bring it around here?"

As Clara rolled the chair out from behind the bank of equipment, Leslie returned to her desk. On her way out she passed Al, who had returned with a reel-to-reel tape, which he handed to Seth before leaving again. Seth put the tape on a reel-to-reel player to his left, part of the bank of equipment separating his section of the studio from the corner with the guest mic. The time on the Kenny G CD was counting down as Seth put the pot for the reel player in cue and rolled the tape back and forth across the tape heads until he found the beginning of the sound. He turned back to the board just moments before the song came to an end.

"Kenny G and 'Sentimental' from the album *Breathless* on your light rock, more music station RTV." Seth glanced out the window to the sign on the bank clock across the parking lot, which flashed the time and temperature. "It's 9:12 and 67 degrees."

Seth's voice hovered somewhere between tenor and baritone, masculine and friendly, not the deep, "the new Ford truck," type of voice. It was the same as his everyday speaking voice, but with a slightly elevated energy, as someone might speak when greeting an important person he was meeting for the first time.

"Lots of great music coming up this hour, Richard Marx, Celine Dion and a solid gold oldie from the Dave Clark Five. But, even more exciting, at 10 AM we're welcoming a new RTV DJ, Clara Jane, to the airwaves.

You won't want to miss her debut. First, though, it's time for the RTV traffic update brought to you by Saturn Tire."

Without looking, Seth reached out his left hand and hit the button to fire the reel player. It started with a clunk and then he quickly potted up the appropriate channel on the board. A traffic report, which sounded like it had been recorded over the phone, started to play. Seth pushed one side of the headphones off of his ear and turned to Clara, "Al records the traffic reports in the news studio with a guy from the Michigan Department of Transportation who calls in a few times each morning and afternoon."

Seth turned back to the board, and put the headphone back in place, as the traffic report reached its end. As he potted the feed down, he reached up and hit play on the second CD player. He adjusted the pot for the player so the red arrow of the VU meter was just below the red zone. As some tinny electronic drums began to play, Seth opened his microphone, and spoke over the song's intro. "Rod Stewart, 'The Motown Song,' on Saturn's Favorite Music, RTV." He closed the mic, took off his headphones and swiveled in his chair to face Clara.

"Where should I start?" Seth asked. He picked up the clip board from the console in front of him. He took the stapled stack of papers off and flipped to the first page. Printed on a dot matrix printer, it had the date and the words "Title Page" at the top and then a grid which acted as a time sheet. This was followed by a series of abbreviations that would be used throughout the log, ID for station identification, CM for commercial, Net for network, Rec for recorded and so on.

"So at the beginning of your air shift you sign in here," Seth said. "This is the time you're operating the board, not your time sheet. You fill this in with your real name, not your air name."

"Well, it's the same really," Clara said, "except in real life I have a last name."

"Do you think that's wise?"

Clara laughed and squinted at Seth. It occurred to her that he might have developed his sense of humor as a way to counteract the effect of his naturally melancholic eyes. Clara looked down at the paper. Seth seemed to notice that she was reading his real name, Seth Butkiss.

"Yeah, my real name isn't that radio friendly," he said.

"When did you come to that conclusion?"

"On the playground in first grade, probably. Anyway," he flipped back to the current time in the log. "This shows you everything you have to play in the hour, you see the legal ID at the top."

The legal ID was another FCC requirement. At the top of every hour, or as close to it as possible, every station had to broadcast the full call letters of the station followed by the city of license.

"You'll usually just play a liner." Seth reached up to a small rack above the reel to reel player. He spun it around so the carts with the station IDs faced them. Carts were rectangular tape cartridges. They resembled 8-track tapes and were designed to cue up after use and play short content as soon as the button was pressed. He then continued to spin the rack to show the public service announcements (PSAs) and then other station liners. "But if you do end up speaking the legal ID, be sure to include the W. The rest of the time it's just RTV."

"Why?"

"I don't know," Seth said. He glanced up at a stand above the console, then took an index card from a box to his right, glanced at it, and got up to find a record. "I think Ed thinks it sounds like one of those old stations, like WJR or WGN. You know, those venerable old brands."

Seth put the record on the turntable, put on his headphones and bent over to cue it up. He made a note on the index card in front of him, then reached over and grabbed a liner from the rack. He slotted it into a spot on the board and potted up the corresponding channel.

He turned back to the log, showing Clara the commercial breaks, weather forecasts, and other show elements. "You just follow along," he said, "and check things off as you complete them. If something doesn't play for some reason, you make a note. If you miss a commercial for some reason, you have to fill out a discrep sheet." Seth stood up and reached over for a manila folder that was leaning against the wall. He pulled out one of the green forms inside.

"OK," Clara said. Already she felt a tension behind her eyes, a full-blown migraine would not be far off. Seth hit the button to fire up the cart, and then potted down the first song as he potted up the next. When the cart had rolled to its end, he took it out of the slot and put it back on the rack.

"So up here," Seth said, flipping through an open three-ring binder on the stand in front of him, "You have all of the sponsorship messages. Anything you need to read live on air will be here."

At this point Bill came back into the studio with a small stack of carts which he put into an empty side of the rack with the IDs and liners. Seth flipped back to the first page in the binder to a pie chart with a series of round stickers in different colors with letters on them. "This is the clock hour," he said. "Yours will be a little different from mine." He flipped to the next page, which had a second chart labeled "Midday and PM drive."

"You have the Superstar Seven in a Row. Be sure to always call it the Superstar Seven in a Row, or as we sometimes refer to it, the Jesus Christ Superstar Seven in a Row."

"Not on the air," Bill said, raising a finger.

"Definitely not on the air," Seth said.

"Superstar Seven in a Row," Clara said. "Your Light Rock More Music Station."

"Light rock, more music station, or Saturn's Favorite Music," Seth said.

"I think I'm going to have to write this down."

"Have you told her about the Popsicle report yet?" Bill asked.

"Not yet," Seth said.

"Popsicle report?"

"The radio obits," Bill said. "Around ten the funeral home faxes over the names of the dead people."

"We're not up to that yet," Seth said.

"OK," Bill said. He started to inch his way behind the bank of equipment to the guest mic when he noticed that Clara had taken his chair. He left the studio to find another place to sit.

"OK," Seth said, gesturing towards the clock hour, "The Superstar Seven in a Row. So here are the cards." He pulled two wooden boxes full of 5x7" index cards organized into sections with tabs indicating various letters from A to D. Seth explained that the round chart represented the face of the clock, and the jocks played music corresponding to the colored and lettered dots as they circled the hour. "The As are your currents," Seth said. "We have about a five-hour rotation on currents. By the time they drop off and become Bs, you'll despise them."

The further along in the alphabet, essentially, was further back in time. A's were at the top of the adult contemporary charts, B's were hits from the past couple of years. The biggest sections were the C's, which were light hits of the mid-'70s and '80s and D's, which were from the '60s and early '70s. Those were called "solid gold oldies."

Each song in the RTV rotation had a card. At the top was a round sticker with the color and letter corresponding to its category, and in large letters were the title and artist, then whether it was on an LP, 45, CD or, occasionally, a cart. This was followed by the running time of the song and the length of the intro so the DJ could "post" it, that is, speak over the intro without stepping on the opening lyrics. There was also space for any notes, for example, if it started or ended cold or had a false ending. Under this header was a grid, with lines corresponding to the various day parts.

"You're supposed to draw the front card in the section, and then put the card in the back," Seth said, demonstrating. "But you can change it up a little bit for timing and to give the show a better flow. You just have to check the grid and make sure that two other airshifts have played it before you play it again." He showed her how to make a notation on the card, indicating when it was played. "And that's it," he said.

By now Clara's head was swimming, and she was giving serious consideration to running out the door. Seth must have sensed her thoughts because he said, "Don't worry. It sounds like a lot when you're saying it, but when you're doing it, it will make sense. Just follow the log and the clock hour and you'll know what to do." By now it was only ten minutes until the beginning of her first show. Clara looked out the studio window. Everyone was hanging out by Leslie's desk pretending to be talking or drinking coffee, but really they were standing under the speaker waiting to hear the new girl. "Do you have any questions?"

The only one that came to Clara's mind was, "What am I doing here?" "No, I-- I don't think so."

The first track in the Superstar Seven in a Row, a string of seven songs before the first commercial break, actually began in the last five minutes of Seth's show. Seth handed Clara the card and suggest she cue it up.

Cuing records was one of the first things that Clara had learned to do at the Harrison School. You turned the slider or pot into the cue position, and then placed the stylus in the blank groove before the beginning of the audio track. You let the record play until you heard sound, and then, by spinning the disc back and forth a few times, you could stop the stylus right at the first note. At that point you turned the disc back a half turn or so. (Different announcers had different preferences for how far back to go and developed their own feel for how soon to fire up the turntable) If you didn't turn a record back, the turntable wouldn't have time to get up to speed before the song began and you'd hear a dramatic "woosh" on the air.

On her first day at WRTV, this elementary skill seemed impossible. Every time she tried to turn the record back, her shaking hands knocked the stylus out of the groove. Seth watched for a moment, then he came up behind her and put his hand on her shoulder, nudging her gently out of the way. "It's OK," he whispered. "I couldn't cue up my first record either."

When he had finished cuing the record, Seth pushed the extra chair back into its place behind the guest mike. "Go ahead," he said to Clara. "Sit in the driver's seat."

Clara sat facing the board with the microphone in front of her. She had sat at a microphone in the studios at the Harrison School many, many times. "I know how to do this," she reminded herself, but she felt as though she was sitting at the crest of the first hill on a roller coaster.

Clara fired the turntable and potted up the channel, keeping a close eye on the VU meter to make sure her levels were not too hot. So far so good. Seth came up beside her and slid the card for the record into view. "This one is technically my show," he said, "So I'll mark the card here." He wrote his initials on the grid and placed the card in the back of its category. "Now it's all you." Clara looked at Seth with an expression of sheer panic. "You've got it," he said in a gentle voice. "Look at the clock hour. What is next?"

"An A."

"Right," Seth said, "but you're going to need the legal ID for the top of the hour."

Clara took one of the legal ID carts from the rack and slotted it into one of the cart machines in the board. Then she took a card from the front of the A section. Because the As were the most current, they were almost always on CD. Clara went to the CD rack, found the disc, and slotted it into the player. As the song on the record started to fade, Clara hit the legal ID and then cross faded into the A.

"You got it," Seth said. "I'm going to get some more coffee. I'll get out of your way, but I'll be around if you need me."

Clara was both nervous and relieved that Seth was leaving her alone. She wasn't sure she was ready to take the training wheels off, yet she was glad she would not have someone looking over her shoulder as she fumbled around. Clara made it through the Superstar Seven in a Row without incident. When it came time for her to speak on the air, she opened the mike and said, "Good morning, this is RTV, Saturn's Favorite music, I'm Clara Jane, it's my first day, so be nice to me."

By now Clara had moved out of the block of solid music and into some of the special programming features. The break included something called "Good News," a folksy recorded feature with upbeat observations by a local 73 year old. According to the log, "Good News" was recorded onto a labeled and dated cart. Clara found the spinner with the carts for the short recorded features. The same shelf had a space for compact discs in paper sleeves. These were mostly syndicated programs.

Clara would have to play the "Good News" feature, then read the obituaries live, and then go into "Casey's Biggest Hits," a daily anecdote about an adult contemporary song which was provided to stations that subscribed the weekly syndicated show Casey's AC Top 40. It came as a bonus CD along with the programming discs.

Clara cued up both the Good News and the Casey Casem disc and then went to the back room to find the fax from the funeral home, which would include the list of the day's deceased. The fax had arrived on time, and there was only one name. The name was "Johan Csikszentmihalyi." The funeral home had not provided any information on how to pronounce it.

Johan had apparently been a popular guy because as soon as Clara finished reading and hit "Casey's Biggest Hits" the phone lit up with irate mourners who couldn't believe how badly she'd butchered the poor guy's name. (The studio phone literally "lit up." To keep it from ringing on the air, it was fitted with a large red light that flashed when there was an incoming call.) Clara wanted to tell the callers it wasn't her fault. How on earth was she supposed to know how to pronounce it? But she could not argue with people who had just suffered a loss. All she could do was let them yell at her.

In the heat of the moment, Clara had forgotten to cue up another record. The Casey Casem segment ended with a four-tone jingle, and then there was silence, a full 15 seconds of **Dead Air. Dead Air**-- having no sound on your airwaves-- was the cardinal sin of radio. Whenever the sound on the broadcast speakers stopped, everything stopped. Conversations stopped mid-word. People who were walking stood still, for a moment everyone looked up as if they could *see* the silence. Then the running would start. Anyone with an FCC license would head for the studio. If someone was lying unconscious on the studio floor, they would step over the body, jam a PSA into the cart machine and turn up the pot before checking his pulse to see if he was alive.

Clara grabbed a :60 PSA from the rack, but the "Good News" was still rolling to its cue tone in the closest cart slot. In a panic, Clara hit play on the CD again, starting Casey Casem's segment for the next day. Clara felt faint. When she turned around Seth was standing there. Everything seemed to swirl around his calm presence.

"Take a breath," he said. "What's happening?"

"I need to cue up a record," Clara said, wiping her brow. She leaned across the console and grabbed a card.

"Here, give it to me," Seth said. He took the card, looked at it and seeing that it was an LP, went back to the box to find something on a CD that he could cue up more quickly. As he was doing that, Ed appeared in the doorway.

"What is going on?" he shouted. "Why did we have dead air, and why are we playing Casey Casem twice in a row?"

"I-I messed up the obits," Clara said. "I didn't know how to pronounce this name, and then everyone was calling and the track ended."

"You messed up the obits?" Ed said in an elevated voice." You can't mess up the obits, people are very sensitive about that."

"I-I found that out," Clara said. She tensed her muscles as though preparing for a blow. Seth started laughing.

"What's so funny?" Ed asked. His face was flushed.

Seth had picked up the fax from the funeral home. "She got a great one on her fist day," he said, handing the paper to Ed. Ed looked at the fax, and then he started laughing. "Yeah, OK," he said. "Look, don't answer the phone when you're busy. It can wait."

"Yes, sir," Clara said.

"Ed," Ed said. "Ed is fine." He left the studio.

"OK," Seth said, "The B is in CD 1. You OK now?"

"Yes, thank you."

"Don't panic," he said. "You're doing great."

Clara appreciated the sentiment, but she knew that she wasn't. Her nerves gave her a nasty case of hiccoughs, and her next break sounded like: "It's 10:40 (hic) on RT (hic) V.. Your light r- (hic), rock, more music (hic) station. Coming up.... Um, more music. (Hic) Stay tuned..."

At about 1 PM, Clara looked out the window was relieved to see the next DJ walk in for his shift. It was the heavy-set guy with the spiky mullet who had been operating the board when she came in for her interview. He had a bag slung over his shoulder. He stopped at Leslie's desk and she could see them laughing, but something about Leslie's smile seemed artificial. As soon as the man turned away, her laughter stopped. Clara hit the button to start Gloria Estefan, walked to the studio door, and peeked around the corner. The man had set his bag down on the desk and was pulling out a stack of music reference books and copy of the industry journal *Radio & Records*.

"You must be Rad Farr," Clara said, with a smile.

"You're the one who likes Casey Casem," said Rad. He was not smiling.

"What?"

"Casey Casem back to back?"

"Oh, right," Clara said. Her cheeks turned crimson. She headed back into the studio and cross faded into Mariah Carey's "Vision of Love."

Rad came into the studio and started rummaging through the cards, "So you're Clare?"

"Clara."

"You know, you should try not to play two female singers back to back. They blend together."

"Right," Clara said.

"I'm the music director," Rad said. He took out cards for the remaining letters on the clock hour and set them on the console. "I'm going to take these," he said, picking up the card boxes.

"Uh, OK," Clara said.

"You'll get better," Rad said as he walked out the studio door.

"Thanks for the pep talk," Clara thought, but she said nothing. By the time her airshift ended she had a splitting headache.

"If you'd like I can critique your airchecks for you," Rad said when he returned to the studio. "I'm sure it would be very helpful to you. Just bring them in one afternoon and we can go over them and discuss what you're doing on the air. I've done this with a couple of the young part-timers and they found it to be helpful."

Rad seemed to be about her age, maybe even a bit younger. Clara was so flustered that at the moment she could not be sure if her first show had been disastrous enough to warrant this condescension or if Rad was just an arrogant jerk.

"Have a good show," she said.

Clara was relieved that it was finished. She walked to Leslie's desk, ready to collapse.

"You were great," Leslie said. "For a first day, you were great."

"Do you have any aspirin?"

Leslie reached into her desk and pulled out a bottle of aspirin. She opened it and handed two tablets to Clara. "There's a lot to learn," she said. "It'll get easier. You'll be doing this in your sleep. I'm pretty sure Seth does."

The intro to Rad's show began to play over the speakers. It had a special theme featuring overly dramatic music and snippets of women's voices saying "Rad Far out!" "Good afternoon, everyone," Rad said. His radio voice was nearly an octave deeper than his high tenor speaking voice. As Clara started to walk to the kitchen to get a glass of water, she caught a view of Rad through the window. Instead of sitting like the other announcers, he stood at the mic with his hand over one of the ears of the headphones, as if he were playing an announcer in a movie. "Congratulations to the new girl, Clare James on her first day." He played a sound effect of applause. "We're looking forward to lots of great things from Clare."

"It's Clara Jane," she said to the speaker. Rad's voice continued to play through the station as Clara went to the kitchen, filled a glass with water, and swallowed the aspirin.

"Coming up we'll have music from a musician born Reginald Dwight, a band with three musicians named Taylor-- all unrelated, and a song that was named 'The Best Song of the 70s.' But first we'll kick off another Superstar Seven in a Row with Rick Astley: 'Never Gonna Give You Up.'"

There was something familiar about Rad's cadence, but Clara couldn't quite place it. A phrase would steadily and slowly rise in pitch, then a pause, and Rad would begin lower and ramp up again, always maintaining the same moderate pace. Seth sounded conversational on the air. Rad sounded like he was announcing. Clara just hoped she had not sounded like an idiot.

On the way home, Clara felt like one raw nerve. She was sweaty and her cheeks were flushed. She stopped at the gas station store and picked up a box of wine. She thought a cheap rosé might pair well with her fast food take out. The cable company was not slated to come to her apartment and hook her up for another week, so she stopped at Hollywood Video. Clara loved movies about counter cultures. She envied the people in them who were bold enough to rebel against everything safe and respectable. She had three days to watch before the late fees kicked in, so she settled on two films. The first was "Alice's Restaurant," a 1960s bohemian slice of life based on Arlo Guthrie's anti-Vietnam anthem and starring the folksinger himself. The second was the musical "Cabaret."

When she got back to her apartment, she decided she was more in the mood for 1930s Berlin than 1960s hippies. She put "Cabaret" in the VHS player, and sat down with her fast food. She could not taste anything or concentrate on the film. She felt as though her entire life depended on the next day's performance. If she got fired from a station in little Saturn, she was sure she'd never get a second chance. She did not have a plan B for her career and could not imagine anything else that would make her happy. The only alternative, as she saw it, was a life devoted entirely to paying the bills-- a desk job, a family with 1.5 kids, and a home in some suburb with a white picket fence which would serve as her prison bars.

That night Clara lay on her air mattress listening to RTV's overnight man. Clara had never met him, but she knew from the logs that his name was Grant Camano. On air he went by General Grant. His voice was like molasses. He spoke in a deep, laconic half whisper as though he were trying to seduce the song titles he announced. Clara imagined the audience of Grant's show must have been made up of middle aged, bored housewives who wished they were brave enough to have an affair. It was not long before Clara was asleep.

That night she had a radio nightmare. She dreamed she was doing her airshift completely naked. She was playing a record that kept skipping. She was embarrassed when Ed came in to scold her for not changing the song and noticed she was naked. "I can't believe I forgot to wear clothes."

WAPED

Clara was sitting at a desk in the station's back room. Her left hand was simultaneously propping

up her head and covering her eyes. In her right hand was a telephone receiver. She had been listening to the same instrumental version of The Beatles' "Yesterday" on an endless loop for ten minutes. She had thought, by coming in early, she could take care of a few personal tasks before her airshift.

Bill came out of the studio and sat down at his desk. "You're still on the phone?"

"No," Clara said holding up the handset, "I'm fly fishing." Bill started to write something on a sheet of paper. "I've been on hold for fifteen minutes," Clara said. "Fifteen, no, sixteen minutes." A liner played over the speakers and Bruce Springsteen's "Human Touch" started to play. A few seconds later, Seth was standing in the studio doorway.

"You still on hold?"

"I'm trying to get my phone service set up. I would do it at home but-"

"No phone service," Bill and Seth said in unison. Seth continued down the hall towards the kitchen where he could get a fresh cup of coffee. Suddenly "Yesterday" cut off mid-line.

"Hello?" Clara said. It was a false alarm. The song resumed. Clara gave a deep sigh.

"Besides the phone, are you getting settled in?" Bill asked.

"Now that it's pay day, I'm finally going to have some furniture," Clara said. "They're delivering a bed this afternoon. I hope the weather is good."

"Well, the cold front is moving to the south, and the cloud cover is going to move down with it. The clouds will break up as the dry air moves in." Clara stared at Bill. "You were just making small talk?" he asked.

"Yeah," Clara said.

Out of the corner of her eye, Clara saw Seth meandering back to the studio just moments before the end of the song. He did not pick up his pace. He went through the door as the song reached its softest fade. Through the speakers she heard the song transition into the next without any discernible gap.

"Hello. This is Michigan Bell, how can I help you?"

"Hello," Clara sat up straighter. "Yes. I'd like to get a phone hooked up please."

"Your address please"

"3900 N. U.S. 101, Saturn, South Apartment."

"Hold on, that's not here in the book, I'll have to look it up."

The line went silent. "Hello?" There was a click. Clara put down the receiver. "They hung up on me." She was talking to no one because Bill had returned to the studio.

It was now only ten minutes before her airshift. As Clara walked into the studio, Seth was finishing cuing up a record. It was second nature to him. No, it was first nature. All of those little tasks that came up on three-minute intervals, the cuing, the logs, the liners, the feeds, Seth performed them like a seasoned driver who arrives at his destination without ever having been conscious of the individual turns. He could go from sitting slumped on his elbows straight into a lively break as though a switch had been turned. Watching how unconsciously he performed these mundane tasks, Clara wondered if any of this would ever seem natural to her. As she was having this thought, Seth fired the turn table. It was still set on 33 and Elton John's "Goodbye Yellow Brick Road." 45 sounded like "Wh-eeeeeee-nnnn aaarreee..." Seth flipped the turn table into 45, and the record sped up right on the air.

"I meant to do that," he said.

"Like those artists from cultures that put an intentional flaw in their work to show they're not gods?" Clara asked.

Seth laughed. "I doubt there's much confusion in this case." Seth took the other record from its turntable and put it back in the jacket "Oh well, I don't think I've ever had a perfect show. Some are just less screwed up than others."

Clara noticed a 45 with the card in its sleeve sitting on the stand with the clock hour. "What's that?"

"Oh, do you mind putting that on Rad's desk?"

"Sure." She took the record off the stand and looked at the card. She noticed that Seth had written "Waped" on it.

"What is 'waped'?" She asked.

"Huh?"

"You wrote waped. W-A-P-E-D."

"It's a radio term," Seth said, taking the card back.

Bill had extracted himself from the corner. "Yes," he agreed. "Only morning shows use it. It's a very special word."

"I see," Clara said. "What does it mean?"

"What does it mean, Bill?" Seth asked.

"It means FUBAR. It's the morning show equivalent of FUBAR."

"Yes," said Seth. "As in, 'this whole music library is totally waped.'" He inserted the" r" above the word with a little carrot. "It's late," he said, handing the card and the warped record back to Clara.

"It's, like, ten in the morning."

"When you start work at 5:30, that's late." Clara left the studio and put the record on Rad's desk. She came back with only one minute to go before her shift.

"Did you get your phone?" Seth asked.

"They hung up on me." She shook her head and muttered, "What do I need to do first?"

"You look a little keyed up," Seth said. "I can get your first tracks set up. Why don't you go get a coffee and relax for a minute?"

"Really? Thanks." Clara walked to the restroom waving her hands in front of her in an attempt to shake out the tension. She used the restroom, then threw some water on her face and returned to the studio. The legal ID had played and Annie Lennox was on the air.

"Better?" Seth asked as she walked into the studio.

"Yeah, thanks."

"OK," Seth said, standing up. "I've got you set up for a while. You have the A on CD1." He pointed to its card, sitting on the console. "After that, I cued up the C, that's on turntable 1. The B is on turntable 2 and then the next A is on CD2."

"Thanks," Clara said, leaning in to look at the cards.

"Good luck with the phone," Seth said on his way out the door..

Clara sat down and tried to get her bearings. She wondered what new and humiliating mistakes she was going to make today. In the second hour of her show, Clara glanced out the window and saw a 300- pound man in torn clothing enter the lobby. His face was almost invisible behind an uncontrolled beard, and his scraggly hair was covered with a worn baseball hat. Clara thought he must be a homeless man who walked in off the street. But Leslie smiled at him in a familiar way and handed him a windowed envelope. Leslie pointed up at the booth, and she and the man started walking in the direction of the studio.

"Knock knock," Leslie said, peeking in the door. "Safe to come in?"

47

"Yeah," Clara said.

"Grant came in for his paycheck, and I wanted to introduce you," Leslie said. "Grant, this is Clara Jane, the new midday girl. Grant does overnights, so you probably won't cross paths that often."

Grant stepped forward and extended a dirty hand. Clara shook it. "I've listened to your show," Clara said, hoping her expression did not reveal her shock at his appearance. "You have a soothing voice."

"Grant gets the most fan mail of anyone at the station," Leslie said. "Mostly women. Women love him."

"Good luck with your show," Grant said, and left the studio. Clara exchanged a look with Leslie.

"I know," Leslie said. "He really does get the most love letters. We try to keep his face a mystery."

There were, in fact, a number of "mysterious" co-workers whose paths only occasionally crossed Clara's. There was a team of three sales people who popped in and out on their way to schmooze clients. The sales staff, Leslie told Clara, had expense accounts for martini lunches and a budget to cover their gasoline. Their shared office was as far from the studio as possible, in a room across from the kitchen. Clara generally only saw them if they dropped off commercial copy. There was also an engineer, a friendly guy named Max, who occasionally rummaged around in a strange, dark back room during Clara's shift, but who mostly worked at night.

By now Clara was starting to feel comfortable at the board. In the third hour of her show she decided to use the relative calm of the Superstar

Seven in a Row to call the phone company again. She was sure she would mostly be on hold anyway,

She lined up a couple of tracks in the CD players and dialed. She put the phone on speaker and let the "Yesterday" hold music play as she cued up a single. The track on the second CD was just finishing when someone finally answered the phone.

"I'd like to set up phone service please," Clara said, removing a single from its sleeve. She placed it on the turntable, and with half of the headphones to one of her ears she cued the record while still listening to the call.

"Address please."

The record was now cued and ready. "3900 N. U.S. 101, Saturn, South Apartment."

"OK, I'll have to look that up. It's not in the book."

"As long as you don't hang up on me, last time I was disconnected."

"One minute ma'am." The woman put Clara on hold just as the track on the CD was reaching its end. Clara threw a liner into cart player, and transitioned to the single.

While she was on hold, Clara had time to fill in the card for the single and pull out the next card. It was for an artist named Lee Michaels. Clara had never heard of him. As she was taking the LP off the shelf, the agent came back on the line.

"I'm sorry, that address doesn't exist."

Clara came in close to the phone, holding the album in her hand. "What do you mean the address doesn't exist? I live there."

"You must have the wrong address ma'am."

"The address is printed on the card my landlord gave me."

"Well, he must have given you the wrong address."

"Look, there is a phone jack in there already. You must have been there before." Clara set the record on the turntable, and started cuing with one half of her brain while she argued with the other.

"You'll have to call your landlord and get the correct address."

Clara had finished her cue and she turned her full attention to the call. "OK, now, when I call my landlord, and he tells me that this is the correct address, are you saying that I can't get phone service?"

"No, you'll just have to find out what the address is."

By now the previous track was reaching its end. Clara hung up on her call, jumped into the driver's seat and threw on her head phones. "You're listening to another Superstar Seven in a Row on Saturn's favorite music, RTV. Here's Lee Michaels with 'Do You Know What I Mean.'"

Clara started the turntable. She felt proud that she was now comfortable enough to multitask in the studio like Seth. The song began with a jangly, blues inspired piano. Clara was pleasantly surprised that this was part of the RTV playlist. She was even more surprised when the chorus rolled around. It was a joyous celebration of being stoned. She could see Leslie through the window, grooving and laughing at her desk. That was when Ed rushed through the door. "What is this?" he shouted.

"It's, um," she looked at the card, "Lee Michaels, 'Do You Know What I Mean.'"

"No, it isn't," Ed said. He went over to the turntable. "You cued up the wrong track!"

Clara panicked and potted down the song just as it was reaching its second drug filled chorus. "What are you doing?" Ed shouted. Clara threw an AIDS awareness spot into the cart machine and played it. Ed shook his head. "You should have just let it play out."

Clara picked out another card from the D category. She had trouble cuing it up while Ed was yelling at her. "Pay more attention next time," he said. After Ed had left the studio Leslie came in laughing. "Good song," she said.

Clara explained that she had been distracted because she could not get anyone to come out and install a phone. "How can they not find it? It's on the road. The one road in town."

"What address are you giving them?"

"3900 N. U.S. 101."

"That's your problem," Leslie said. "In town it's called Main Street. Next time you call, tell them it's Main Street."

Clara thanked Leslie for giving her what she believed would be the key to the telephonic life. It would have to wait for tomorrow, though. Clara didn't dare multitask again. When Rad showed up for his shift he came into the studio and, by way of greeting, said "What was that drug song you played half of?"

"It was the wrong track."

"You have to pay attention to what you play," Rad said. "You stepped on the vocal of Celine Dion at 1:37."

"Thanks for listening," Clara said.

That night Clara got to sleep in a brand-new bed, but she was still restless. She could not stop seething about Rad. He seemed to go out of his way to make her feel like an idiot. It was not as though she needed any help on that score. She had excelled at Harrison, but what if she could not cut it in the real world? What would she do? There was no way she could go crawling home and admit she had no talent. Seth never tried to make Clara feel worse about her mistakes. What was Rad's problem?

In truth, Clara had never heard Rad make a mistake on the air. Seth was the one who had played a record at the wrong speed. Rad was rehearsed, and he sounded rehearsed. Seth sounded like he was making things up as he went along, it was spontaneous and that was more fun to listen to. It was Seth, not Rad, who Clara hoped she would become.

That's when she had an epiphany. Rad was artificial because he didn't have the confidence to be natural. Rad's arrogance and condescension grew out of social awkwardness and deep insecurity. Clara decided that if she made an effort to get to know him better, he might stop trying to impress her with his "superior" knowledge. If she could pull that off, maybe she would have at least one less source of stress in her life.

Professional

The next day Rad arrived about 15 minutes before the end of Clara's shift. He dumped his bag on his desk and came into the studio to collect the music cards. Even when he did not need to update the cards as music director, he liked to plan out the first hour of his show in advance. Rad went to his desk and spread out his books and papers. He subscribed to a number of radio prep sheets. These were weekly newsletters full of trivia, weekly events and one-liners. Prep sheets were not cheap. Unless he was getting a lot more than she was, Rad probably used half of his salary on prep materials for his show. He was circling one of the bits with an orange highlighter, when Clara came out of the studio and leaned against the door.

"Hi, Clare," Rad said.

"Clara," she said.

"Have you thought of using Clare?" Rad asked, "I think it would sound good on the radio."

"My name is Clara."

"Sure," he said, looking back down.

Clara bit her lip and reminded herself of her mission. "You do a lot of prep," she said.

"It's professional," Rad said.

"Right," Clara said. She retreated into the studio and wrapped up her show. She handed the reins over the Rad, and went back to her desk to try, once again, to get herself a phone. As Clara waited on hold, she heard Rad's overly dramatic opening theme. As the first of the Superstar Seven in a Row played, Rad came out to his desk to pick up some papers. Clara, dogged in her mission said, "So Rad, what made you decide to go into radio?"

"I grew up listening to Casey Casem," Rad said. "Every weekend, the American Top 40. I thought, 'that's what I want to be.'"

That is when it dawned on Clara, Rad's cadence, it was Casey Casem. He used a different register of his voice, but he'd adopted every inflection and pause.

"Did you go to broadcasting school?"

"I did college radio," Rad said, "Community college. Just a semester. No one cares about your degree in radio. They just care what you sound like. So I taught myself everything I could learn about music and radio. I'm a musical autodidact."

At that point, the representative at the phone company picked up. "Hello?" Clara said, pointing to the phone and waving Rad off. "I am calling to get my phone service hooked up."

"Your address?"

"3900 N. Main St."

"Is that a house or an apartment?"

"It's an apartment, the south apartment."

"What is the apartment number?"

"It's the south apartment."

"Well, we don't do it that way. Is the apartment on the first floor?"

"See, it's a house divided into two apartments, mine is on the left-hand side. It's the south apartment."

"So it's on the first floor?"

"It's on the only floor."

"And which side of the hall is it on?"

"There is no hall; it's just the door on the left."

"First floor, left."

"Yes."

"We can have a crew out to your apartment on Friday."

Victory! Clara ran into the studio, "I'm finally getting my phone hooked up!"

"Oh," Rad said.

"Of course," Clara thought to herself. "That was not about him." Clara regrouped and decided to try again with the previous conversation. "So Casey Casem was your teacher?"

"In a way. What I learned from Casey," Rad said, "is that anyone can billboard a song. To keep your listeners, you can't just tease the name of the song; you have to tease a fact, a story. Like this," he pointed to one of the cards for his show, which he had fanned out on the table. "I've got Eric Carmen, 'All by Myself' coming up, right?"

"That is such a depressing song," Clara said.

"That's not the point," Rad said.

"Just making conversation," Clara said, shaking her head.

"It doesn't matter what we like," he said, "Everything we play is someone's favorite song."

"Fair point," Clara said.

"So I know I'm going to play this, so I go to my books," he said, flipping through a well-worn tome. "I get these at garage sales and stuff. So this one has a blurb on the song. It says the melody is based on Rachmaninov, but everybody knows that."

"Of course," Clara said, hoping he could not see that she did not.

"Here's something: he taught himself guitar by listening to Beatles songs. So maybe I'll use that, I'll tease 'a song by an artist who taught himself guitar by listening to Beatles songs.' It makes people curious who it is, so they keep listening. You could do that. You'd sound more professional."

Clara clenched her fists again, "Good idea," she said with a tight smile. She left the studio without saying goodbye to Rad. Befriending Rad was clearly not going to work for Clara. Her new strategy was to avoid Rad as much as possible.

Emergency Broadcast System

With its powerful signal, WRTV was a "primary" Emergency Broadcast System station, which meant that in the event of an emergency, it would be the station that would transmit the information to the public. Next to the transmitter was a shelf with an EBS monitor. Next to the EBS monitor, hanging from a nail, was a binder that included emergency information and, in the front, a sealed envelope that contained a sheet with activation code words. Updated monthly, the code words would be used in the worst-case scenario to determine that an emergency message was authentic. If the station received an emergency message, and the authenticator code matched, something major had just happened. All the other stations in the area would tell their listeners to tune to RTV and then go dark. RTV would continue to broadcast the emergency information. Once a week, at random times, the FCC mandated that radio stations conduct a test of the system. This was, arguably, the biggest responsibility to the public that a radio station had. When Clara looked ahead in the log and saw that a test would be coming up in her first hour, it seemed straight forward.

Clara turned up the fourth pot on her board, and then played the opening EBS cart with a message in Al's voice: "This is a test of the Emergency Broadcast System, this is only a test..." She went over to the

EBS machine and flipped two toggles on a section of the machine labeled "tone generator," but there was no ear-piercing screech. There was nothing but silence. Clara's pulse began to race as she looked at the flat meters on her console, scanned the steps written on the log in front of her, and tried flipping the toggles again. Still nothing. Not knowing what else to do, she fired the closing cart. "This was a test of the Emergency Broadcast System, if this had been an actual emergency..."

The phone started to light up. Clara had never seen Ed arrive in the studio so quickly. "What just happened with the EBS test?"

"It-- I don't know. I pushed the button and it didn't do anything." Clara fired the turntable.

"We have stations all across the state that monitor our EBS signal," Ed said. "You can't mess with the EBS tests, they're an FCC requirement."

"I know," Clara said. She pressed her lips together, hoping it might hold back her tears. By now Seth had come into the studio. He was examining the EBS monitor. "We can get big fines for not keeping up with the tests," Ed said.

"I don't know why it didn't play," Clara said, trembling.

Seth continued to examine the monitor, but over his shoulder he called out to Clara, "You'd better catch your record there, it's ending."

With all of the commotion, Clara had failed to properly cue the album, and it ramped up on the air with a whoosh. Clara burst into tears. Ed took a step back. He looked startled, as though Clara had suddenly changed the rules on him. Seth put a hand on Clara's shoulder, "Don't worry, you're doing fine," he said in a gentle voice. Then to Ed, "Give me the pie song."

Ed hardly had to look to find the album he needed in the stacks. Seth took the record from Ed. "Side one, track one," he said to Clara, handing it to her. She looked up at the clock hour. "It's not the right..."

"Don't worry about it," Seth said.

Clara wiped her nose with the back of her hand and then cued up the track on turntable one. As the Eagles got close to its end, Clara turned towards the board preparing to give the weather, the next element on the log.

"Just play a liner and go into the next song," Seth said. Clara glanced over at Ed, who nodded.

Clara hit the cart; there was a sound like a mini explosion and then a nondescript tune with three women singing in harmony, "Saturn's Favorite Music, RTV FM." She potted up Don McLean's "American Pie."

"8:28," Seth said with a smile.

"What?"

"8:28. The length of 'American Pie.'"

"You know that by heart?" Clara sniffed.

"It's the longest song in our rotation," Seth said. "When all hell breaks loose, ignore the clock hour. Play a long one."

Ed was still standing with his hands on his hips, "What happened with the EBS test?"

Seth gestured past the monitor to a piece of equipment that looked like something you'd see an old-fashioned telephone operator working on in a black and white movie. "She didn't re-patch the board," Seth said. "Before you run a test you have to re-patch it." Seth demonstrated, moving the patch cords into the proper position for the test, and then back to the default. "Did anyone explain this to you?"

"No," Clara said.

"No," Seth said. Then he turned to Ed. "*Someone* should have told you that before they gave you an EBS test for the first time." Ed, now satisfied that the equipment still worked, mumbled something inaudible and went back into his office.

"It's OK, you're doing a good job," Seth said. "It's a lot to learn all at once." He looked at the log, then reached over and started the reel tape to catch a news feed that Clara was about to miss.

"Oh God," Clara said. "This is a total disaster."

"Everything's under control here," Seth said. "Why don't you go to the kitchen and get something to drink. Calm down a little bit, and I'll run things here for a little while."

Clara looked at him for a moment without moving. "It's OK," Seth said. "Go on."

Clara went into the bathroom. She splashed her face with cold water. Then she went to the kitchen and poured a coffee to bring back to Seth.

Seth had already dug through the box to find the card for "American Pie." He was writing the date on the card when Clara walked in.

"Thank you," Clara said, holding out the coffee. Seth got up from the chair. Taking the mug he said, "A gift for me? You shouldn't have."

Don McLean was still only up to the part of the song about James Dean. Clara sat back down took at quick look at the cards and what was coming up in the logs, then swiveled back to Seth, who was leaning against the wall of LPs.

"Do you know the lengths of a lot of songs by heart?"

"The long ones," he said.

"Like what?"

"'Deacon Blues,' Steely Dan, 7:36. Al Stewart's always good. 'Time Passages' and 'Year of the Cat' are both right around 6:40. Then you've got your 'Beginnings' by Chicago, 7:41. 'Hey Jude,' 7:27. Those two are good because they've got the long fade outs. You can cut out when you need to."

"I'm never going to know all of this stuff."

"Sure you are," he took a sip of his coffee. "When you've been doing this for 18 years, you'll know exactly how long it takes to get to the kitchen and refill your coffee, or go to the bathroom, number one and number two. Believe me."

Clara started to smile, just a bit. "How long is that?"

"That's private." Seth's face stretched into its elongated smile. "Anyway, it'll probably be different for you. Results vary."

"You've been at RTV for 18 years?"

"No, I've been here... eight? I think eight now. I've been in radio for 18."

"You must have been 12."

"Nineteen. Don't do the math." Clara sighed as she took the EBS cart out of the board and put it back on its spinner. "Look," Seth said, taking the EBS book off its nail, "This, today, was not a disaster. You know what would be a disaster?"

"What?"

"The day that these authenticator codes match," he put a hand up to his ear imitating headphones and affected a radio announcer voice. "This station has interrupted its regular programming at the request of the United States government to participate in the Emergency Broadcast System. This is not a test. I repeat, this is not a test. During this emergency we will stay on the air delivering news and official information. You are now listening to the Emergency Broadcast System."

"That's intense."

"Told you. It puts playing records at the wrong speed in perspective, huh?"

"You have an interesting way of looking at the world," Clara said.

"We'll probably spend our final moments on earth patching cables into the EBS machine."

"I think you just found a flaw in the whole EBS system."

"What?"

"The entire fate of the planet depends on people like you and me following the instructions in a book instead of saying, 'the world is ending, I'm out of here.'"

"Would you run?"

"Nah. I have nowhere to go. Nowhere I could get to in time. What about you?"

"I'd stay on the air. I'd like to spend my last time on earth doing something that matters."

"You do a lot of stuff that matters."

"Oh, yeah?"

"You rescued me."

"Least I can do if we're going to spend Armageddon together." By now Clara had almost forgotten about the EBS debacle.

"I should find an appropriate song for this occasion," Clara said. She started digging through the cards. "I got it," she said, holding up the card for Seth to see. It was R.E.M. "It's the End of the World as we Know it." On the speakers Don McLean was still crooning about the music dying, with at least two minutes still to go.

"Seth Jones and Clara Jane," Seth said, "the last two witnesses to a world that died."

Crosstalk

"Hello? I'm calling... No, wait, don't put me on hold. I already..." Clara sighed. "They put me on hold," she said to no one in particular.

Clara had come in to the station early again. She was sitting at one of the desks in the back room, tapping a pen. Friday had come and gone and she still had no phone. A song by Sting (Clara had trouble telling one from another) started playing over the speakers. A moment later Seth came out of the studio holding his RTV coffee mug. "I'm going to get some coffee," he said. "You want some?"

"I'm never getting a phone," Clara said. Seth shrugged and headed off to the kitchen. As Clara listened to "Yesterday" through the telephone, she heard a female voice in the lobby. When Seth reappeared, he was walking with Leslie. Seth had a coffee mug in each hand. Leslie had a bundle of newspapers under her arm. "It's always so interesting how your day is wrapping up just as everyone else is just coming in," Leslie said.

"Still have a bit to go," Seth said. He put one of the coffee mugs on the desk in front of Clara and went back into the studio.

"I'm never getting a phone," Clara said to Leslie.

"Sorry to hear that," she said. Then she fanned the papers across the desk. It was a selection of the type of tabloids you would find in the grocery store checkout aisle. "It's tabloid day!" Leslie said. "Everyone makes fun of me for buying them, but I notice they all read them."

"Well, sure," Clara said. "Otherwise how would you know what the ghost of Elvis is up to?"

Laid out in front of Clara were *The Enquirer* and *The Star* but by far the most eye-catching cover was that of the *Weekly World News*. It featured a giant image of a wide-mouthed vampire baby with sharp teeth and pointed ears. "Bat Child Found in Cave!" blared the headline.

"The title has an exclamation point on it," Leslie said. "That's how you know it's important." Clara laughed, and with her free hand started flipping through the tabloid's pages.

"How are you settling in?" Leslie asked.

"Well, I still don't have a phone," Clara said.

"How's the show coming?"

"Well, I keep having stress dreams," Clara said. "Last night I dreamed I was in the studio, and Ed was going around telling everyone that I was 'the weakest link' at the station."

Clara was startled by Ed's voice behind her. "I would never say that," he said. Clara turned crimson. Ed had come around the corner while Clara was looking at the tabloid and she had not noticed.

"I- I didn't know you were there," Clara said.

"Who are you talking to?" Ed asked.

"She's on hold," Leslie said.

"Oh," Ed said, "Is it tabloid day?" He picked up a copy of *The Star* and took it with him to his office.

Clara was mortified. "How long was he there?"

"Not very long," Leslie said. "See, he said you're not the weakest link."

"He said he wouldn't *say* I'm the weakest link. He didn't say he didn't think it." A liner played over the speakers and a new track started to play. A moment later Seth was standing leaning in the doorway with the coffee mug cradled in his hands.

"Relax," Leslie said. "You're doing fine. You have listeners you know."

"I have listeners?"

"Sure. The guy at the drug store thinks you're a stitch."

"Huh," Clara said, "I thought my only listener was Rad."

"Rad?" Leslie asked.

"He comes in every day with some critique of my show."

"Rad is a dweeb," Seth said.

Leslie laughed, "He seems like the kind of guy who plays his own airchecks as romantic background music."

Hearing Leslie and Seth badmouthing Rad filled Clara with pleasure. It was a relief to know that she was not alone in her view of him. "He's always offering to go over my airchecks with me and give me tips," Clara said.

"Run," Seth said. "Run fast. You don't want to sound like Rad. Rad takes his sense of humor very seriously, and it shows."

"To be fair, he's not that bad on the air," Leslie said.

"No, it's just in life," Seth said, returning to the studio.

Leslie gave Clara a little pat on the shoulder before heading back to her desk. As Clara continued to hold, she read about Hitler's secret crush on Marlene Dietrich. Then she flipped to the back of the tabloid and saw that they sold t-shirts with some of their most outrageous covers. Clara ripped the order form from the back of the paper and put it in her purse. When hold music finally stopped, Clara was so surprised that she stood up.

"Hello," Clara said, "I was supposed to have phone service installed on Friday but no one showed up."

"Address please."

"3900 N. U.S... I mean 3900 N. Main St."

"Yes, the service people couldn't find that."

"It's right on the main road in town!"

"What is the apartment number?"

"S."

"S isn't a number."

"I know it's not a...," Clara waved her hand in frustration. "It's the south apartment. There's one labeled N for north and one labeled S."

"Now, that apartment is on the first floor on the left?"

"There is only one floor, it's in a house. It's divided into two apartments. They don't have numbers, there's a north apartment and a south apartment."

"OK, that must be the problem. It has to have a number."

"What if it doesn't?"

"We just need a number for the form."

"Can I make one up? It's number one-- no, two. One. If you are coming from the south it's the first apartment. So, let's say one."

"Apartment number one."

"Sure. Why not?"

"Our next service appointment is not until next Friday."

After the call, Clara walked into the studio to pick up some cards to prepare the opening of her show. Seth was in the driver's seat with the headphones hanging down on his shoulders. He was swiveling around in the chair while somehow managing to avoid getting twisted up in his own headphone cord.

"I don't think I am ever going to have a phone," Clara said.

Seth stopped swiveling and put the headphones on his ears. "Stand by." (Stand by is "shut up" in radio.) Clara closed the door behind her and stood still. Seth flipped on the microphone, causing the speakers in the studio to go silent. "Monday Monday on RTV on this Monday Monday."

Al was in the news studio across the hall. From the driver's seat Seth could look out the window and see Al or look to his left and see Bill, in his spot in the guest seat which was wedged into a corner behind the reel-to-reel player. Al and Bill could not see each other.

"This solid gold oldie was brought to you by Saturn Appliance Repair," Seth said. "Bill, have you ever noticed there are no good Wednesday songs? When was the last time you found yourself humming a really catchy Wednesday song?"

"Never," said Bill.

"We have another special guest in the studio this morning," Seth said, turning to face Clara. He waved her over to the mike. Clara shook her head and waved her hands in front of her.

"Clara Jane is here in the studio. Say hello, Clara."

"Hello, Clara," she said. Bill was at the only guest mike, so Clara had to lean in and speak into Seth's mike. She had no headphones, so she did not know how her voice sounded.

"I hope you've been listening to her show," Seth said, "10-2. She's our newest, what do you like to be called jock, announcer, air talent?"

"How about air hostess," said Al from the news booth. To a radio listener, Al sounded lively and engaged in the conversation. In reality, he was more intent on arranging the pages of the copy for his next news broadcast.

Clara leaned in to Seth's microphone again. "Nothing special," she said, "Empress of the Airways is fine." Seth's lips stretched into his distinctive narrow smile and his eyes grew wide.

"Clara has just moved in," he said, "I understand you're having trouble getting your phone hooked up."

"I am having trouble getting my phone hooked up."

"Why won't they give you a phone?" asked Bill.

"They don't like my address for some reason."

"Of course," Seth said, "I mean, on that side of town. How can you trust people out there with a telephone? Imagine all of the nefarious things you could do."

"Call and ask people if their refrigerator is running," Bill chimed in.

"Do you have Prince Albert in a can?" Al asked.

"Don't listen to them, Phone Company," Clara said. "If you're listening, I promise I will not make any crank calls. At this point I'll take a rotary dial if that's all you've got."

"Or one of those party lines where you had to crank the phone," Bill said.

"Two cans and a piece of string," Clara said.

"You know what?" Seth said, "After the news, I'm going to play a telephone song. What's a good one? "Jim Croce, 'Operator.'"

"Is that to make me jealous?"

"That's exactly why. Stay tuned, we'll have Jim Croce coming up, and then the Clara Jane show, but first, Bill, what's it going to be like outside today?"

"Well, there will be cars driving by, people going in and out of stores..."

"I meant in the weather, Bill."

"Oh, the weather. Why didn't you say so?" Seth hit the cart with the Weather Center music bed and Bill spoke: "This RTV Weather Center forecast is brought to you by Jeff Wilson Lincoln Mercury Dealers. Expect cloudy skies for most of the day, breezy with occasional light showers. This will be more of a mist than a downpour." Seth glanced out the window to the bank clock and wrote the current temperature on a scrap of paper. He handed it to Bill, who was not at the right angle to see the sign himself. "High temperatures today will be around 78 degrees. Right now in Saturn and vicinity," Bill glanced at the paper. "It's 70 degrees."

"Thanks, Bill," Seth said, turning to his right to see if Al was ready. "So Al, what are the latest headlines from Saturn?"

As Al read a story about the local library board meeting, Seth jumped up and took the Jim Croce LP from the rack. It took him only a few seconds to cue it up. By the time Al finished his morning report, Seth was back in his chair. He fired the turntable and over the introduction said, "This one is for you Clara. Jim Croce, 'Operator.' It's Saturn's Favorite Music, RTV."

When the On Air light went off, Seth turned to Clara. "That was great. We should do more of that. What do you think Bill?"

Bill was on his way out the door to start recording weather inserts for the later day parts. "It's fine with me," he said.

Seth walked out of the studio, "Hey Al," he called out, "What do you think of having Clara do some cross talk each morning when she comes in?"

"I'm busy," he replied and shut the door of studio B.

"He loves the idea," Seth said. "Come here," he said, and led Clara to Ed's office. Ed was reading *The Star*. His face flushed as set the paper down.

"Did you hear the bit with Clara?" Seth asked.

"What bit?"

"The stuff about the phone."

"It wasn't a bit," Clara said.

"What do you think?" Seth asked, "I'd like to do more of that. Have Clara do more cross talk when she comes in. Give it that major market sidekick feel."

"It's fine with me," Ed said, "Might carry some of the audience over." He looked to Clara, "There's no extra pay for it. It's up to you."

"I'll get another guest mike in there." Seth gave Clara a friendly punch on the shoulder. "Welcome to the morning show."

Five Hands

When Clara arrived at the station, Leslie was at her desk holding up a copy of the *Weekly World News*. "It's tabloid day!" she said, shaking the paper from side to side.

"Space Aliens Meet with Ross Perot!" Clara read. "And it has an exclamation point, so it must be true. Speaking of tabloid day..." Clara opened her flannel shirt to reveal the t-shirt underneath. It was a reproduction of the tabloid's "Bat Boy" cover.

"That's amazing," Leslie said. "Only you could pull that look off."

"Put those away. You know Norton doesn't like seeing tabloids lying around." Ed had come up the hall from the kitchen and stopped just behind Clara, who had not heard his approach. She jumped and gave out a little scream.

"You've got to stop doing that," Clara said. Then to Leslie, "He's like a stealth program director."

Leslie hid the tabloids away in her desk. "The owner, Mr. Norton, is coming to the station tomorrow."

Ed was staring at Clara's shirt. "Look, I don't have a problem most of the time with your... self-expression, but tomorrow when Mr. Norton is here, would you mind dressing a little more..."

"Less Bat Boy?"

"Yes, please." Ed continued into his office.

Leslie leaned over her desk and said in a stage whisper, "Ed gets anxious when the owner comes in."

"Why is he coming in?"

"I don't know. That's above my pay grade. If I find out though, I'll let you know." Clara heard banging on the studio window. She turned and saw that Seth was gesturing for her to come into the booth. She walked into the studio as the song was fading and sat at the microphone Seth had set up especially for her.

"That was the Little River Band with 'Cool Change' on your light rock, more music station," Seth said. "It's 9:37, and walking into the studio now is someone cool."

"For a change," Al chimed in.

"It's Clara Jane, also known as CJ the DJ, the coolest DJ on our air." Seth pushed a button, and a cart with an applause effect played. "Say hi to the people, CJ."

"Hi, people."

"What am I, chopped liver?" asked Bill.

"You're the coolest meteorologist on our air," Seth said.

"I'm the only meteorologist on our air."

"Bill is cool," Clara said. "His street name is Cold Front."

"Thank you, Clara," Bill said.

"I'm secretly cool," Seth said, looking at Clara.

"Secretly cool?"

"People meet me and they don't realize I'm cool. It's not visible on the outside."

"It's a very well-kept secret," Bill said.

"That's the idea," said Seth. "I try to be stealth about it. Stealth cool."

"Stealth cool. That sounds like a jazz record," said Clara.

"It does, doesn't it?" said Seth. "Well, we don't have any jazz coming up, I'm afraid, but we do have Rod Stewart, Wilson Phillips and Sting."

"What more could you ask for?" asked Clara.

"Was that a rhetorical question?" Seth asked.

"Would I ask you a rhetorical question?"

"Good one," Al said.

"Well, we've got all that plus the RTV traffic report, right after this," Seth said. He hit a commercial cart, and one by one each of the announcers switched off their microphones and the "On Air" light went off. As soon as it did, Leslie entered the room. She pointed at a flashing line on hold on the telephone.

"I've got a lost pet on the line, who wants to take it?"

"CJ can get it," said Seth, as he fired the next commercial.

Clara came out from behind the guest mic and picked up a lost pet form. It was a photocopied sheet with spaces for the type of animal, its color, whether it is was male or female, its name, and then lines for the name, address and phone number of the person who had lost it. As Seth started the recorded traffic report on the reel-to-reel player, Clara pushed the button to put the caller through the speaker phone so she could have her hands free to fill out the form.

"I'd like to report a lost pet," the caller said.

"OK."

"It's a bay mare, five hands."

"So, it's a horse?"

"Yes, it's a bay mare, five hands."

"What color is it?"

"It's a bay mare"

"Oh right"

"And she's lactating."

"So, it's a female?"

"I said it's a mare."

"That's right, you did. Um how big is it?"

"It's a bay mare, five hands... Can you say lactating on the air?"

Seth had his hand over his mouth so the caller would not hear him laughing. When she got off the phone, Clara handed him the lost pet report. "They didn't teach you about farm animals at broadcast school?" Seth asked, finally releasing his suppressed laugh.

"Pets are dogs and cats. Maybe a gold fish."

"You know," Bill said with a pensive expression, "we don't get a lot of lost fish reports. I wonder why that is."

"You could leave the bowl somewhere," Clara said.

"Do you go out walking your fish a lot in Detroit?" Seth asked.

"Only on Wednesdays."

"You might want to learn a little bit about horses," Bill said.

"It's not very rock n' roll, is it?" Clara asked.

"I don't know," Seth said. "I was in 4-H when I was a kid. It was fun." Clara was afraid to ask if Seth grew up on a farm. His answer could force her to re-examine her pre-conceived ideas about Seth or about farmers, and she didn't want to do either.

"You were a 4-H kid?" she asked.

"Sure. We even got to name a cow."

"What did you name it?" Clara asked.

"It doesn't matter."

"Oh, this is interesting," Bill said, "What did you name the cow?"

"Just a cow name," Seth said.

"Which was?" Clara asked.

"Bessie," Seth said.

"Bessie?" Bill asked.

"Bessie the cow?" Clara asked.

"Yes," Seth said.

"You really named your cow Bessie?" Bill asked.

"We were kids."

"So creativity, that wasn't one of the merit badges," Clara said.

"That's Boy Scouts," Seth said, "Boy Scouts have the badges."

"Bessie," Clara said, shaking her head.

"Hey, at least I know what a cow is, city girl."

"That's the one with spots that gives you milk, right?

"Very good," Bill said. "And a bay mare?"

"I don't know," Clara said, "but apparently it has a lot of hands."

Seth played a liner, and then hit play on the first CD player. Wilson Philips' "Hold On" came through the speakers. Seth then picked up a piece of paper from the console and handed it to Clara. "Can you pin that up on the board?" He pointed to the bulletin board next to the door where notices were posted. Clara looked at the paper. It was a photocopy of a quote from Alice in Wonderland.

But I don't want to go among mad people,' Alice remarked.

'Oh, you can't help that,' said the Cat: 'we're all mad here. I'm mad. You're mad.'

'How do you know I'm mad?' said Alice.

'You must be,' said the Cat, 'or you wouldn't have come here.'

Clara shrugged and pinned it to the board. Al nudged her out of the way in order to come into the room and hand Seth a reel-to-reel tape. Ed came up behind him. There was a small traffic jam at the door. "It's crowded in here," Ed said.

"I have to record the midday report," Al said, and ducked back out of the room, creating a space for Ed. "Look," Ed said, "I just came in to remind everyone that Mr. Norton is coming in tomorrow. So could you please be on your best behavior?"

Seth gave a mildly mocking salute.

"OK, good talk," Ed said, turning to leave. He spotted the Alice in Wonderland sign on the board and tore it down on his way out.

"He seems worried about Mr. Norton coming in. Is he scary?"

"No," Bill said, "I've always gotten along with him."

"He doesn't come in much," Seth said. "Just pops in from time to time to remind us that he owns us."

"He doesn't own us, he owns the station," said Bill.

"You say tomato," Seth said; then to Clara he added, "We try to act like adults for a little while when he comes in. It's mostly to make Ed look good."

"Strong leader," Bill said. Then he and Seth laughed. Clara didn't get the joke.

"The problem with people like Ed is they think being mad is a bad thing," Seth said. He tore a blank sheet of paper from the back of the log and, with a sharpie, wrote "Madness is Cool" in big letters. Before he left for the day, he pinned the sign to the bulletin board.

Later that afternoon, in the last hour of Clara's show, Ed walked in and asked if he could take the boxes with the music cards. He carried the boxes into the back room, and a moment later came back in and tore the "Madness is Cool" sign down. He left the studio door open, and Clara could hear Rad's voice.

"See this is what I told you," he said. "Seth isn't following the card system. Look, I've been recording the shows and keeping a journal of what he plays. He's just skipping songs he doesn't like and putting them in the back of the box without playing them." Clara could not hear Ed's response.

Line 2

Clara listened to the station as she drove to work. She usually pulled into the parking lot just as the "solid gold oldie" was playing, which was about 20 minutes before the top of the hour when her airshift began. As she parked, she heard the opening cackle of The Surfaris' "Wipeout." Instead of immediately turning off the car, she sat drumming on the steering wheel for a moment. When she entered the station, she found Leslie was also drumming along on her desk. "Hey," she said, giving a little wave. As Clara walked into the back room she caught Ed in his office out of the corner of her eye. He had a pen in each hand and was absentmindedly playing air cymbals.

Clara set her purse on her desk and walked into the studio just as the second drum solo began. Bill was behind the guest mic, and Seth was leaning over in his direction. They were both drumming on the desk near the guest mic, far enough from the turntable to keep the vibration from traveling over to the record. Clara burst out laughing.

"What?" Seth asked.

"Everybody's drumming. Leslie, Ed."

"You can't help it with this song." Bill said. When the last drum solo rolled around, Seth stood up and looked out the window at Leslie's desk.

He mimed the drums in the air to Leslie, who did her own drum solo back to him as Bill hammered out the rhythm on the desk. There was no surface that Clara could hit without risking the record skipping on the air so she could only watch and laugh.

When the song ended, Seth turned to Clara, "Why the librarian look?"

Clara had come in dressed in her interview power suit, "I wanted to look serious for the big visit by the boss."

"So that's your best-behavior suit," Seth said.

"Yeah," Clara said. Seth already had cards laid out in front of him for the last tracks of his show. "Do you mind if I take the cards?" Clara gestured towards the wooden boxes.

"Go ahead," he said.

Clara took one of the boxes out of the studio and set it on her desk then went back into the studio to collect the second. "Can you hand me the 10 AM clock hour?" Seth reached up and opened the three- ring binder on the stand in front of him, slipping out the midday page and handing it to Clara. "Here you go. We're about to go to break, so in or out."

Clara quickly left the studio and closed the door behind her. As Seth, Bill and Al bantered about traffic and weather, Clara started picking out cards for her first "Superstar Seven in a Row." By the time she had selected her songs, the morning show was wrapping up. Al had already run out of the news booth into the production studio. Bill headed into the production studio to record an updated weather forecast onto the RTV weather line.

"That's it for me for this Friday," Seth said. "Clara Jane, CJ the DJ, is coming up next to take you through your morning." The intro of the next track began to play under Seth's voice. "I'll leave you with a change in tempo from some real rockers, Extreme, 'More than Words.' See you on Monday." The vocals began and the ON AIR light went off. Clara picked up one of the wooden boxes, balancing it on her left arm. She used her free hand to pick up the stack of cards she had selected and the clock hour and took them back into the studio. Seth was making a note on the card for Extreme.

"Excuse me," Clara said, squeezing around him to put the box back in their corner. As she did she brushed his arm. There was a small shock. With all of the electronic equipment, the studios were always prone to static. "Sorry," Clara said.

"Shocking," Seth said, moving away from the chair. Clara responded with an artificial laugh. "It's all yours," Seth said, pointing to the console.

"Thanks," Clara said. She picked up the last of Seth's cards and put them into the back of their respective categories in the box. She clipped the clock hour back into its place in the binder, and then stacked the cards she had selected on the console in front of her so the names and letters of each were visible. As she went to the CD rack to pick out the A, Seth asked, "Have you heard any of Extreme's non-wimpy stuff? The guitarist can shred."

"Not my thing," she said, removing the disc from its plastic case and placing it in the CD player. "That guitar virtuoso stuff, too much showing off."

Seth walked out of the studio for a moment and came back with the second card box. He leaned in and set it beside the other box.

"Thanks," Clara said.

"If you could do that, wouldn't you show off?"

"Oh totally, but that doesn't make me want to listen to it. I actually like this song though. I like the sentiment. Reminds me of that song off the Martin Gore EP, 'In a Manner of Speaking.' Do you know it?"

"Who's Martin Gore?"

"Depeche Mode."

"British synth pop isn't exactly my core competency. We might be from different musical planets."

"What's your planet?"

"Planet classic rock, British invasion, Motown. I like a lot of different stuff. What's your planet?"

"Not Saturn."

"If you could slip one thing on the air, what would it be?"

"Hmm. Maybe Nirvana, 'Lithium.'"

"That would blow their minds."

"What about you?"

"The Kinks. 'Shangri-La.'"

"I don't know that one."

"What? Heresy. You must be educated. I'm going to make you a Kinks tape."

"OK. And I'll make you a tape of my stuff."

"Deal."

Clara hit the start button on the CD, then fired a cart to play the legal ID over the introduction to Elton John's "The One."

"You're right about the As," Clara said. "I would be happy if I never heard this song again in my life."

"Yeah, most people only listen to the radio for a little while on their commute or something. We're the only poor saps who have to listen to it for hours at a time day after day." Seth had glanced through Clara's cards, and he went over to the rack of 45s, pulled out the C and handed it to Clara who started to cue it up. Through the window she saw a short man in a tan suit enter the lobby.

"Is that him?" Clara asked, taking off her headphones.

"That's the boss man," Seth said.

"He's shorter than I pictured him."

Seth leaned back against LP rack. "So has Rad still been giving you a hard time?"

"Actually, I think he's letting up on me. I think you're his new target."

"Me?"

"He said he's keeping a log of what you play and checking it against the cards." Clara had enjoyed the gossip about Rad, and she expected Seth to make a joke about this. Instead, he shook his head and looked disgusted. She had, unknowingly, struck a nerve and she instantly regretted sharing the information.

"What a little weasel," Seth said. "He knows absolutely nothing about putting together a morning show. You know when I started out, I worked at an AOR station. We had some freedom. There were some things we had to play, but you could throw in all kinds of stuff, album cuts, whatever you thought the audience would like. Now you've got Rad pitching a fit if you shuffle the cards a little bit. They want to take away even the tiniest bit of creativity and dumb it all down. You know they used to call the AC format 'chicken rock'."

"Really? Why?" Clara took a cart of the rack of liners and slotted it into the board. She then sat down in the chair. Seth stopped talking as Clara performed a cross fade from the A to the C. As she made notes on the A and C cards, Seth continued the conversation as though there had been no interruption.

"Not sure," he said. "Maybe because they're chickens. They're afraid of anything too loud, too sexy, too political. I can't believe Rad. You're not going to play ballad after ballad on a morning show. Who's inspired to jump out of bed by Air Supply? If Rad had his way, we'd put everyone to sleep and no one would show up for work. The whole economy would break down."

"I know your show is popular and all," Clara said, "But you don't think you might be overestimating your power a little bit?" She got up from the chair, and stepped towards Seth, who was blocking the path to the LP she needed. She gestured for him to move aside.

Seth chuckled, "I'm pretty sure I cause the sun to rise. I come in to the station, no sun. I start talking, the sun comes up."

Clara selected her album and put it on the turntable. "The sun comes up on Sunday too doesn't it?"

"It's a fluke."

"Ah, OK. Well, I'm sure you're right."

"That's just science."

As Clara started to cue the next track, Leslie appeared in the door. "Seth, there's a call for you from Helen on line two." Seth rolled his eyes and let out a heavy sigh.

Clara stood aside for Seth to pick up the phone. He shook his head. "I'll take it in the newsroom," he said. Leslie and Seth left the studio and Clara closed the door behind them. No sooner had she sat down than she started to hear voices. At first she thought it must be coming from the back room, but the door was closed, and everything was soundproofed. She looked at the board, but there was nothing potted up that should not be.

"I really need that document," said a female voice.

"I looked. I haven't got it." That voice was Seth. Through the window, Clara could see Leslie was standing and looking up at the speaker. After a moment, she started running toward the back room.

"Well, you must have it." said the woman's voice.

"Why would I lie to you?"

Clara stood up and in a panic started touching the pots to see if something was in cue. Nothing. She started to sweat. She looked through the window to the news booth and saw Seth on the phone. She ran to the door, and as she opened it she saw Leslie running to the news booth.

"If you can just find it, we don't have to keep having these conversations," the woman said.

Leslie threw open the news booth door and started pointing, "You're on the air." The conversation stopped. Ed ran into the studio, "What is going on?" Mr. Norton was standing in the back room with his arms folded across his chest.

"I don't know," Clara said. She could feel tears welling in her eyes. "The news studio isn't potted up. I don't know how that got on the air. Seth went in the newsroom to take the call and all of a sudden..."

Ed left the studio. Clara went over to the side window and saw Ed walk into the news booth. She could not hear anything, but she could see Seth holding the receiver and Ed and Seth gesturing at each other. While this was going on, Clara looked through the front window and saw Mr. Norton leave the station. A few minutes later, Ed came back into the studio followed by Leslie. His face was red. "Where is Mr. Norton?" he asked.

"I think he left," Clara said.

"Great," Ed shouted, and stormed back to his office. Leslie came into the room, and shut the studio door behind her.

"Well, that was interesting," she said.

"I don't know how that happened."

"I don't think it's your fault," Leslie said. "Seth said it was something in studio B."

"Stand by," Clara said. "I have to do a break." Leslie stood still as Clara put on her headphones and opened the mic. "Your light rock more music station, Saturn's Favorite Music, RTV. Good morning, I'm Clara Jane and I hope you are enjoying our first Superstar Seven in a Row of the day. It's 10:12 and 73 degrees, we're going to have a beautiful sunny day ahead, so keep it here for a great summer soundtrack. Curtis Stigers, The Doobie Brothers and Swing Out Sister are all on the way, but right now it's the Bangles and their cover of 'Hazy Shade of Winter.'" Clara flipped off the microphone and took off her headphones. She picked up the next card, then turned to Leslie, "Who was that on the phone anyway?"

Leslie lowered her voice, "His ex-wife."

"Oh my god."

The door opened and Seth walked in, "That was embarrassing."

"I'm sorry," Clara said, "I don't know what I..."

"It wasn't you," Seth said, "Al left the phone up after his interview with the head of the board of supervisors."

"Come here," Leslie said. She gave Seth a hug. Separating, she rubbed his shoulder. "I don't think anyone actually heard what you were saying."

"No," Clara lied.

Seth rubbed his forehead. "I don't know why she keeps calling me at work."

Clara was caught off guard as "Hazy Shade of Winter" ended cold. "Ahh," she said, running back to the board to fire the next track.

"Come on," Leslie said, "Let's go talk at my desk and let Clara do her show."

Clara watched Seth and Leslie through the window. Seth kept looking down and shaking his head. They spoke for about five minutes before Seth left for the day. An hour later, Ed came into the studio and asked Clara to pull the last card Seth had played from the back of the box.

"Who played that song last before Seth?" Ed asked.

"I did," Clara said.

"And who played it before that?"

Clara felt a knot in the pit of her stomach. She had played the track out of sequence. Two other airshifts should have played the song before she played it again in her time slot, but it had been played twice in her daypart. Clara still believed she had been responsible for putting Seth's call on the air and she could not bear the thought of being in trouble again, so she lied.

"Well, they were both in my shift, but this one," she pointed a shaky finger at the card, "that isn't my handwriting. Someone else must have played it."

Ed looked at the card. It was an incompetent lie. He should have been able to see that the handwriting in both squares was the same. "Is it Seth's writing?" he asked.

"I- I don't know."

"I knew it," Ed said. "Seth wrote that in there so he could play it again. Rad was right. He's fudging the cards."

"Rad?" Clara said, "No, I don't think..."

Ed took the card and left the studio.

That night Clara, once again, found it hard to sleep. She didn't understand herself. She had to believe she was a good person, a person with integrity. Yet she had let someone else take the blame for what she had done, and why? To avoid being scolded, a little discomfort that would have lasted a moment. She tried to justify her actions to herself. She had not said Seth played the track out of sequence. She had not actually put the blame on anyone else. Ed had done that himself. Her crime was just that she did not correct him. It was an innocent lie. She hadn't known, at that moment, that Seth was Ed's target. But now she did know. There was only one answer. She would have to go in and tell the truth. But she ruminated over what that would mean. She could not help but imagine the worst case scenario. She understood her own mind, and how she had been pressed by circumstances, how she panicked. To everyone else, she would just be a liar. Would she ever be trusted again?

Counting Them Down with Casey Casem

After her shift on Friday, the Michigan Bell workers finally showed up to install Clara's phone. After almost a month, Clara's apartment was starting to shape up. In addition to her real bed and telephone, she had managed to secure a used couch, a coffee table and a table cloth to cover the burn on her card table. She should have felt settled and secure, but she couldn't shake the feeling that this was all for nothing because she was about to be fired over her lie about the cards.

Clara tried to distract herself by calling her Harrison School friend Julie. "Clara! Tell me about your glamorous radio life!"

Clara felt an obligation to present herself as a success, but she had little "glamour" to report, only stress. At the modern rock station where she interned Clara had met rock stars, she'd been given free concert tickets, she even once helped emcee a punk fashion show. At RTV, she had not even received a coupon for a free pizza. Clara decided to tell Julie about Seth inviting her to speak on the morning show.

"That is so cool," Julie said. "I'm so jealous. But if you can do it, maybe the rest of us will too. So what is it like up there?"

"Oh, yeah," Clara said. "It's nice. The weather has been nice. The air is clean. It's where people go to get away from it all, you know."

In truth Clara knew very little about her adopted town. Each day she drove from her apartment to the studio, and the buildings along that stretch of Saturn were all that she saw. As far as she knew, Saturn consisted entirely of the inside of the grocery store and Hollywood Video.

"So what is happening in Detroit?" Clara asked.

"Oh, not much," Julie said. "A bunch of us are going to Lollapalooza tomorrow at Pine Knob."

Clara was, at that moment, wearing the Nine Inch Nails t-shirt she had bought at the first Lollapalooza a year before. It had been an eye-opening experience for her. She had never realized how many misfits there were who loved the kind of music mainstream radio rarely played. The experience had sparked her imagination and left her vibrating on a higher plane for a week. "Lollapalooza?" she said, "I didn't think you liked alternative music."

"I don't really," said Julie. "But there's a whole group going."

"Who's playing?"

"You know, I don't even know," Julie said. "For me it's more about who's going than what we're seeing."

By the time Clara hung up the phone, her old life seemed impossibly distant, yet her new life seemed equally out of reach, hidden somewhere over the horizon. Clara sat on her couch looking out the window. The room was quiet, no music and liners, no news feeds, no cheery voices selling cars, just silence. "Dead air," Clara thought.

Clara worked six days a week. The morning team had a full weekend, which meant that her schedule was slightly different on Saturdays. Her shift started two hours earlier than it did during the week, after a teen-aged part-timer who ran the board from 5-8. Saturday was a leisurely day. Clara packed a small black backpack with snacks and a book. When she arrived, the lobby was dark, illuminated only by the glow coming from the broadcast studio. After the part-timer handed the studio off to her, Clara was all alone in the building.

Clara dug through the box with the music cards to find a long Al Stewart song. She found the card for "The Year of the Cat" first. Because she was in at a different daypart than usual, she needed to look at the 6-10 time slot to see if she could play it. Seth had played it three weeks before, and Rad two days ago, so one more shift had to play it before it could run again in what was normally Seth's slot. She dug around until she found "Time Passages." Grant had played it last and she had played it the week before. So, it was good to go in Seth's slot. Clara had never heard of Al Stewart before she started at RTV, and she found it hard to believe his music had ever been cool. It was, however, long, which made it popular with the staff. Clara suspected that the trend towards long songs in the 1970s had something to do with lazy DJs wanting to take naps. Clara pulled a packet of Pop Tarts out of her bag. She had time to go to the back room, heat them in the microwave, come back and eat half of one before she had to hit a liner and fire her next song. Clara sucked the crumbs off her fingers and put the "B" in the CD machine.

Clara took out a stack of the cards from the C and D sections and started looking through them. She noticed that there were songs that Seth almost never played. He avoided Air Supply, Captain and Tennille and Abba, among others. With only four airshifts, if one jock decided not to play something, it could slow down its circulation for months as two of the other shifts waited for the third to play it. This observation brought back Clara's anxiety. As a form of penance, she decided to help Seth by playing as many of his hated tracks as she could between the hours of 8 and 10.

"Barry Manilow and 'I Write the Songs' on Saturn's Favorite Music, RTV. Coming up another Superstar Seven in a Row and we're counting down to Casey's Countdown at 10 O'clock. Don't go anywhere."

Casey's Countdown was the best part of Saturday. It came from the Westwood One Radio Network on a set of four CDs. The first three were for each hour of the three-hour broadcast. The last CD was full of liners and the five-minute Casey's Biggest Hits feature, the same one she had played twice in a row on her first show. She separated the bonus disc from the others and put it in its slot next to the liner rack.

Clara flattened out the log that came with the discs. The program was divided up into ten 18-minute segments each with a couple of songs and a block of national commercials. At the top of the hour, Clara fired the legal ID and then the first CD. The dramatic opening music of the countdown began to play. Clara looked ahead to her next local break and slotted the corresponding carts into the board. She would now have a good eight minutes until she had to return to the studio. She took her book out of her backpack and plopped down on the orange couch.

The gates at Lollapalooza were probably just opening. There would be a local opener who would not be getting enough love, and a sea of young people finding their places, dressed up and dressed down for each other. Clara's friends would probably not have sprung for the theater seats and would be putting down a blanket on the hill.

Clara opened her copy of Anais Nin's *Henry and June*. It had a cover tying it into the film of the same name, which Clara had found artistic and sexy. Nin's life did not resemble Clara's, but her thoughts were familiar. They made Clara feel less alone. "I seek life," Nin wrote, "and the experiences I want are denied me because I carry in me a force which neutralizes them."

Clara did not aspire to the kind of erotic freedom Anais Nin craved, but she shared her longing to be more fully alive. "I am a woman!" she wanted to say. "I enjoy being alive and I'm not ashamed!" She believed the Clara who longed for passion and adventure was her true self, but was it? Or was she really the person who hid behind a microphone and watched movies about other people's adventures as she let her life pass by? Could both be true?

Clara found herself thinking about Seth and wondering about his ex-wife. She wondered what she looked like and how they had met. This reminded her that Seth would probably hate her soon. She took some deep breaths. It was Saturday. She had another full day before she had to confront that. She would try to stay calm.

The first national commercial started to play, and Clara put a bookmark in the page and walked back to the studio. She sat down as the last spot was playing. "1-800-Operator. There's no cheaper price for a long distance call from payphones." Then there was a four-note Casey Casem

97

sting. Clara hit pause on the CD and played the local spots. When the last of the local spots had run, she unpaused the CD and went back to her book.

The next song on the countdown was by the squeaky-clean Amy Grant. "I can't believe I'm missing Pearl Jam and Jesus and Mary Chain for this," Clara thought.

The Cards

Clara woke up on Monday feeling nauseous. She considered calling in sick, but she knew that would only postpone the confrontation. On her drive into work, she imagined Seth yelling at her, "Why did you tell Ed that I fudged the card?" Clara steeled herself as she walked into the studio.

"Hey CJ the DJ," Seth said with a broad smile, "I made you a tape." He tossed a cassette tape to her.

"Wow, already?"

"I said I was going to."

"Did Ed say anything?

"About what? Hold on," he said, putting on the headphones. Seth went into a break. Coming out he said, "9:54 on your light rock, more music station RTV, playing Saturn's Favorite Music, like this one from Billy Joel."

Billy Joel's "A Matter of Trust," usually opens with a countdown that goes "one, two; one, two, three, four." But it had a skip in the introduction; it skipped in just the right spot for the opening to become "one, two, three, four." Seth and Clara looked at each other and both broke out laughing.

"That was amazing," Seth said. "I don't think we should tell Rad it skips."

"No," Clara said, "It's just so perfect."

"RTV has its own, exclusive version of 'A Matter of Trust,'" Seth said. "It exists on RTV and nowhere else on earth. Let's see how long it takes Rad to notice."

By then Seth had forgotten Clara's question about Ed, and Clara did not bring it back up. "Have a good show," he said as he left the studio.

Clara started preparing her show. Looking forward in the log, she saw that she would need to run a contest that involved putting callers on the air to answer trivia questions. She looked through the window and saw Seth about to leave the building. She ran out of the studio. "Seth," she shouted as she rounded the corner, "Hey, Seth, can you help me? I've never run this contest before. I don't know how to put phone calls on the air."

"Well, I'm the expert in that," he said, returning to the studio, and between records he tutored her in the mechanics.

"So you don't want to put a caller on the air accidentally, right?"

"Yes, we've established that."

"Right, so that's why you have a toggle here under the board. If you want to pot up the call, first you have to switch this toggle. Once you've done that, you just pot it up like any other source. You'll hear the caller over the air and they'll hear you over the air. Be sure you do it in the right order. If you try to toggle on when you've already potted up you'll get feedback, and probably dump the caller."

Clara nodded with her brow furrowed. "OK, pot down, toggle on, pot up, caller on air."

"You got it. Now this is important: Remember to switch the toggle back after." Clara laughed. "So you take caller ten, or really whatever caller, and just call them number ten." He reached behind the binder with the clock hours and pulled out a pocket folder. The pages inside were lists of contests with names of winners and dates. "Be sure to check against this log. This is all the people who have won each week. They can only win once every 30 days. The contest geeks will mark their calendars and call exactly 30 days later. You'll see the same names a lot. Like Jason Briggs, who won yesterday, he's a 30-day guy. So before you put them on the air, make sure they're eligible. This cart has the music samples...."

Through the window, Clara saw Ed walking into the studio. He looked at the booth and pointed at Seth, then started walking with purpose. He appeared in the studio door a moment later holding a song card. He waved it at Seth.

"At the end of your show yesterday, did you play this?"

Seth took the card from Ed's hand. "It looks like it," he said, "Yeah."

"Um, Clara said, "This contest is about to come up..."

Ed ignored her and continued on his mission. "Look," he said, pointing to the grid on the card. "This is not Clara's handwriting."

"And?"

"Are you doctoring the cards to play what you want?"

"We're busy here," Seth said sensibly.

"Just look at the card," Ed said.

"What's the problem? Two shifts played it before me."

"Two of the same shift."

"Why is that my problem?"

"Hey, um," Clara said, "the song is going to end here soon."

Ed grabbed Seth's arm and pulled him into a corner, as far from the mike as he could get, which was not very far. "We have a format for a reason," he said. "Just because you have the highest rated show doesn't mean the rules don't apply to you."

"OK, first of all," Seth said, "I'm not doctoring the cards. Where did this come from?"

"Rad has been keeping a log of what you're playing. He says you're not following the format."

"Rad. You've got to be kidding me."

"Stand by," Clara said, but no one stood by.

"Rad is the music director," Ed said.

"Stand by!" she shouted, then put on her headphones. "That was Richard Marx on Saturn's Favorite Music, RTV. It's 10:23. I'm glad you're listening because it's time for the song of the day contest brought to you by Cal's Carpet Cleaning." She flipped through the binder looking for the right copy. "Cal's Carpet Cleaning..." She could not find the page with the commercial tag line. "The... sponsor of this contest. I'm going to take caller ten right now on the RTV contest line." She fired turntable 2. The phone line had already started lighting up as she spoke over the musical introduction. "Give us a call now for your chance to win." She turned off the microphone.

Clara answered the phone. "Hello, you're caller 10," she said to the woman on the line. She could hear Seth in the background, "Rad is a sniveling suck up who has nothing better to do than monitor other's people's shows. Anyway, you told me when I came here that I would have autonomy."

"Um, if you can just hold the line," Clara said to the caller, "I'll put you on the air at the end of this song." She put the line on hold. Then to herself she muttered, "if I can figure out how."

"You're not helping things by undermining his authority."

"Can you guys get out of here, please?" Clara called over her shoulder.

The two men left the studio. Clara was shaken. She started shuffling through papers, trying to find the contest rules. Her hand shook as she flipped the toggle under the console. The record was running closer and closer to its inner groove. Clara took a deep breath, and tensed as she potted up the phone line, ready for the high pitched squeal of feedback. There was none.

"Supertramp 'Take the Long Way Home' on Your Light Rock, More Music Station RTV. Hi, you're caller number 10- what is your name?"

"Carol." She was there!

"OK, Carol, for your chance to win free carpet cleaning from Cal's Carpet Cleaners, I'm going to play you a piece of a song." She reached for the cart with the music samples and realized that Seth had it in his hand when he stormed out to argue with Ed. "...Um, and you'll have to... identify it..." She looked around for anything, any piece of music that she could cue up in a split second, while reading the contest rules to... what was her name? "Are you ready... Carol?"

"Yes, I am, Clara Jane."

"Wonderful!" Wonderful. In a flash of inspiration Clara turned back the song that had just finished and let it roll up right on the air. "Carol- can you name that song?"

"Uh, I know it, I know it, um was it..."

Hadn't she just told everyone what the song was?

"Uh, is it..."

"Oh, I'm sorry Carol, your time is up. Thanks for playing, and keep listening for your next chance to win free carpet cleaning from Cal's Carpet Cleaners on WRTV." She threw in a liner, and as it was running, quickly put a CD into player one. And then Ed and Seth came back in the studio.

"I don't care. I don't care," Seth said, as he put the contest cart down on the console.

"Look, you don't know anything about how to run a business, OK?"

"Stand By!" Clara shouted again. (The "damn it" was merely implied.) With that Ed and Seth left the studio, closing the door behind them. A few moments later, Clara saw Seth storm out the front door.

That evening Clara paced her apartment. She couldn't bring herself to eat anything because her stomach was in knots. She had let it go too far. She had to confess to Ed about the card. She tried to prepare herself again by imagining the worst case scenario. It was not that she would be fired. That would be too easy. The worst case was that she would be allowed to stay but everyone would hate her. She got herself worked up enough that she was flush and felt like she was running a fever. She tried to watch television, but the images on the screen appeared as fuzzy abstractions. She turned off the TV and tried to go to bed, but it was another sleepless night.

The next day Clara took a deep breath before she opened the station door. When she did, she heard laughter. Seth, Bill and Ed were standing around Leslie's desk joking with each other. The song "September" by Earth, Wind and Fire was playing through the speaker.

"Hi, Clara," Leslie said. "We're having a coffee party."

"Does anyone know what the words to this song are?" Bill asked. "I only know it says 'September' because that's the title of the song.

"I think the word 'remember' is in there somewhere," Leslie said. "La di da...da dee dee... Remember... La di da... Da da dee September."

"The word 'in' is in there too," said Bill. "In September."

Through the studio window, Clara saw Al putting a fresh reel on the tape machine. Seth inched back towards the studio, ready to run in when the song ended. Clara was confused. All of that worry, and everything seemed to be back to normal. Seth and Ed bantered together about mis-heard song lyrics until a smiling Ed finally said- "What would your boss say if he caught you all sitting around like this?" Seth and Bill returned to the studio, and Ed went back to his office. Clara was distracted. "I don't get it," she said. She had not quite realized that she was speaking out loud and was surprised when Leslie answered.

"Get what?"

"Well, yesterday I thought Seth and Ed were going to get into a fist fight over the cards, and today it's like nothing."

"It's a penis thing," Leslie said in a stage whisper.

"Oh yeah?"

"Men have to establish dominance."

"Haven't they sorted that out by now?"

"I think sometimes they need to recalibrate."

"Who's winning?"

Leslie looked back and forth to make sure no one else could hear. "Seth," she said. "Definitely Seth. He has a high PIA factor."

"A what?"

"You don't know the PIA factor? It stands for 'Pain in the Ass.' The more valuable you are, the more of a PIA you can be. If you surpass your PIA factor, you get fired. Seth has the top rated morning show in the market, so he has a high PIA factor."

"And me?"

"Well, you're new. Let's just say, I'd try to be agreeable."

Clara shook her head. She was relieved now that she had not made a confession. "It's just weird how everything just blows over."

"You know how it is with men," Leslie said, "They're so emotional."

"Irrational creatures."

"Here," Leslie said, handing Clara a copy of Weekly World News. The headline read "Mom Gives Birth to 12 Babies at One Time." "Some light reading," she said.

"Anything good in it?"

"I like the article about the psychiatrist who says happiness is a form of mental illness. Also there's a follow up on the Ross Perot alien story and a bull that got injured trying to mate with a statue."

"Those are some serious stories." Clara's muscles finally untensed.

"What's it like being in the middle of all that testosterone?" Leslie asked.

"You're here too."

"Yeah, but I'm not a DJ. I'm not competing with them."

"I'm not sure I am either. I don't think they see me as competition. I'm a different category."

"The female voice," Leslie nodded. "When they were filling your slot, Norton said they needed a female voice."

"Right. The guys aren't competing to be that. So I'm over here in my own lane."

"But are you competing with them?"

"Oh, I don't know. Like you said, I'm new. I just want to get better."

Erickson Hardware

"Good morning, 8:30 on Saturn's Favorite Music, RTV. If you're supposed to be at work at 9 and you're still in bed-- GET UP!"

"Nag, nag, nag," Bill said.

"It's my job to nag. It's right in my contract." Seth shuffled some papers. "The radio announcer must nag the public. When it's snowy we say 'drive safely,' when it's late we say 'get out of bed.'"

Seth raised a finger, and then Bill, Clara and Seth said in unison, "Get out of bed."

"That'll do it," said Bill.

"Another thing to nag about," Seth said. "It's election day. Go vote. Who do you think will be the next president?"

"It's a local election, Seth," Clara chimed in.

"Didn't they teach you anything in civics class?" Bill asked.

"Civics class? Listen to Mr. Vocabulary here. I know the Constitution guarantees free speech, which is about what I get paid for it."

"Civics class-- where they explain what different elections are for." Bill said.

Clara jumped in, "In a *presidential* election you vote for the president. A local election is when you stay home and then complain for the next few years about the condition of the roads and the school board your neighbors voted in."

"Don't do that," Bill interjected.

Seth raised his finger again and all three said, "Vote."

"Call me old fashioned," Seth said, "but I'm voting for the Free-Soil party because no matter what any of the Whigs say, slavery is wrong."

"That is old fashioned," Clara said. "Sounds like you should vote for the Know-Nothing party."

"Oh, I always vote for the no nothing party, I don't mean to do it, it just always seems to work out that way."

"Ba-dump-dump," Bill said, imitating a rim shot.

"Tuesday Trivia is coming up in the next half hour," Seth continued. "Your chance to win a free pizza from Arlo's Pizza. Stick around for that. Now it's time for the local traffic report."

Seth simultaneously potted his mike down and hit a button on the reel-to-reel tape which started with a thunk. He closed the mic, and the "on air" light went off.

"Good one," Clara said, taking off her headphones. "Do you think anyone got it?"

"Nope," Seth said.

Seth was already cuing up the next record. As he spun it back he muttered, "Paul is Dead man, miss him, miss him."

"Rumors of Paul's death have been greatly exaggerated," Bill said as he left the studio.

Clara looked over Seth's shoulder at the record he was placing on the turntable. "Oh look. It's the Bloody Moos."

"Hey, I like the Moody Blues!"

"You obviously have no taste."

"What have you got against the Moody Blues?"

"Nothing, except they're boring."

"I used to think this song was "Knights in White Satin," with a K," Seth said when he had finished cuing the record. "You know, like a guy on a horse with a lance all draped in white satin."

"That's why you don't think they're boring," Clara said. "Your lyrics are better."

Seth sat back down. "Did you listen to the tape I gave you? 'Shangri-La'?"

"Yeah, I did," Clara said. "It's interesting; I had to listen to it a few times because I wasn't sure if it was making fun of the guy in his little suburban castle or if it's supposed to be sympathetic to him."

"That's what's so great about it," Seth's face lit up. "You can read it either way. And the music, how it builds and swells. It's just great. The Kinks should have had way more success than they did. Ray Davies writes these little three-minute dramas. Even the stuff we play, like 'Come Dancing'... Actually, I want to play that."

Seth jumped up, took the Moody Blues record off the turntable, and put it back in its sleeve. "Can you find the card for me?" He slotted the Moody Blues back into their place on the shelf and looked for the Kinks album.

"Come Dancing?"

"It should be a C." As Seth picked out the record, Clara thumbed through the file looking for the card. It was about a third of the way from the back.

"You played it last," Clara said.

Seth put the record on the turntable. "Well, I just won't sign the card," he said. He put a finger up to his lips in a "Shhh!" gesture and then cued up the new track.

Seth slid back into his seat just as the traffic feed was ending. He put on the headphones, then used his left hand to toggle on the microphone while he used his right to slot a station liner into the board. He potted up the mic, "Good morning, 8:45 on your light rock, more music station RTV." Clara could see the turntable starting to run, but could not hear the music as Seth spoke over the introduction. "Here's a pop hit about nostalgia for the big band era. It's the Kinks and 'Come Dancing.'" Seth turned off the mic, and the "On Air" light went off.

"You really light up when you talk about the Kinks," Clara said.

"They're up there with the Beatles in my book."

Leslie walked into the studio. She looked uncharacteristically sheepish as she waited for Seth to cue up his next track. "I need you to cut a spot when you're done," she said, handing him some copy and a production slip. Seth looked at the copy. His brow furrowed.

"They asked for me specifically?"

"No," Leslie said. "But it needs to run today, and you're the only one."

"Clara's here," Seth said.

"She's never done one before," Leslie said.

"She has to start some time," Seth said. "I don't need to be the voice of…"

Leslie cut him off, "Yeah, no. Sorry." She handed the copy to Clara. "Congratulations. Your first production."

Clara took the copy, and sat on the orange couch to read it. "The friendly folks at Erickson Hardware would like to remind you that autumn is coming. Erickson has everything you need to make your fall go more smoothly, and right now they're selling all rakes and leaf blowers at 10 percent off. That's right, 10 percent. This deal won't last. Get them before they're gone. Hurry in now to Erickson Hardware, two miles north of the airport in beautiful downtown Saturn." The spot had to time out at exactly :30. At a maximum it could be a second over or under. She practiced reading the text over, modulating her pacing, to get it to come out just right.

From time to time Seth popped his head out of the studio to see if Clara was still practicing and he'd laugh. When Clara got embarrassed enough by this, she went into the production studio where she spent another 15 minutes listening to music beds to find just the right one. Then, in a fit of inspiration, she decided to add a wind effect. In a closet just outside the production studio was a long rack of LPs full of tracks with names like "door slamming," "scissors cutting," and "dog growling." There were entire discs of different laughs and different crowds and three full discs of types of weather. She selected the track called "steady wind under pine" and cued it up.

She cued up the musical track on the CD, ran a reel tape as a backup, just in case, erased a cart and put it in the cart machine. She hit the yellow button which started the record process and placed the stop tone on the tape, hit the green button to start recording then went to hit the CD player when she got a shock. She hit stop on the cart.

She checked her copy again, hit the yellow button on the cart machine and started over. As she read the first line, she fired up the wind effect. The levels were right and the reading went flawlessly. She stopped the recording, satisfied with the performance. When she went to play the spot back, instead of hearing her voice, the cart rolled for a few seconds of silence then stopped. By stopping and starting, Clara had put an extra cue tone on the cart. She hit play again and listened to the result. She thought it was good enough, but she wanted confirmation. She took the cart into the studio and asked Seth if he could listen to it. He glanced up at the clock, and at the time still remaining on the CD on the air. "Sure," he said. He slotted the cart into the board and then put it in cue. He hit play and the false start ran.

"You have an extra cue tone," he said.

"Yeah," Clara said. "I'll redo that."

Seth hit play again and listened to the spot. "No, it's good," he said. "Write 'warning, extra cue tone' on the label. That should be fine."

"So it's OK?"

"Yeah," he said. "It's good. So your first production, how do you feel?"

"I feel like I'm part of the team," Clara said.

"Of course you're part of the team," he said. "You're CJ the DJ." Seth touched Clara on the shoulder as he left for the day.

The Erickson Hardware spot ran for the first time two hours later. A few minutes later, Leslie came into the studio. Clara was taking her meter readings, which involved standing at a giant grey box of a machine that monitored the FM and AM signals. She pushed a button and the meters fell down and sprung up again with a buzz. Clara recorded the values on a log on a clip board.

"I can't believe you know how all this stuff works," Leslie said.

"Well, I know how to work it," Clara said. "I don't really know how it works." She hung the clipboard back up on a nail on the same bulletin board that displayed everyone's operator licenses and then sat back down in the driver's seat to check where she was on the log.

Leslie looked to the left and the right as if someone might suddenly appear to overhear her. "You know that Erickson Hardware?"

Clara's heart skipped a beat. "Yeah?"

Leslie spoke in a stage whisper. "Seth's ex-wife is Mrs. Erickson Hardware."

"Oh, thank God," Clara said. "I thought you were going to tell me something was wrong with the spot."

Leslie laughed. "No, don't worry. It's fine."

"Hold on a second," Clara said. She put a liner into the board and played it as she transitioned from one song to the next, then took the CD out of machine A and put it back in its case.

"Mr. Hardware is 25 years older than her," Leslie said, "and he was married to someone else, too. Small town, big news."

"No wonder he didn't want to do the spot," Clara said. "Wait, Erickson Hardware sponsors Eye Opener Trivia."

"Yep."

"She cheated on him with the hardware guy, and the hardware guy buys spots in Seth's show?" Leslie nodded.

"Harsh."

"To be fair, I think the sponsorship deal came before the... other thing."

"Still."

"He hasn't really dated since then, I don't think," Leslie said.

"That's too bad." Clara was only half listening, making notes on the programming logs and figuring out what to play next. She had to ask Leslie to move so she could put the next song on the turntable. When she had finished, Leslie leaned against the console again.

"We all went to high school together," Leslie said. "Me and Seth. Ed too."

"Really? That's interesting."

"Well, Seth sort of got me the job here," Leslie said.

"Huh. Was Seth popular in school?"

"Not really. I mean, it was a small school. He was really skinny."

"He's skinny now."

"Not like he was then." She made a pulling motion with her hands. "You know how teenage boys are all stretched out. I always thought he looked kind of like a bird, you know, with these skinny little legs and the big beak."

"Wow."

"I mean, I didn't tell him that."

"Good call."

"He was mostly just quiet."

"Quiet? Seth Jones?"

"Most DJs are quiet, don't you think? They'd rather talk to the air than face to face. If you want to have a good time, you need to hang out with the sales people. They're the extroverts."

"Yeah, I can see that."

"Seth got in trouble sometimes though."

"Why?"

"He'd talk back to teachers and stuff. Get sent to the office."

"He was quiet and he mouthed off to teachers? That seems like a contradiction."

"Well, people are contradictory, aren't they?"

"Yeah, I guess so." Clara started pulling the carts with the commercials for her next break and stacking them up on the console.

"You and Seth sound good together," Leslie said. "It seems like you have the same sense of humor."

"Yeah, I think so."

"Hmm," Leslie said.

"What?"

"Well, it's interesting," Leslie flashed a conspiratorial smile. "You asked me what Seth was like in school, but you didn't ask me about Ed."

"Oh, yeah, I guess I didn't. What was Ed like?"

"Good student. He didn't get sent to the office."

"OK, then."

"Interesting," Leslie said again, as she walked out of the studio.

Remote Broadcast

A remote broadcast is when a radio station sends its on-air personalities out with a bunch of equipment to do a show at an outside location. Sometimes a remote is connected to a local event like a county fair, but more often they are elaborate commercials. Businesses book them to drive traffic. The irony is that they are expensive, and the only businesses that can afford them are the kinds with very little impulse shopping, usually car dealerships and furniture stores.

RTV's remotes usually took place on a Saturday, which meant that a relaxing day of watching the board and playing syndicated shows on CD was replaced by an elaborate affair. Everyone grumbled about having to do them, but once everything was set up, they were usually fun. It gave the jocks a chance to meet listeners and play celebrity for a little while.

The Bob James Chevrolet remote was not usual. To begin with, it came as the station was being rampaged by a flu that spread quickly in the airless confines of the radio studios. The on-air voices were dusky, and the banter was punctuated by pauses as the jocks potted down the mic to cough or sniffle. The sales executive who sold a remote usually went along with the talent to make sure everything went well for the client. But the salesman who sold the Bob James remote had a fever of 102, so

Seth loaded up the Incredible Broadcast Machine and headed to the dealership on his own. Clara remained at the station to run the board.

During the remote, Clara would be able to put Seth in cue, and he could speak to her between breaks, but he would only hear her when she spoke on the air. They each had copies of the log to follow. To set up for the remote, Clara had to re-patch the audio board. Once that was set up, broadcasting was a simple matter of potting the remote up on what was normally one of the cart's channels. As she was patching, the phone flashed. Clara picked up the receiver. "WRTV," she said.

"Hey, it's me," Seth said.

Clara cradled the receiver on her shoulder and stretched the cord out to where she was patching the board. "How's it going out there?"

"Everything's set up except for the big RTV banner. I can't find a place to hang it. They have me outside, there's no wall behind me."

Clara finished patching, walked back to the board, and put the pot in cue. "I'm patched; do you want to give me a level?"

"Testing," Seth said. There was a sharp whistle. Clara heard the phone being set down. "Sorry," Seth said over the mic. "I had the phone too close. Testing, testing, one, two, three, four, five six. This is Saturn's Favorite Music, RTV. We're here for a great day..." He paused to sneeze. "It's a great day at..." a second sneeze. "Bob James Chevrolet." Seth came back to the phone. "How was that?"

"Good. But next time try less sneezing."

"What do you think I should do with this banner?"

Clara tried to picture the remote set up. There was a long table with a table cloth and a WRTV sign, a remote antenna, a small board for the microphone, and two speakers on stands which stood on each side of the table.

"What if you string it between the speakers?" Clara asked. "Wouldn't that be about the right length?"

"Oh yeah, that's a good idea. Thanks."

Clara kept the remote in cue in case Seth had to tell her anything. This meant that she could hear him interacting with the customers. "You don't look like your voice," a woman said.

"What does my voice look like?" Seth asked.

Clara took the channel out of cue as it came up to the time for the first break. "Good morning. It's a great Saturday at Saturn's Favorite Music, RTV. If you're out and about today, be sure to head over to Bob James Chevrolet. They're having a fantastic sales event with popcorn and balloons and our own Seth Jones is broadcasting live." Clara potted down her mic for a second, sniffed, and then turned it back up. "What is happening out there, Seth?"

"That's right, Clara," Seth said, "It's a lot of fun here today at Bob James Chevrolet. We have some folks here at the RTV table. What's your name?"

"Jason," a boy's voice said.

"Jason, are you having a good time today?"

"Yeah."

"Did you want to say hello to anyone?"

"I want to say hello to my dog because he died."

"OK," Seth said. "Thanks, Jason. There are a lot of reasons to come to Bob James Chevrolet today. They have incredible prices on these cars; you won't believe it until you come down and see it for yourself. They've got a Geo Tracker 4 x 4 for just 12,450. There's a beautiful S10 Tahoe Pickup VC for 9,695. Or you can test drive the Geo Prizm, it's just 9,495. Today only, everyone who comes in for a test drive will get a coupon for a free pizza from Arlo's Pizza. So stop by, look for the Incredible Broadcast Machine, and say hello. Now back to the music at your light rock, more music station RTV."

Clara hit play on CD1 and put Seth back into cue.

"Note to self," Seth said into the mic. "Don't put kids on the air. Otherwise it's going well." Then he moved away. Clara could hear the voices of people at the table. "I like it when you have that woman on in your show," a man's voice said. "It's really good; you sound like you're having a good time."

"Thank you," Seth said. "CJ's great. We do have a good time."

The unexpected compliment was almost enough to make Clara forget her sinus headache. This was how it felt, she thought, when you have arrived. People liked what she was doing. She had become an undisputed professional.

"Whoa," she heard Seth say. "Yeah, can you pick that up? Thanks." Then he spoke into the mic directly to Clara. "It's getting a little windy here;

the box of contest entries blew off the table. I put a rock in it. I'm ready for the next break after this song."

Clara put on her headphones and opened the mic, "Mariah Carey on Saturn's Favorite Music, RTV. It's a great day to be out and about." Her throat started to burn as she tried to suppress a cough. "Seth Jones is out with the Incredible--" her voice cracked and a tear started to run down her face "Broadcast Machine. How are things at Bob James Chevrolet, Seth?"

She potted down, and fell into a fit of coughing.

"It is a great day out here at Bob James Chevrolet. Come down and enter to win free Carpet Cleaning from Cal's Carpet Cleaning. We're having a great time meeting everyone. There are some great deals on..." Seth's voice became muffled by the sound of the wind across the mic. "Brand new Silverado for only... 99..." Clara potted her mic up, "Seth, we're having a little trouble hearing you. There's a lot of wind blowing across the mic. Is it possible to move to a less windy place?"

"Of course, CJ," Seth said. "I was just talking about the great deals on... Look out!"

Clara heard a bang. "Is everyone OK?" Seth's voice said.

"Seth?" Clara said over the mic. "Can you tell me what's happening?"

"I think it's broken," said an unfamiliar voice.

"It sounds like we're having some technical difficulties right now," Clara said. "We'll get back to Seth and the Incredible Broadcast Machine as soon as we can."

She threw a PSA into one of the open slots and hit play, then put Seth into cue.

"The speakers blew over," Seth said. "Everyone's OK. The wind went through the banner and it acted like a sail. One of the speakers is cracked, and it's not working anymore."

Predictably, the phone lit up.

"What is going on out there?" Ed shouted down the line.

"Seth says the speakers blew down."

"Why would they blow down?"

Clara felt her cheeks go red. "I don't know," she said. "Everything's fine, but Seth says one of the speakers broke."

"The speaker broke? What is he doing out there? Do you have any idea how much those cost?"

"Um, they're probably expensive."

"They're $800 each," Ed said. "I've got to call Norton." Ed hung up.

Stringing the banner between the speakers had been her idea. She told herself being fired wouldn't be so bad. She would probably find another radio job eventually. Maybe she could start a mobile DJ service or something. She could always get a job delivering pizza. Maybe she'd make manager in a year or two if she went to pizza college.

The phone lit up again. This time it was Seth. "Ed just called," Clara told him. "He's calling Norton. He's really mad."

"Great."

"Just tell them it was my idea, with the banner."

"Don't worry," Seth said. "We moved the table to a place with a little more shelter, so we're ready for the next break."

After the remote, when the Incredible Broadcast machine pulled into the parking lot, it was followed by Ed's and Mr. Norton's cars. Clara watched through the window as the three men argued in the parking lot. Finally, Seth walked in the door followed by Ed and Mr. Norton. Clara stepped out of the studio to listen.

"But what made you come up with a bonehead idea like stringing something between the speakers?"

"Where would you have put it, Ed?"

"Not on a pair of $800 speakers."

"I made a mistake."

"It's coming out of your salary," said Mr. Norton.

"Yeah, yeah, yeah." Seth said. "Are we done now?" He started to walk out. When the managers turned away, Seth looked back and smiled and winked at Clara as he walked out the door.

Fan Mail

On Monday Clara arrived at the office and stopped at Leslie's desk. "You have a letter," Leslie said, handing Clara an envelope.

"Me?"

"Probably fan mail."

"Huh. Is he in?" Clara asked, gesturing towards Ed's office.

"He's on the phone," Leslie said.

"Did you hear about the remote?"

"The speaker?"

"Yeah." She looked around and then in a low voice said, "I'm the one who told Seth to hang the banner that way."

"He didn't say anything."

"They're docking his salary."

"I heard."

"I feel guilty. "

"I'm sure it's fine."

"I don't know why he just didn't tell them it was me."

Leslie sat back in her chair. "Really? You don't know?"

"Know what?"

"Let me put it this way," she said, glancing down the hall to make sure she was not overheard. "Can you think of any reasons why a man might do something nice for a woman?"

Clara turned and looked at Seth through the studio window. "No, it's not like that."

"Are you sure?"

Clara turned back to Leslie. "We hit it off, but..."

"Do you think he would have said something if it was Rad's idea?"

"I don't think he would have done it if it was Rad's idea," Clara said.

"See," Leslie said. Clara turned to look at Seth again. He noticed, and waved. Clara blushed as she waved and quickly turned back to Leslie. In spite of herself, Clara felt a giddy excitement welling within her. "It's nothing," she said, and walked to the back room. She hesitated before entering the studio. She had never imagined that Seth might have that kind of interest in her. Was there something to it? Had he said something to Leslie, or was it all in her imagination? Maybe it was just Leslie's idea to play matchmaker.

Clara leaned into the studio, "Hi," she said, trying to be nonchalant.

"Hey," Seth said. He smiled at her. Clara scanned his face trying to detect any surplus of emotion, but she couldn't. It was just the same old Seth with his big eyes and long nose, but his face filled her with affection. Clara became nervous and backed out of the studio. She sat on the orange couch to read her mail. She did not recognize the name on the return address. On the back someone had drawn a series of triangles. She opened the envelope and pulled out a five page letter. As she read, Seth came out of the studio.

"I'm getting some more coffee," he said. "You want some?"

"This letter is so weird," Clara said.

"What is it?"

"I guess you'd call it a fan letter," she said glancing up with a furrowed brow. "Listen to this: 'I am from the exoplanet 16 Delphani. I have been monitoring your broadcast, and I know that you are from my planet too. I have received your signals on...' And then he's got a list of times and dates and things I said on the air. And then there are three pages of diagrams of something."

"Can I see that?" Seth asked.

"Sure," she handed him the letter. Seth read a bit and then went to Ed's office and knocked on the door. He disappeared inside, and after a couple of minutes Ed and Seth both came out. The letter was now in Ed's hand.

"Have you gotten letters like this before?" Ed asked.

"No, I mean, I get some fan letters occasionally. Paula from Roscommon sometimes sends me things."

"I mean from aliens."

"This is a first."

"It's up to you," Ed said. "But I think we should let the police know about this."

"The police?" Clara said. "It's just a weird letter." The song was ending, so Seth went back into the studio.

"It's more than weird," Ed said. "He's writing down everything you say. It's obsessive. It's probably nothing, but I'd rather do something and have it be nothing than do nothing and have it be something."

Seth came back out of the studio and leaned against the door frame. He was nodding. "You should listen to Ed," he said. "You're right here, live on the air. Every time you do your show, people know exactly where you are."

"You think this guy is going to try to beam me back to the mother ship?"

"I don't know," Ed said. "But I'd be more comfortable if we let the police know, and if you made sure someone was with you when you leave the station to go home for a while."

"You think that's necessary?"

"Probably not," Ed said. "People who think the radio is talking to them are normally harmless, but just to be safe."

"You don't need to be scared," Seth said. "Just careful."

"Can I show this to the cops?" Ed asked.

"Yeah, OK"

"Good." Ed went to his office, got his jacket, and then walked out of the station, taking the letter with him. Clara followed Seth into the studio.

"I really think you guys are overreacting."

"Probably. I hope so."

"I don't want to feel like a weak little girl who needs to be protected by the big men."

"Ed's not so big."

"I mean you, too."

"Are you talking about the speaker?"

"I wasn't, but now that you mention it, yeah, that too."

"I wasn't protecting you because you're a girl. It was my remote. It's my responsibility."

"Is that the only reason?"

"Well, no," he said with a serious expression. "There is one other thing."

"What?"

"I was afraid you'd zap me with your ray gun."

"We call them phasers."

"My mistake. Nanu Nanu," Seth said, putting out his hand for a "Mork from Ork" handshake.

"Live long and prosper," Clara said, making the Vulcan hand gesture.

"You're a pro," Seth said. "You don't have to prove you're one of the guys. You're one of us. But it *is* different for you. You have to be a little more careful about the creeps. It's not fair, but it's true. It doesn't make you weak, just smart."

"OK, well, then, thank you for not telling on me."

"I'm not a snitch," he said. He gave Clara a gentle punch on the shoulder.

Later that day, during Clara's airshift, Ed came into the studio and pinned a memo to the bulletin board. "Don't let Seth take this down," he said.

"It's not my day to watch him," Clara thought, but she just nodded. After Ed posted the memo, he left for the day. Clara was occupied with a break, and did not read it immediately. When she finally had a moment, she was surprised that Ed would announce something like this in a memo instead of telling everyone face to face. It said that the station no longer had a custodian and that the staff would now be expected to help keep the place clean. "Cleaning supplies are located in..."

The song was ending, so Clara played the cart with the legal ID, started up "Bennie and the Jets," cued up the next record and then went out to Leslie's desk, taking Ed's memo with her. Leslie was typing up a production order.

"Have you seen this?" Clara asked, waving the memo. "What is this all about?"

"You've heard that this place is up for sale, haven't you?" Leslie asked. Clara hadn't. "Norton doesn't want to spend any money on the place because he wants to unload it. So if he can cut corners..."

Her voice trailed off in mid-stream. The two women both looked up at the speaker. They had to listen for a moment before they were sure Bennie and the Jets was actually skipping.. "B-B-B-B-B-B-B-B-B-B-B-B" Elton John was singing. On such occasions no explanation was needed to break off a conversation. Clara ran to the studio to advance the stylus. Leslie followed. Once Elton had moved on to the next syllable, they resumed their conversation.

"What happens when he sells the station?" Clara asked.

"It depends on who buys it," she said. "Rumor is..."

Elton had become repetitive again. "Bennie, Bennie, Bennie, Bennie, Bennie, Bennie, Bennie..."

Clara sat down in the chair, threw on her headphones, potted the record down and said, "That was, of course, the dance remix of "Bennie and the Jets." Now here's the new one by Celine Dion." And she fired the next song. As Leslie started talking again, Clara wrote the word "Skips" on the card for "Bennie and the Jets," put the card inside the record jacket and handed it to Leslie to put on Rad's desk.

"Rumor is that the guy who owns WGGB Country is looking at it," Leslie said.

"You mean... We could go country?" Clara sat slack jawed.

"Hope y'all have your boots ready."

Dancing Past the Graveyard

Clara listened to the RTV morning show in the background as she put on the Halloween costume she had bought from the drug store, a long black witch dress with frayed sleeves and skirt. She paired this with some torn fishnet stockings she already owned and her best imitation of Tim Curry's Frank N' Furter makeup from "The Rocky Horror Picture Show." She added a pair of fingerless lace gloves to highlight her black nail polish. On the radio, Seth gave a werewolf howl. "Michael Jackson's 'Thriller' with the inimitable Vincent Price."

Someone, probably Bill, gave a high-pitched Michael Jackson "Woo-hoo."

"Happy Halloween on your light rock, more music station, RTV."

"What do you think was a better move," Bill asked, "Getting Vincent Price to put his voice in the song, or the choreography for the 'Thriller' video?"

"A lot of good moves there," Seth said. "By the way, if you've never seen the movie 'House of Wax' with Vincent Price..."

"That's a great movie," Al said. "Did you see it in 3-D?"

"You have to see it in 3-D," Seth said. "So Bill Katz, what will the weather be like for the trick or treaters tonight?"

The Weathercenter music bed started to play. "The trick-or-treat weather will not be scary," Bill said in his best vampire voice. "Partly cloudy skies and a high temperature today..."

Clara walked away from the radio to check her look one more time in the mirror. When she was as satisfied as she would ever be, she turned off the radio. It was only when she had gotten into her car to drive to the station that she started to worry that maybe she would be the only one in a costume. She was relieved when she walked into the station to see Bill was wearing a sweatshirt with an H in the center with wavy circles around it.

"Let me guess," Clara said, "High pressure system?"

"You got it," Bill said. Then he pointed at her, "Witch?"

"Nah," Clara said, "Just my normal outfit." Bill gave an odd little laugh that suggested he was not entirely sure if her response had been a joke.

Clara headed to her desk. Leslie had left some production copy for her, but there was no cart label attached. "Leslie forgot to do up the label," Clara said, more to herself than to Al, who rushed past wearing a trench coat and a hat with the label "press" in the brim.

Clara went into the studio so she could glance through the window at the bank clock. Seth was spinning the rack to find the commercial carts for his next break. He was dressed in faded black jeans and an Aerosmith t-shirt with a flannel shirt over it. "What are you supposed to be?" Clara asked him.

"Sexy morning show DJ," Seth said.

Clara gave him a thumbs up, "Nailed it." She noticed that there were a few records leaning against the window without the normal station markings on them. "What are those?"

"A few special things for Halloween." As he took one of the albums out of its jacket and put it on the turntable, Clara spotted Leslie coming through the door. Clara went out to meet her at the front desk. She was costumed with large pointed ears.

"Star Trek?" Clara asked.

"No," Leslie said. She took a pair of plastic vampire teeth out of her pocket and put them in her mouth, then opened her mouth wide and tilted her head back.

"Bat Boy!"

"You got it," she slurred around the plastic teeth. She took the teeth back out of her mouth.

"Hey, I got some production copy, but it's missing its cart label."

"It's not missing," Leslie said, taking off her jacket and sitting down at her desk.

"No, I didn't get it."

"I mean, it's not missing, there just isn't one. I can't do cart labels, we're out of them."

"We're out of cart labels?"

"We're out of a lot of things. Norton hasn't paid the invoice on the supplies we ordered two months ago, so they won't give us any more until the past due bill is paid."

"When will that be?"

"I wouldn't hold your breath. I have no typewriter ribbon anyway. I had to call the electric company and beg them not to turn the station's power off yesterday."

"Jeez. I didn't know it was that bad."

"Hopefully somebody will buy us before we're repossessed."

"So what should I do about the cart?"

"I don't know."

Clara shrugged and went back to her desk. A few minutes later Leslie appeared and handed Clara a bottle of White Out and a sharpie. "Maybe this will work," she said.

The on-air light above the studio door was illuminated, and through the speakers came Seth's voice over the intro music to "Zombie Jamboree." "Dancing past the graveyard on your light rock, more music station, RTV."

The light over the door went off and Bill came out of the studio. He was doing a little calypso shimmy. Leslie laughed and started to sway along with Bill. Clara joined them from her seat, clapping along with the music. This made Leslie and Bill dance more. Clara stood up and joined in. When Seth stepped to the back of the studio to put an LP back on the shelf, he saw the impromptu party and he sashayed out into the room. He took both of Clara's hands and they started to dance together, turning back to back and then belly to belly with the chorus. At this point Ed walked into the room. For a moment everyone stopped and waited to see how he would react. He paused, then laughed and started to dance. Leslie went over to dance with Ed, as Seth led Clara back into the studio. In the studio their bodies drew close as partners might stand when doing a waltz. As the end of the song approached, Seth inched over to the board, and as it faded, he pushed the button for a liner cart while striking a zombie pose from the Thriller dance. When he potted up Bryan Adams, Clara heard a disappointed "Awww," from the back room.

Ed clapped his hands together. "OK, back to work."

Seth smiled as he wrote the date on the card for "Do I Have to Say the Words" and put it in the back of the A's. Clara was still standing close to Seth. "That was fun," she said. Seth turned to her. He didn't say anything, but he held her gaze, and his smile became more gentle the longer he gazed. Clara felt herself mirroring the smile, and did not look away.

"Excellent choice," Bill said, entering the studio. Then to Clara, "Are you going to hang out and do the next break with us?"

"Oh yeah," Clara said, turning to Bill. "Yeah, I'm ready."

Coffee

Six months into her tenure at WRTV, Clara's student days belonged to a strange and distant past. She occasionally got calls or letters from her Harrison friends, but she had not heard of any of them being hired by radio stations. One or two were doing radio-adjacent things, production, club DJing, but as far as she knew she was the only one on the air. In November, she got a letter from Joe. He had taken a desk job at a radio station doing marketing. "I want to enjoy myself," he wrote."So I need a job that provides me with enough money for all the things I need. I believe the road to moderate success is easier behind the scenes than on air. This is my personal view."

Clara was floored. God had gifted Joe the ideal radio voice. He was supposed to be a star. In Joe's letter Clara caught a glimpse of her greatest fear, waking up one day with a mortgage and giving up on her dreams because she could no longer afford them. She suddenly felt grateful for the Superstar Seven in a Row, the weather center forecasts, the Incredible Broadcast Machine and even Michael Bolton. She was poor, sure, but she had chosen her life. She was one of the lucky ones.

Yet she couldn't shake the feeling that Joe might be right, and this radio dream might be folly. After Clara paid the rent, her car payment, the electric, cable and phone bills she had barely enough left for food and the occasional solitary movie ticket. As she racked up debt on her credit cards, she worried about what would happen if her period of poverty and dues-paying was not as brief as she planned. Seth had been working in radio for 18 years. Based on the AMC Eagle he drove, she guessed he didn't have a lot to show for it. Meanwhile things at the station continued to deteriorate as Norton refused to pump money into a property he was trying to unload.

One morning Clara came into the station to find Al and Bill cowering on the love seat in the lobby. "Watch out, he's on a rampage," Bill said.

"Who, Ed?"

"No, Seth. It's safer out here."

Seth's voice came across the speakers. "That was Dolly Parton, "9-5," a song about drinking coffee to survive the work day. It's 8:46. I hope you've got your coffee brewing. We'll get you through your commute with more of Saturn's Favorite Music by Lionel Richie, Peter Cetera and Shawn Colvin on your light rock, more music station."

When the "on air" light went off, Clara went to the studio, opened the door and stood in the doorway. Seth was drinking from a Styrofoam cup with a gas station logo on it. He stood up to change the CD.

"Bill said I should be afraid," Clara said.

Seth picked up a piece of paper from the console. "Have you seen this?" He handed it to Clara. It was one of Ed's memos. It said that due to budget cuts, the station would no longer be providing free coffee in the break room.

"Cheap, petty bastards," Seth said.

"It's not that surprising," Clara said. "They haven't replenished the toilet paper for a week. Leslie's been stealing rolls from the gas station."

"It's the principle of the thing. If you ask someone to get up in the morning before God does, you have an obligation to give them coffee. That's just being a responsible member of society. Mutual obligation."

"I could bring in some coffee tomorrow."

"*I* could bring in coffee," Seth said. He was trying to get a ball point pen to work, and was scribbling with it on a piece of scratch paper. He had no success and he threw it into the trash can with great force. Clara walked out to her desk, found a functioning pen, came back and handed it to Seth. "Thanks," he said. "The point is, the man's going to make millions selling the station. He can't spend $2.50 for a can of coffee?"

"That's probably how people get to be millionaires," Clara said. "Is it possible, just hear me out here, is it possible you're overreacting just a little bit about the coffee?"

"What time do you get up in the morning?"

"Fair enough."

Bill came to the studio door and peered over Clara's shoulder. "Is it safe to come in?"

"Are you going to kill the weather man?" Clara asked Seth.

"No."

"I think you're safe," she said, and stepped aside for Bill to make his way to the guest microphone.

140

When they had finished their break, Seth took a sheet of copy from an early weather report and started scribbling on the blank back side. When he had finished, he tacked his sign up on the bulletin board where the coffee memo had been.

"News Update," the sign read. "Station Denies Caffeine to Morning Staff. Five Things The Morning Team Would Rather Be Doing at 5 in the Morning: 1. Sleeping. 2. Dreaming. 3. Catching Some zzzzzs. 4. Snoring. 5. Drooling on our Pillows."

Clara left the studio to prepare for her show. A few minutes later, Ed walked in. Clara felt like she should warn him. "Ed, um, you should... I think Seth is a little..."

Ed nodded, "The coffee?"

"Yeah."

"Is that Ed?" Seth's voice came from the studio. Bill ran out first, he looked at Ed, "Good luck," he said as he made a bee line for the lobby. Seth emerged from the studio with the memo in his hand. He held it up and raised his eyebrows.

"It's not me," Ed said, throwing up his hands, "I don't control the budget. Don't shoot the messenger." Seth went back into the studio. He shut the door and the "On Air" light came on.

"Good morning, it's Saturn's Favorite Music, RTV. And we have a treat for you, a song from Genesis about how the world feels in the morning before you've had your coffee. It's 'Land of Confusion.'"

Ed sighed and went to his office. Clara went into the studio to start pulling her cards. A few minutes later, Ed came back to the studio.

"Good news," he said. "I talked to Norton and he's restoring the coffee budget, so you can end your protest." Ed turned and looked at Seth's sign. He tore it down, and left the studio.

That afternoon, Clara was coming back from the restroom when she nearly collided with Ed. He was heading to the kitchen carrying a plastic bag from the grocery store. Clara could see that it contained a can of coffee. "You bought that yourself, didn't you?" she asked.

"You didn't see me," Ed said, and continued walking to the kitchen.

Snow Day

Clara did not usually listen to General Grant's overnight show. The last thing she wanted to do when she got home was to tune in to her workplace. But the station was gearing up for a major snow storm. Bill had been so certain that it was going to be a big one that he and Seth were both camping out at the station to avoid getting stuck on the road at 4 AM. So Clara switched on her clock radio and listened in her bed, hoping to get a sense of how bad the storm was going to be.

Grant's was the only show that took requests, and when she turned the radio on, there was a caller saying, "We've been married for 40 years tomorrow, so could you play 'I Will Always Love You' for my wife, Paula?"

"Absolutely," Grant said in his treacle voice. "Here's 'I Will Always Love You' going out to Paula on Saturn's Favorite Music, RTV." People were always requesting "I Will Always Love You" for their sweethearts. It was one of Clara's pet peeves. She shouted at the radio, "It's a break-up song!" No one ever listens to lyrics.

Just as Whitney was reaching her crescendo, the song was interrupted by a short tone, then Grant came on the air, "We interrupt this program for important information from the National Weather Service. Important information will follow this tone."

Then there was the long, high-pitched wail of the EBS tone. It was followed by an unfamiliar voice on a tinny audio feed. "The National Weather Service has issued a winter storm warning for the counties of Northern Lower Michigan. Heavy snow and blowing snow are expected overnight with dangerous drifts followed by freezing rain. Accumulations of up to 8 inches are expected..." Clara turned off the radio, and reset her alarm for a few hours earlier than normal.

In the morning, Clara found one side of her car almost obscured by a large snow drift; the other side was essentially uncovered. Clara entered through the passenger side, turned on the car and let it run while she went inside to find the snow shovel Ed had lent her. It took about twenty minutes to shovel out. Clara lived on Saturn's main road, which had been plowed throughout the night, but the snow continued to fall and blow. The short drive to the station was more like aiming her car and skiing than driving. Fortunately, at that hour, she was the only one on the road.

When she got to the station, all of the phone lines were lit up. Bill was going through them one by one. He waved to Clara briefly and started writing something on his notepad. Clara went to another phone and started picking up lines. Most of the callers were kids asking "Is there school today?" Occasionally though, there would be someone from a school calling to announce classes were canceled or delayed.

"I'm calling from Saturn Country Day School, and the password is..." Clara flipped through a book. The schools all had a password to prevent deep voiced kids from calling with false cancellations. "The password is... Oh here it is. Elephant. We're going to be closed today." Clara wrote this down and handed it to Bill who was gathering various scraps of paper together.

"Isn't this fun?" Bill said.

Leslie arrived a few minutes later. She stamped her feet and shook off the snow. With her was a boy who appeared to be 7 or 8 years old. Leslie started peeling off his coat. "School is closed and I couldn't get a sitter," she said.

"What's your name?" Clara asked the boy.

"Kevin."

"Nice to meet you, Kevin."

"Don't worry," Leslie said, "He won't be in the way. I'll set him up in the kitchen with some Legos."

"Bill- the break's coming up," Seth shouted from the studio. Bill handed his phone to Clara and ran into the studio. Clara finished writing down the information on a nursery school closing.

"RTV Saturn's Favorite Music," Seth's voice rang out over the speakers. "Good morning, it's ten minutes to seven, and yes, we do have some school closings to tell you about. If you're wondering if your school is closed, please don't call the station. We'll be announcing all the closings we have right after this weather center forecast. Good morning, Bill."

As Bill was giving the weather, Clara tip toed into the studio with three more closings. Seth reached out for them with one hand. With the other he was flipping through the sponsorship book. School closings got an even bigger audience that the obits, and they were, naturally, sponsored. Bill finished his forecast.

"Thanks, Bill. And because of the weather we have a few closings to tell you about," he was still searching for the sponsorship copy. "This morning's school cancellation and delay report is being brought to you... By the wonderful folks at..." Ah-ha, he had it! "Erickson Hardware. Mention this advertisement and receive 10 percent off your Ames snow shovel purchase. Erickson Hardware, two miles north of the airport in beautiful downtown Saturn..."

Al was in the newsroom talking to someone on the traffic tip line. When he got off the line he waved through the window of studio B as Seth was wrapping up the list of school closings.

"It looks like Al Lear has joined us in the studio. Al, what have you got to report?"

"Good morning, Seth. There is a traffic tie up to report on south bound I-30. An RTV traffic spotter called to report that there is an overturned truck near the junction with Maple Drive blocking traffic. Gawkers are slowing traffic on the northbound side as well. Drivers are advised to find an alternate route. Traffic conditions are dangerous through the region with drifting and blowing snow and occasional white outs. If you do not absolutely have to travel this morning, please stay off the roads."

"Thank you, Al," Seth said. "Coming up, more great music, and we'll be back very shortly with more school closing announcements plus the news, obits and more. Stay tuned."

He closed the mic and hit the commercial cart. It was Clara's Erickson Hardware spot with the extra stop tone on it. Whoever had used it last had not cued it past the extra tone. There was a moment of dead air while the cart rolled through the silence to the real start point.

"Damn it," Seth said, and fired the cart again. "Someone needs to put that spot on another cart. Good morning, CJ." He wasn't looking at her; instead he was sorting through the pile of papers in front of him.

"Bill- what does this say- the Swines aren't holding ponchos at the Yuca?"

"Swimmers aren't holding practice at the YMCA."

Seth hit two more carts, then a liner and Patty Smith's "Sometimes Love Just Ain't Enough" was playing. "OK, I have to get organized here," he said. "I'm getting the dead people all mixed up with the school closings."

Leslie popped her head into the studio. "That was Ed on the phone," she said. "He wanted to know why we had dead air a minute ago."

"Did you tell him it was a low-pressure center?" Seth grabbed the Erickson Hardware spot. He had not cued past the stop tone either. He handed it to Clara.

"Can you go recut this? I need some more coffee." Before he could get out of his chair, Kevin came bounding into the studio.

"Kevin," Leslie scolded. "I told you to stay in the kitchen."

"It's OK," Seth said. "He wants to be where the action is, don't you, Kevin?"

"I'll get him out of your hair," Leslie said, putting her hand on the boy's back.

Seth leaned down to Kevin's level, "Do you want to watch us doing a radio show?"

Kevin's eyes lit up. "Yeah," he said.

"You have to be really quiet," Seth said, "Can you be really quiet?"

"Yeah."

Seth extended his pinky finger to Kevin, "Pinky swear?" Kevin wrapped his tiny pinky finger around Seth's and pulled. Seth looked up at Leslie, "Why don't you get him a chair, he can sit behind me over here."

"You don't have to..."

"It's OK," Seth said. "He'll be fine. Can somebody get me a coffee?"

As Leslie was getting Kevin seated in the studio, Bill poked his head in. "Hey, Seth! I think you should take this call." Clara squeezed her way out of the crowded studio, and sat at a desk to answer the phones. Looking through the open door, she could see Seth on the phone writing something down on a scrap of paper. He got off the phone and called out the door– "Thirty seconds, guys!" Bill and Al ran to their places and two doors clicked shut.

Then Seth's voice rang out over the speakers: "WRTV, Saturn's Favorite Music. Yes, there are school closings. Be patient. We will be listing them after the commercial break, but first, we have an unusual lost pet report this morning. I just got a call from Brenda Smith. She woke up to find 7 cows standing in her yard. This is not what I would consider an everyday event."

"Seven cows?" Bill asked, as though he had not heard this before, but of course he had given the news to Seth.

"Seven cows, and we are now on a mission to stay with this story until the cows come home," Seth said.

"Boo," said Bill. "Or should I say, 'moo.'"

"Where did the cows come from?" Al asked.

"She doesn't know," Seth said, "but it may be that sign saying 'Cows Eat Free' that she put up. Actually, she was expecting eight tiny reindeer, but she got cows. Don't know how."

"How now brown cow," Bill added.

"So if you have cows, go out in your pasture now. Count your cows, please. If you seem a little low in the bovine department, give us a call and we'll tell you where they wandered off to," Seth said. "OK, so lost cow people, go ahead and call. If you're wondering about the school closings don't call, we have them for you right after this."

As soon as he had hit the first spot, Seth jumped up, opened the door and shouted, "Hey Clara, while you're in the production room, could you make up a lost cow update music bed?"

Clara went into the production room and closed the door. It was still and quiet. Clara had become much more proficient with production. It took her only a minute to transfer the Erickson Hardware spot to a reel-to-reel tape. She then put the cart on a magnetic device and slid it back and forth a few times, erasing it. She put the blank cart, with the Erickson Hardware label, into the cart machine and recorded the old spot back on the cart with a clean stop tone. With a marker, she covered up her old warning about the extra stop tone.

The cow report bed was a bit more challenging. But she was now familiar enough with the sound effects LPs to go right to the disc with the farm animal noises. She grabbed a CD of generic music beds. On the turntable she quickly cued a track called "cow barn." She chose a music bed at random, and did a quick mix of the two onto the reel. When she had enough, she rolled back the reel tape and recorded the result onto an old commercial cart she had erased. Over its old label she scribbled COW in big letters. Then Clara opened the production room door and returned to the chaos.

Kevin had apparently gotten bored with radio. He was sitting at one of the desks in the back room building a tower with yellow and red Legos. "Nice tower," Clara said, walking past the desk. She went into the studio and handed Seth the carts. Someone had brought him a coffee, and the snow closings were now in a single, alphabetical list, in Leslie's handwriting. "I think we found the owner of the cows," Leslie shouted from her desk.

"I'll get it," Clara said. She left the studio and headed to Leslie's desk to get the bovine information. As she arrived, Ed was coming in the door. He stomped the snow off his feet and put his hood down. "I didn't think I was going to make it in," he said. He was holding a box of donuts, which he set on the ledge in front of Leslie's desk. "They're gas station donuts," he said, "but they should be edible."

Kevin came running around the corner, "Mom, can I have a donut?"

"Only one," Leslie said, She looked at Ed and shrugged, "I couldn't get a sitter."

"That's fine," Ed said, unzipping his coat. "It's great that everyone managed to get here early. I was listening on the way in, when I wasn't pushing my car out of the snow drifts. You're all doing a great job."

Clara took a glazed donut and placed it in a napkin. She carried it in one hand, and the cow information in the other hand, and returned to the studio. Seth was gazing out the window with a blank stare. "You look exhausted," Clara said, handing him the paper.

Seth rubbed his forehead. "I'm holding up OK."

"Ed brought some donuts," Clara said. "Why don't you take a little break. I can run the board for a while."

"Yeah?" Seth sat up straighter.

"Yeah. Go get a donut. Sit for a while."

"Thanks," Seth said. He pointed to the clock hour, "We're on the C. The B is cued up on CD 1." He stretched as he stood up to leave the studio. As he walked out, he passed Bill, who was on the way in. Bill was full of energy. "I love snow days," he said.

"It is kind of fun," Clara said.

As the morning wore on, and the time that school would have started passed, the phone calls slowed. There were occasional notices of afternoon events that had been called off, but for the most part, the pace reverted to something like normal.

Seth returned to the studio with cinnamon crumbs on his cheek. "That hit the spot, thanks."

Clara made a flicking motion against her own cheek.

"Mm," Seth said, wiping the side of his face. "How do you know I didn't want that there?"

"Just a guess."

"Is it gone?" Clara gave a thumbs up.

"I'll tell you what," Seth said, looking back and forth between Clara and Bill. "We make a good team."

That's when Ed came into the studio and leaned against the door. His eyes were lowered and his hands were in his pockets. "Great job this morning," he said. "Listen, I'm going to be posting a memo, but since I have you all here, I'm just going to give you a head's up that there is going to be a mandatory jock meeting on Tuesday."

"What is it going to be about?" Bill asked.

"I think that's something that's going to have to wait until Tuesday," he said. He shuffled out of the studio, went into his office, and closed the door.

Jock Meeting

Since the members of the airstaff all had such different hours, staff meetings were always held in the afternoon. In this case, 2:30 PM, just after Clara's shift. To Grant, the overnight man, this was early morning and to the morning team it was already dinner time. Bill had decided to stay at the station, and he had fallen asleep on the orange couch. Al had spent the entire morning writing copy and doing production. Seth had gone home, and come back towards the end of Clara's shift, around 1:30. He walked into the studio and sat down at the guest microphone. "I hate jock meetings," he said.

"What do you think the meeting is about?" Clara asked him.

"It can only be one thing," Seth said, "Norton must have sold the station."

"That's good, right?" Clara asked, as she pushed record on the reel to reel to catch the news feed. "The new owner will start spending some money on this place. We'll get the custodian back, and the cart labels."

"Maybe," Seth said.

Clara slid over to the turntable and cued up her next record. When she looked back at Seth he had a pensive, worried expression on his face. "You don't look like you think it's good news," she said.

"New owners usually mean new formats," he said. "New formats usually mean new air talent."

Clara was just starting to get comfortable on the air. "You mean we could all get fired?"

"Yep," he said. "I'd put the chances at 60/40. Maybe 80/20."

Rad came stomping in, carrying his shoebox of liners and material, which he dropped on the console next to the cards. A little cloud of dust flew up when he did this. "They always have these meetings during my shift so I have to keep running back and forth and I miss half the stuff."

"What do you think the meeting's going to be about?" Clara asked.

Rad looked straight at Seth. "How some people are screwing up the format by not playing what they're supposed to."

"Could be," Seth said as he got up from the guest mic. "Or it could be about how certain people spend their time spying on other people instead of doing their own jobs."

Rad signed the log and took over at the board. Clara and Seth went into the back room. Al had come out of the production studio, and was sitting at one of the desks reading a newspaper. Seth shook Bill awake, and he and Clara sat down beside him on the ugly furniture. Grant came in muttering under his breath about having to get up early for this stupid meeting. No one offered him a place on the couch.

Leslie came around the corner, "Is this where the party is?" She sat on the arm of the couch beside Seth. In spite of the uncertainty, and the annoyance of having to be at the station outside of their normal work hours, there was, indeed, a bit of a party atmosphere because, with the exception of the morning team, most of the announcers worked pretty much in an empty station. It was a rare, and fun, thing to see everyone together.

To kill the time Bill decided to lead the group in a chorus of the theme song to the television show WKRP in Cincinnati, which every DJ knew by heart. "Come on, everybody, sing along!" Bill said. Everyone but Al joined in. "I have work to do, someone come get me when the meeting starts," Al said, retreating to the news room.

"You ever notice those WKRP guys never wore headphones?" Seth asked. "And, they only had two DJs. What did they do the rest of the day?"

"And why were the overnight guy and the morning guy always hanging out at the station in the middle of the afternoon?" Clara asked.

"Probably had a lot of staff meetings," Grant grumbled.

Finally Ed arrived with Mr. Norton and another man in a suit who no one recognized. The man was tall and heavy-set with thinning dark brown hair. His chin was tilted up in a stance of extreme confidence. His posture was erect, but with a slight forward slant. He was never still, but shifted from side to side in an impatient rocking motion. Leslie yelled for Al. As they waited for the newsman to arrive, the stranger looked at the motley assemblage as if he was assessing them. Rad leaned against the studio doorway so he could run in and change the tracks as necessary.

"Mr. Norton has an important announcement," Ed said.

"Thank you, Ed," Mr. Norton said. "Last Wednesday I sold WRTV. This is Frank Kirchner. He will be the new owner as soon as the FCC approves the sale. This can take anywhere from a few weeks to a few months.

During that time, I will still be the owner and things will continue as they have been. We want you to continue doing things as you always have. I asked Mr. Kirchner to come to this meeting so he could have the opportunity to meet you and vice versa."

Kirchner spoke as though he were at a podium, "I'm sure you all have a lot of questions," he said. "There are a lot of things I will not be able to answer until the sale is final, but please ask any questions you have and I will answer what I can."

"Will there be a change in format?" Grant asked.

"I can't answer that now," Mr. Kirchner said.

"What are your plans for the station?" Leslie asked.

"It's really too soon to go into that," he said.

Seth asked the question that was on everyone's mind. "Are you going to be making staffing changes?"

"I have no plans to do that at this time," Kirchner said, leaning back. Somehow the answer did not seem especially re-assuring. After another 15 minutes of questions and non-answers, the three suited men left, and the DJs sat in stunned silence.

"First time someone asks me to play 'Achy Breaky Heart' I'm out of here," Rad said, before he disappeared back into the studio.

The day after the official staff meeting, in the last hour of the morning show, Leslie held an impromptu, unofficial staff meeting of her own in the kitchen. Seth put on "The Pie Song," and everyone gathered at the table. Leslie looked as though she had come from a funeral. "It's not good news," she said. Frank Kirchner owned five radio stations in Michigan and two in Canada. Unlike the current version of WRTV, his stations were all making a profit.

"He comes in, and he cleans house," Leslie said. "Last three stations he bought, he put in automation systems and fired half the people there. One of the stations, he fired everybody, and now it's just a repeater for his big country station."

There was a long silence. The only voice was that of Don McLean, whose lyrics about the music dying seemed suddenly prophetic. Finally, Bill spoke. "We don't know that's what will happen here just because he did that before. WRTV is a bigger station than those other ones, isn't it? We're popular. Why mess with something that works?"

"It may be popular, but the station is losing money," Leslie said. "Has been for months. People call Norton every day about past due bills."

"Well, whatever format they go with, they're going to need news," Al reassured himself. Everyone agreed that there was no one the station could do without, but they all looked worried.

Later that day, Leslie was in the studio with Clara sharing some new intelligence about Kirchner Broadcasting as Rad came in to prepare for his show. Overhearing the conversation, he glanced at Clara and said, "Last hired, first fired."

"Shut up, Rad," Leslie said. Then to Clara, "You don't have anything to worry about. You're a commodity around here."

"A commodity?" Clara asked.

"The girl," said Rad. His back was turned as he rummaged through the card boxes, but Clara imagined a sneer on his face.

"There are other women with voices in the world, you know," Clara said. "Some of them even have demo tapes." Rad grunted, and took a stack of cards out of the studio.

"Never mind him," said Leslie. "He's just jealous because you have more listeners than he has."

"I do?"

Leslie patted Clara on the shoulder as she stood up. "You have nothing to worry about," she said. Then why was Clara so worried?

TPB

Clara's notion that the sale of the station would mean more money for day-to-day operations had been sadly mistaken. They had entered a period of limbo. The station had theoretically been sold, but nothing could happen until the FCC approved it. If Norton had been reluctant to sink money into his dying station before, he was not about to start now with the sale pending. A week after the jock meeting, Ed put up one of his famous memos. It announced that due to the pending sale, there would be no holiday party or bonuses. Clara had not been there long enough to expect either, but the situation had prompted Seth to replace Ed's sign with one of his now-infamous counter memos.

"From the Bah-Humbug Department. Due to the pending sale of WRTV, management has declared that no Christmas cheer is allowed this year and any presents exchanged shall be WAPED."

Ed had torn it down and put up a sign of his own reading, "Do Not Post Signs-- Management." The sign had been up for about three days when Clara arrived for her airshift to find Seth tacking a piece of paper to the bulletin board. It read: "Protest Sign-- Morning Team." Clara looked at the sign and shook her head.

"Ed loves it really," Seth said.

"That's not my impression."

"Well, sometimes you have to rebel a little bit to show you're still alive," Seth said. Clara slid into the chair to take over at the board. She flipped to the title page of the log to sign in. "By the way," Seth said, "have you looked at the log lately?"

"What do you mean?"

Seth pointed at the "abbreviations" notice that appeared on the page just below the signatures. It was a boilerplate section of the log that Leslie printed out each day. After the notice that "All times are Eastern Standard Time" there was a series of abbreviations that would be used throughout the log. There were timing abbreviations (Sec and Min), program source abbreviations "L-Local, Net-Network, Rec-Recorded" and then a section labeled "Announcements." It was usually one line long. Now, after the standard abbreviations, "ID-Legal Station Identification, CM-Commercial Matter, PSA-Public Service Announcement," were some creative additions: "TPB-This Place Bites. WIT-When is the Takeover, NM-No Money, NCS-No Cleaning Supplies, NTP-No Toilet Paper, NTR-No Typewriter Ribbons, NC-No Coffee, NR-No Raises, NCL-No Cart Labels, NCP-No Christmas Party, NF-No Future, NJ-No Janitor, NW-No Water, NE-No Electricity, NH-No Heat, NN-No Nuttin'!"

Clara laughed. "It looks like Leslie is still alive too." Clara flipped ahead in the log and saw that she had an EBS test coming up in her first hour. "I have an EBS test coming up," she said to Seth, "Would you mind getting the board patched for me while I get set up?"

"Can't do it," Seth said.

"Why not?"

"Take a look," he said. He pointed to the bank of equipment where the EBS monitor was supposed to be. It was gone.

"Where is the EBS monitor?" Clara asked.

"It's been gone for a week," Seth said. "It broke down and Norton's too cheap to fix it."

"But... Don't we need an EBS monitor?"

"Yep," he said.

"What am I supposed to do? Do I check it off that I did an EBS test?"

"Can't do an EBS test without the machine," Seth said. "Just leave it blank."

"Don't we have a bunch of stations that monitor us for the tests? Couldn't we get in big trouble for not running them?"

"If the FCC found out," Seth said, putting on his coat. "Luckily, in the 18 years I've been in radio, I've only had the FCC visit once."

"What did they do?"

He thought for a moment. "They checked the logs and had me do an EBS test," he said. Then he shrugged and left for the day.

Christmas

Beginning in December, Rad clipped a new set of clock hours into the binder and put a third small box of cards next to the two larger wooden boxes. The clocks had a new category X for Xmas music. In the first week, only two dots an hour were replaced with Xes. Every few days Rad added a couple more until in the week leading up to Christmas the clock hour looked as though every category had been crossed out and every program was playing nothing but Christmas pop classics. By December 24th Clara felt as though she was being strangled by jingle bells and reindeer references. Clara was not much in the Christmas spirit anyway because no matter what day of the year it was, WRTV's meter readings would have to be taken, someone would have to be on hand if the EBS system was activated, and the board would not run itself. Christmas was just another work day for most of the air staff. Only Al and Bill had the day off. Their voices would be on the air in the form of pre-recorded "reindeer reports" tracking the movements of Santa Claus around the globe. Clara had tried to make it sound as though being selected to work on Christmas was a radio honor when she called her parents to say she would not be home that year.

On Christmas morning, Clara put a red and green ribbon in her hair and drove to the station at the normal hour. En route, she stopped at one the few businesses that was open on Christmas, the gas station. She bought a couple of candy canes. The cashier wished Clara a "Merry Christmas," but she looked glum. Clara thought that if she had to work on Christmas, at least she was doing something like working in radio, not a gas station. She wondered, though, if the gas station or the radio job paid more. She had a strong suspicion it was the gas station.

As Leslie and the sales staff were on vacation, RTV's outer office was dark, except for the blinking of Christmas tree lights. The illuminated studio was glowing like a stage, or a giant fishbowl. Stevie Wonder's "Someday at Christmas" played through the empty halls. Through the window Clara saw Seth leaning back in his chair with his eyes closed. Clara took off her coat, and went to the dark back room, where she hung it over the back of the chair.

"Merry Christmas," Clara said, entering the studio. She held out a candy cane to Seth.

"Merry Christmas," he said, taking the candy and setting it on the console. "I like your..." he pointed at the ribbons in her hair.

"Thanks," she said. "I thought I should do something to celebrate."

"Your first time working on Christmas?"

"Yeah. Probably not yours, huh?"

"I haven't had a Christmas off in a long time." Seth yawned and stretched. "But I'm on early, so it's not so bad. Most of the day is free. I always hated missing the Santa thing, though. Helen would try to keep Ashley from going to look at her stocking before I got home, but it's hard. It's like holding back the running of the bulls or something." He leaned into the board to fade into the next Christmas hit. Both of the discs in the players were made up entirely of Christmas songs, so Seth could cue from one to the next without changing the discs in the machine. It made for a light work day.

"Helen is your wife?"

"Ex," Seth said, and then more to himself than to Clara, "My ex-wife."

Clara was still new enough to being an adult that having a friend who was married, much less, married and divorced, was novel. She didn't know what to say.

"Ashley's with her mother today," Seth said. "I got her on Christmas Eve. So we already did Christmas."

"How old is she?"

"She's eight."

"Nice."

"Yeah," Seth said. "She wanted a California Roller Baby doll. Do you know these things?"

"No."

"It roller blades," he said, pumping his arms back and forth to demonstrate. "It's this doll that actually skates. I mean, in the commercial it skates. On the box it says it skates. In reality it mostly falls down."

"That's cute," Clara said.

"Yeah," Seth's face relaxed into a warm smile and his eyes glanced upwards. He looked back to Clara, "I think it's the kind of thing that's probably going to be fun for about a week."

"Is this the first Christmas you've..." She trailed off, unsure of how to ask the question, or whether she should.

"It's been a couple of years," he said with a shrug. Then he stood up and reached over to the counter near the guest mic. He handed Clara a small wrapped gift. "Merry Christmas," he said.

"Is this for me?"

Seth looked around, "I don't see anyone else."

"You didn't have to get me anything," Clara said, taking the gift.

"I know, if I *had to* it wouldn't be fun." he said. "Open it."

Seth had used so much tape Clara had to tear the wrapping to shreds to get to the gift. Little by little the bits of paper tore away to reveal a lime green mug with cartoon skiers and the words "I'd Rather Be Skiing" across the top.

"Do you like it?"

"I'd rather be skiing?"

"Yeah," he moved in close to point to the cartoons on the side. She could feel the warmth from his body. "See the little guy with his ski poles there?"

"Yeah, OK, Seth, I've never skied once in my entire life."

He burst out laughing. "I know! Get it? That's the point!" Clara didn't get it at all, but for some reason it made her laugh. It was very Seth.

"I didn't get you anything," Clara said.

"Tell you what," he said. "Why don't you invite me over one day and we'll rent a movie or something."

"OK," Clara said. "It's a deal."

"What kind of movies do you like?"

"I only watch black and white Norwegian films with subtitles."

"What a coincidence. Me too. But just in case Hollywood Video doesn't have a big Norwegian section, do you have a second choice?

"You choose."

"OK," Seth said. His narrow smile spread across his entire face. "We'll have to make a plan."

"Absolutely."

"OK," he said again. "Well, I guess I will leave you to do your show. Merry Christmas."

"Merry Christmas, Seth."

And then it was very quiet at RTV, just a lazy day of Christmas songs and board watching. Clara put her new mug on the console. She looked at it and grinned. She wondered when Seth had gone out and bought it for her. Then again, maybe he hadn't bought it at all. Maybe he was re-gifting it. Maybe he'd decided at 3 AM to get her a gift, and it was all he could find at the gas station at that hour. If it were anyone else, she would assume that was probably the case, but with Seth's sense of humor she was not so sure. Maybe this was a gift that allowed him plausible deniability, a gift that was personal but could appear impersonal. Clara had to laugh at herself. It was a cheap Christmas gift. He was not playing three dimensional chess. Yet how much forethought he had put into his gift was a question that continued to intrigue her. Whatever it meant, without any great fanfare, they had just agreed to have a social relationship outside of work. As Clara sat gazing through the window at the flashing lights of the lobby Christmas tree, she felt less alone.

Seth's Visit

"Nice place," Seth said.

He had arrived with a bottle of red wine and a bag from Hollywood Video. Seth handed Clara the wine. As Clara took it, she put a hand on Seth's arm. "Come on in."

Seth stomped his wet feet and took off his coat, which she hung next to Clara's on the wobbly coat rack she had bought at the Goodwill store.

"My decorator thought I should go with late 20th Century Garage Sale," Clara said extending her arm behind her to showcase her décor.

"A fine aesthetic choice."

"I'll give you the tour," she said, putting the wine down on the counter. "Livingroom/kitchenette."

"Nice."

"Back there is the bathroom and the bedroom."

"OK, nice tour."

Clara rummaged in the drawer for a bottle opener. "I'll have to get out my fancy wine glasses for this," she said, pulling out two drug store glasses with different floral patterns. She poured the wine, and handed one of the glasses to him. "I've got popcorn, should I make popcorn?"

"Sure."

Clara took a bag out of the cabinet and put it in the microwave. As it popped, Seth put his glass of wine down on the coffee table, and walked over to glance through Clara's record collection. He pulled out an LP and glanced at the back cover.

"Do you like the Stone Roses?" Clara called out to him as she pushed the stop button on the microwave.

"I prefer the Stone Poneys," he said, putting the LP back in its place. Then taking out another album he said, "You like Bowie."

"Doesn't everybody?" she said, taking the popcorn out of the microwave. "I have some white labels."

"I like the picture disc."

"When I was in school I used to save up my lunch money. I'm kind of addicted to ads for all the rare records in Goldmine magazine."

"Me too," Seth said, still glancing through the records. "Don't you love the smell of the record store? All that vinyl."

"Ouch!" Clara had tried to pull the bag open too soon and burned her fingers. She dropped the bag on the counter.

"You okay?"

"Yeah," she said. She sucked on one of the steamed fingers.

"You have some interesting stuff," Seth said, pulling out a rare Doors LP.

"You sound surprised." Clara poured the popcorn into a large plastic bowl.

"I thought it would be all dark and moody alternative stuff."

"Well, yeah, obviously I have a lot of that. But it's all music. If you put Jim Morrison in black, The Doors are an alternative band, right? I have a mix tape where I put 'The End' next to 'Bela Lugosi's Dead' and it totally works."

"You're not a dark person, though," Seth said, moving on to her CD rack. "What's the attraction with all this dark stuff?"

"I don't know. I just like it," Clara said. She picked up the bowl and her glass of wine and walked over to the couch, placing the bowl and glass on the coffee table beside Seth's glass. "I get tired of all of the same clean, mass-produced pop stuff. I guess I don't find that poppy ideal that you should be celebrating and having a good time at every moment that appealing. You have to get scared out of your comfort zone sometimes." She took a sip of her wine. "Who knows," she continued, "I'm just making this up. You're making me think about something I don't usually think about. It's like falling in love, isn't it? The music you're attracted to. There's a mystery in it."

Seth spun the CD rack. "I think there are probably two kinds of people," he said. "People who fall in love with music and people who don't. Helen never cared that much about music."

"Probably a bad sign," Clara said.

Seth continued his inventory of Clara's collection. "Yeah," he shrugged, "People like us probably have more in common with the kind of people

171

who fall in love with music than with people who happen to like one or two of the same bands we like."

"I'll buy that."

Seth took a disc off the rack. "This one doesn't seem like your taste."

"Oh yeah," Clara said. "I forgot to send the card back to the CD club saying I didn't want the featured selection. Do you like Damn Yankees? You can have that if you want."

"Really? Thanks," Seth said. "He took the CD with him and sat down beside Clara on the couch.

"Should we have a toast?"

"To radio."

"To radio."

"Do you know, I just found an old cassette in a box of stuff. When I was a kid, my parents got me one of those portable Sears cassette players. You know, with the little microphone on a cord? Maybe you're too young."

"No, I remember those."

"I made tapes pretending to be a DJ."

"Oh my god, I did that too. My friend Beth and I, we did parodies of the stuff on MTV."

"Do you still have it?"

"Probably in a box somewhere. Can I hear yours? I totally have to hear Seth Jones before his voice changed."

"You show me yours, I'll show you mine." He waggled his eyebrows.

"It's early for that isn't it?"

"You'll have to get me drunk first."

Clara took another sip of her wine. "I really would love to hear the tape."

"I'll try to find it."

"What movies did you bring?"

Seth rummaged through the Hollywood Video bag. "We have two choices for our video viewing pleasure this evening." He pulled out the first tape, "If you're in the mood for a real movie, I got *The Player*. It's kind of a thriller. Have you seen it?"

"Not yet."

"Or, the wildcard," he pulled out the second tape and held it up, *Teenagers from Outer Space.*

"*Teenagers from Outer Space?*"

"It is absolutely awful, and you should experience it once in your life."

"Well, we should go with awful then."

"Yes!"

As Clara put the cassette in the machine she said, "I bet we would have been great friends as kids."

"Girls? Yuck."

"Don't you think so?"

"Well, when I was ten, you were what?"

"Less than zero, I think."

"Right, so probably not."

The video for *Teenagers from Outer Space* began with the original 1959 trailer promising a "Fantastic Ray Gun Rampage!"

"Oh this is going to be good," Clara said, sitting down next to Seth. "And it's in black and white, so it must be an art film."

The film began with a space ship that looked like a cross between an amoeba and a cork screw landing in a field and transforming into a saucer. Out of its hatch climbed one of the alien teenagers who immediately zapped a dog with his ray gun and turned him into a skeleton.

"The alien technology looks a lot like the stuff in the RTV studio," Seth observed before taking a handful of popcorn.

"You can tell they're aliens because they have perfect hair," Clara said taking a sip of wine, which she immediately spit out when they started acting. Somehow they managed to be melodramatic and wooden at the same time.

"We live like machines," emoted the alien called Derek.

The aliens had come to earth to farm giant human-eating lobsters called gorgons, and the mission involved vaporizing a lot of people and turning them into skeletons. The climax involved a special effect that even by 1950s standards was comical. Someone held a lobster in front of a camera like a puppet so it appeared to be bigger than the people in the background.

"You know, I think this screenplay was based on *Hamlet*," Seth said,

Clara's sides hurt from laughing. "Stop it," she said, trying to catch her breath.

"No really, this was how Shakespeare originally wanted to do it."

"I think I am getting a little drunk, you're actually sounding funny to me," Clara said, and rested her head on Seth's shoulder. He ran his hand over her hair.

"I must be a little drunk too," Seth said, "this movie isn't looking so bad."

"That's it, I'm cutting you off," Clara said.

Seth let out a yawn. "Did you know radio waves travel into space forever?"

"No."

"Thirty years from now someone on Alpha Centauri will be listening to yesterday's show and trying to dial in and win a pizza coupon."

"Oh, they won't get it," Clara said. "Jason Briggs will beat them to it."

"Do you think aliens like pizza?"

"Everybody likes pizza." Seth was having trouble keeping his eyes open. By the time the end credits started rolling, he had fallen asleep on Clara's shoulder. Clara picked up the remote control with her free hand and turned off the TV. For a moment she sat still, watching Seth's rhythmic breathing. His eye twitched. She ran her index finger across his cheek. This roused Seth. He opened his eyes and sat up.

"I'm sorry, it's not the company," he said, rubbing his eyes.

"Why don't you stay here," Clara said. "The couch folds out."

"Are you sure?"

"Of course."

They moved the coffee table aside. Clara took the cushions off the couch. She went to find a pillow and blanket as Seth unfolded the hidden bed. He took the pillow and blanket and curled up on the thin mattress. "Good night," he said. He fell asleep almost instantly. That night, from her own bed, Clara could hear Seth's light snoring. She thought of his "things the morning crew would rather be doing" sign and laughed to herself. She was replaying the evening in her mind and thinking how nice it was not to be alone in the house as she drifted to dreams. Seth was gone by the time Clara woke up. In fact, she woke up to his voice through the clock radio. He sounded pretty good for a man who'd had almost no sleep and was probably hung over.

When Clara walked in to the station the next day she had the strange sensation that Bill and Al were watching her. Bill usually hung out in the studio when Clara came in, but today he announced that he had some weather to check on. He left Clara and Seth alone and closed the door behind him when he left. "I had a good time last night," Seth said. "We'll have to get together and watch a *good* video next time."

"Oh no, I liked the bad one. I can definitely say I've never seen a movie quite like that before."

Later, on his way out of the station, Seth stopped at Leslie's desk for a chat. Clara could see them out of the corner of her eye as she read various public service announcements. Leslie kept glancing up at the studio window. When Seth was gone, Leslie came into the studio.

"So what's going on with you and Seth?"

"There's nothing going on," Clara said with a shrug.

"Are you sure?"

"What do you mean am I sure? He came over and we watched a video. Why, what did he say?"

"He said you watched a video. So, what happened?"

"We watched a video."

"And?"

"And that's it."

"And?"

"And we had wine and popcorn."

"He seemed to be in a good mood this morning."

"It wasn't a date."

"I don't think he's really gone out with anyone since the divorce."

"It wasn't a date."

"He was wearing the same clothes he had on yesterday."

"Oh, well, yeah, he stayed over, but on the couch. It was late."

"So you didn't..."

"We watched a video."

"And had wine and popcorn."

"Right."

"You're just friends."

"I have a break coming up," Clara said, picking up the headphones. As Leslie was leaving the studio, she turned and said, "He seemed like he was in a really good mood."

Before putting on her headphones, Clara shouted to the closed door, "It wasn't a date!"

Friends of Mine

Clara had slept in a little later than normal. She arrived at the station just as the morning show was doing its last break. "Good morning. 9:51 on Saturn's Favorite Music, RTV," Seth said. "That was Clarence Clemons with James Brown, 'You're a Friend of Mine.'"

"James Brown?" Al asked.

"Did I say James Brown? I meant Jackson Browne." Clara laughed at Seth's mistake as she peeled off her damp coat and put it over the back of her chair. She shook her fingers through her hair to get rid of any remaining snow.

"Not quite the same," Bill said.

"No. Do you know happen who sings the backup on this?" Seth asked.

"Is it Daryl Hannah?" asked Bill.

"It is. It's movie star Daryl Hannah. She was dating Jackson Browne at the time."

"Are they still dating now?" asked Bill.

"I don't really keep up with things like that," Seth said.

"Jackson Browne doesn't call you up and gossip about his personal life?" Al asked.

"No, not usually," Seth said. "But if anyone knows the answer, they can give us a call and let us know. But right now it's time for the RTV News. Al, what is happening in Northern Lower Michigan?"

"Thanks Seth," As Al started reading the news, the phone lit up with a call from a listener responding to Seth's request. Clara took down the information and snuck into the studio. Bill waved, and Seth gestured for Clara to take a seat at the second microphone.

"Thanks Al," Seth said. "Guess who just walked into the RTV studio? It's CJ the DJ, also known as Clara Jane. What's happening, Clara?"

"Well, the RTV listening public has an answer to your question about Jackson Browne and Daryl Hannah," Clara said. "Paula from Roscommon says they are no longer together."

"So she's no longer a friend of his?" Seth asked.

"That's right."

"Well, that's too bad," Seth said. "Hopefully Bill Katz has some better news for us in the RTV Weather Center Forecast."

"I certainly do, Seth," Bill said. Seth fired the weather bed. "RTV Weather!"

"This snowy weather is not going to last," Bill said, "The weekend will be much less blustery and billowy, with temperatures going all the way up into the balmy low 20s. Today expect more light, blowing snow and high temperatures around 14 degrees. Right now in Saturn it's 2 degrees on Saturn's Favorite Music, RTV."

Seth started up the first track of Clara's Superstar Seven in a Row and spoke over its intro, "Now here's a comeback single of sorts from a pop band that owned the 80s. It's Duran Duran with 'Ordinary World.'"

"Good show," Bill said, emerging from his spot behind the machines. Seth stood up and gestured for Clara to take the driver's seat as Bill left the studio. As Clara cued up the first tracks of her show, she could hear a buzz behind her as Seth flipped the switches on the meter. He wrote down the meter readings.

"So apparently we're sleeping together," Seth said. He handed Clara the clipboard with the meter reading form, which legally, as the operator now on duty, she had to sign.

"I heard something about that," she said, signing the document and handing it back.

"Yeah. The guy at the gas station this morning, he said, 'So I hear you're doing the midday girl.'"

"Really? The guy at the gas station?"

"It's a small town."

"Did he tell you if I was any good?"

"No, I should have asked him that," Seth hung the clipboard back on its nail.

They went silent as Al came into the studio to drop off the news break he had recorded for the afternoon. Bill followed holding a cart with a recorded weather break. He set it down and headed back into the corner to get his coat, which he had draped over the back of the chair at the guest mic. As he was putting on his coat, Ed leaned in the door, "Al, Bill, can I see you in my office?" Clara and Seth exchanged a look as the news team followed Ed. As soon as he had closed his door, Leslie speed-walked into the studio.

"What's going on," Seth asked her.

"I think he's letting them go," Leslie said. "Until the FCC approves the sale, Norton is losing money. I think he's trying to stop the bleeding."

"No, I don't believe it," Clara said, "Al's been here forever, hasn't he?"

"As long as I can remember," Leslie said.

"I don't think it matters," Seth said, shaking his head. "It's money."

Clara looked at Seth. Leslie had a way of knowing about things, and Clara feared she was right. A moment later Al walked out of Ed's office, put on his coat and walked out without a word to anyone. Bill came into the studio.

"You're just starting out in your career," he said, pointing to Clara. "So let this be a lesson to you. In this business you can get fired and it has nothing to do with your skill. You'll see it happen again and again. It will probably happen to you one day. I hope it doesn't."

He picked up the cart with the weather center music bed and threw it against the wall. He was probably wishing it would explode into shards, but the impact just cracked the corner of the plastic casing. Frustrated with the lack of drama, he gave it a little kick. Then he left. Seth and Leslie followed him out of the studio. Clara wanted to go with them and say goodbye to Bill, but her break was coming up. When she was finally able to get away from the board, she stood by the studio door. Seth and Leslie were standing in the back room discussing the situation. Ed came out of his office with his head down. Mariah Carey's rousing "Make it Happen" played through the speakers in mockery of the prevailing mood.

"What the fuck?" Seth called to Ed.

Ed shook his head and raised his hand in a "stop" gesture, "I can't deal with you today."

"Bill and Al?!"

"Do you think I wanted to do that?" Ed shouted. "That was awful. Did you know Norton wanted to let them go just before Christmas? I held him off."

"Sorry," Seth said. "It's not your fault. Really, I apologize. But what the fuck?"

"I know."

"It's going to change the whole feel of the morning show," Seth said.

"Yeah," Ed said. He sighed. "Just do your best." He turned to Leslie and said, "I'm going home now. If anyone calls for me, just tell them I went home sick."

Mariah Carey's anthem was reaching its end, so Clara returned to the studio to do her next cross fade.

Clara thought about how different it would be in the mornings without a morning team. Where before Clara had been dreading the kinds of changes a new owner might bring, she started to wish that he would hurry up and take over. It could hardly be worse than things were. Even if the new guy announced an all Billy Ray Cyrus Format ("All Achy Breaky All the Time") there would at least be some sense of stability... and toilet paper.

Kirchner Broadcasting

·¦|··||‖··|¦||·||‖··|‖¦·|¦|··¦¦¦

FCC approval of the sale of WRTV to Kirchner Broadcasting finally happened two weeks later. The first thing that Frank Kirchner did as owner of WRTV was to hold another staff meeting. This time there was less of a party atmosphere. Leslie and Seth sat on the couch with their arms folded across their chests. Clara was beside Seth, fiddling with a thread on her jeans. Ed paced back and forth. Rad was, once again, waiting in the studio door. Clara noticed that in spite of Rad's proclamations about not shuffling cards, his music selections seemed to have an edge. He played Lynda Rondstat "You're no Good," "The End of the Road" by Boyz II Men, Madonna, "This Used to be My Playground," and in the D position, "We Gotta Get Out of This Place" by the Animals.

"We're ready to begin," Kirchner said.

"But wait, Grant's not here," Leslie said.

Kirchner told them not to worry about Grant. Leslie and Seth exchanged a look. Then Kirchner started handing out new RTV t-shirts, frisbees and mugs. Designed with a modern look, they were dark purple with RTV and the planet Saturn in gold. Instead of its normal ring, the planet was surrounded with the words "Saturn's Favorite Music."

"No cowboy boots on it," Seth whispered to Clara.

"No accordions," she whispered back.

"This is an exciting time for the New RTV," Kirchner said. He confirmed that Grant and his night time show had been cut. It was to be immediately replaced with a syndicated overnight program on a satellite feed. But all of the other programs would sound just the same- even better- to listeners. He announced that there was not going to be any change to the format. They would remain an AC station. At this news, Rad let out an audible, "Yes!" Kirchner concluded by saying that there would be more news about exciting changes in the future. As the meeting broke up Kirchner said, "Seth, Clara, I'd like to see you in my office."

Clara's stomach tightened. She remembered Bill's words. "You can get fired and it has nothing to do with your skill. You'll see it happen again and again. It will probably happen to you one day." She looked at Seth and he shrugged. Clara felt the sword of Damocles hanging over her as she and Seth walked the now seemingly endless hallway. Kirchner's office was located across from the kitchen next to the sales offices. Before he moved in, he had ordered all new furniture. The chairs were plush leather, the kind with gold nail heads. If the large, polished desk was not mahogany, it gave that impression. Clara and Seth sat down in the two chairs facing the desk. They glanced at each other as Kirchner cleared his throat to start speaking.

"I realize this might be awkward," he said, "but I believe it's important to discuss this situation." Clara glanced at Seth, who seemed to be trying to burn holes in Kirchner's head with his eyes. "Normally at my stations I don't allow... fraternization between employees," Kirchner said.

Clara raised her eyebrows, "Fraternization?" She was so relieved that she was not being fired that she wanted to laugh out loud. Out of the corner of her eye, she could see Seth was also suppressing a laugh.

"I understand that I'm coming into an existing situation," Kirchner said. "So I just wanted to make my position clear. There are many potential problems in work place... involvements. Obviously, since this is an existing situation, I can't make any demands on your personal lives, however, I want to be clear that while you are at work, anything that may be happening outside of work should be left outside. Agreed?"

"I'm sorry, sir," Seth said, then he took Clara's hand, raised it to his lips and kissed it. "It's just that CJ and I are very much in love. I waited a long time to find this woman, and if you're asking me to choose between my job and the woman I love..."

Clara looked away from Seth, pressed her lips together and shook her head. Kirchner was clearly uncomfortable.

"That's not what I'm asking," he said. "I just wanted to make sure that you understood my position. There is no problem as long as it doesn't interfere with your performance."

"I think our performance has been all right, don't you darling?" Seth patted Clara's knee. Clara closed her eyes. "Oh my god, Seth," she thought to herself.

"Well, as long as that's settled," Kirchner sputtered, and motioned for them to leave. When they were clear of his office, Clara hit Seth on the arm. "We're very much in love?"

"Are you saying you don't love me? After I gave my body to you freely. I feel so used."

They were now in front of Leslie's desk, and she was listening with some interest. "What's going on?" she asked.

"Mr. Kirchner doesn't allow fraternization," Clara said.

Seth smiled, "But he made an exception in our case."

Co-Ops

After the takeover, the energy at RTV shifted almost overnight. There was a sense that exciting things really were about to happen. The lobby was repainted with the newly designed RTV logo prominent on the wall over Leslie's desk. The ugly orange couches in the lobby and back room were updated with Scandinavian leatherette models. There was even a brand-new coffee machine for the break room. The station hired a new custodian. Supplies were plentiful. Kirchner did not come in much in those first weeks. When he did, he usually went straight into Ed's office. Clara rarely saw Ed either. He now spent most of his time in his office with the door shut.

One morning in late January, Leslie came into the studio during Clara's show with a revision to the log. "We have some make goods," she said. "You need to add an Erickson's Hardware to each break." Make goods are commercials that run for free because for one reason or another they failed to run correctly when they were originally scheduled.

Kirchner had brought with him a new system for the sales staff to increase their billings-- co-op advertising. With the co-ops, a national company paid a bulk rate to run a certain number of ads for products sold at hardware stores. The sales team spread out across the region offering tags on those spots to local retailers at a fraction of the standard ad rate. For example, after a commercial for a certain brand of snow shovel or fishing pole, there would be a tag saying, "You can find this product at Jim's Hardware in Manistee." The packages were so popular that the ads were beginning to take over all of the commercial avails.

Clara looked down at the log. The unwritten rule in broadcasting was that two commercials for direct competitors should never be played back-to-back. You would not play a McDonald's ad followed by one for Burger King or Coke next to Pepsi. "Where am I supposed to put them?" Clara asked. "It's all hardware."

"I don't know," Leslie snapped. "Play some PSAs in between. Figure it out."

Clara sat back in the chair, stunned. She had never heard Leslie lose her temper before.

"I'm sorry," Leslie said. "I just hate these f-ing co-op spots. Did you know Kirchner is having a contest? The sales person who sells the most co-ops gets a $2,000 bonus."

That was more than Clara made in a month. "Wow, where's our bonus?"

Leslie rubbed her temple. "They just keep selling them and selling them and they have no idea. They don't think about it. They just sell ten spots with the exact same copy. I tell them there aren't enough slots for them. You can't have one break with three of the same commercial with different tags. You can get this drill at Erickson's Hardware. No, get this drill at Jim's Hardware. Maybe you should get this drill at Upstate Hardware. They don't care."

"That sucks," Clara said, tucking a card in the back of the wooden box.

"I told Kirchner, you know. I said, 'They're selling too many of these co-ops. It looks like there are avails, but there aren't. Yeah, there are x number of avails, but you don't really have that many slots because it's all the same copy." She imitated Kirchner, "'That's not your job. Your job is to make sure they all run.'" She sighed. "Maybe I should just let them all run back-to-back, the same spot over and over. But I actually care about doing a good job."

"That's your mistake right there."

"If somebody's getting a bonus for this mess, I should get one."

"I'm with you," Clara said, putting on her headphones. "Stand by." Clara announced the song she had just played and then started the first spot in a break in which four out of five ads were for hardware stores. She toggled off the microphone, and Leslie went back to the conversation.

"There are jobs that get attention and jobs that don't get attention; do you know what I mean?"

"I'm not sure," Clara said, checking the spots off on the log.

"You're on the air, so you have a job that gets attention. The sales people do something you can measure, so they get attention. When you do well in that kind of job you get rewards. Then there are jobs where doing the job well means everything just works and no one notices. It's the opposite. If people notice, you're doing a bad job. That's the kind of job I have. So everyone thinks the job isn't that hard, or important."

"I don't think that."

"Not you. I don't mean you. Have you noticed that it's usually women who have the no-one-notices kinds of jobs?"

191

"Yeah, I think you're right."

"When they do articles on some business tycoon, they never look at the company and say it is successful because of all of the office managers who keep everything organized and functioning. Have you ever seen that? It's just the guy who owns it on the cover. Like the people in the cubicles are nobody." Clara stood up and started putting the carts back on the commercial rack.

"Anyway," Leslie said, "Sorry for snapping. Just do the best you can with the co-ops."

When Leslie went back to her desk, Clara shuffled through the cards and pulled one from the middle of the Bs.

"It's 11:27 on Saturn's Favorite Music, your light rock, more music station, RTV. Stay tuned in the next hour for a chance to win free carpet cleaning from Cal's Carpets. Right now it's a song for all of the unsung workers out there. It's Huey Lewis and the News, 'Workin' for a Livin.'"

Clara looked out the window. Leslie looked to the booth and raised a thumb. As the song played, Clara wondered what it would be like to be a non-Huey Lewis member of the News. She was pretty sure she could not pick any of them out in a lineup. A lot of people have jobs you don't really notice. Clara was thankful she did not have a job like Leslie's. Although that job, at least, had the interest of being in radio. She shuddered at the thought of having the kind of job where you sat at a desk and did inventories of widgets day in and day out. That was her absolute nightmare. She thought she would rather jump off a bridge than be condemned to such a fate.

Fortunately, she was feeling more confident that she would not have to. Things were looking up at RTV. Too many commercials was a good problem to have. As far as Clara could tell, the upheaval of the past couple of months was finally over. That's when Ed came into the studio and posted a memo. There would be a mandatory jock meeting on Tuesday.

Theater of the Air

That Friday Clara flipped through the box of cards, pulling out only tracks that were on CD, while behind her Rad and Seth were crouched down, pulling LPs from a low shelf and putting them into boxes. The vinyl was to be packed away so that over the weekend the studio could be fitted with a bank of CD players controlled by computer automation.

"This is an exciting time for WRTV," Kirchner had said at the jock meeting where he announced the change. Thanks to the wonders of modern technology, many mindless, routine tasks would be eliminated, allowing the DJs more time to focus on the important aspects of their shows. Both the main studio and the production studio were to be equipped with computers. Production would be recorded straight into the system, which meant no more fumbling for carts, no more cutting and splicing reel-to reel-tape. The vocals for commercials could be digitally compressed or expanded to fix a :30 or :60-second time slot exactly. And as soon as a commercial was finished, it could be played on the air, because both studios would share the same computer system. One of the main studio's two computers would be devoted to recording and playing back news feeds. No more back-timing to the news. No more catching feeds on reel tapes. The computer could even play the news back while it was recording. The new system could take meter readings, monitor the EBS signal, and play the music. The DJs could record whole shows in advance and would no longer have to work on holidays. With all of those mundane tasks automated, Kirchner said, "You will be able to focus entirely on making your show great."

As Seth was loading his box, he came across a copy of Bob Dylan's "Highway 61 Revisited." He stood up, glancing at the front and back of the cover. "Is there a card for this?" he asked Rad, who had started packing boxes at the other end of the shelf. "I don't remember ever seeing it come up."

"No," Rad said. "It's not on our playlist."

"Why not?" Seth asked. "It's late 60s. We play that."

"It doesn't fit the format."

"'Like a Rolling Stone' got to, what? Number 2 on the charts?" Seth asked.

"Chart position isn't the only consideration," Rad said. "We're an AC station. We play the pop 60s. Not the countercultural 60s."

"I think you're underestimating the audience," Seth said.

Rad continued to load records into boxes. "It's not about underestimating them. It's about the format. It's giving the audience what it expects."

Seth turned to Clara, "You know it's a serious format when being at Woodstock *dis*qualifies you from the playlist." Clara laughed as she sat down and picked up the headphones. Seth continued his mini-rant, "RTV, conformist radio."

"Stand by!" Clara called out. Rad pulled the studio door shut, and he and Seth stood perfectly still. Clara opened the mic, "You're listening to another Superstar Seven in a Row. That was Pebo Bryson and Regina Belle, 'A Whole New World.' And now something a little bit ominous from Phil Collins, 'In the Air Tonight' on Saturn's Favorite Music, RTV."

Clara removed her headphones and turned around. Seth held the Bob Dylan record out towards her, "Let her play 'Like a Rolling Stone' as the D. No one will run screaming. We're getting rid of the records, what can it hurt to play it one time?"

"Yeah, fine," Rad said. Seth shook the record to indicate that Clara should take it, which she did. Clara was surprised that Rad had given in. She came to realize that for all of Rad's machinations behind Seth's back, he deferred to him when they were face to face.

As Clara cued the record, Rad said, "They're giving me my own computer. I'm looking forward to learning the system. I think it will make it easier for me to program a different mix for each day part."

Seth shook his head as he crouched down to load more records into boxes. "DJs used to do that with their personalities."

"Well, once I have the computer," Rad said, "the DJs won't be able to mess up the system anymore."

Clara did a cross fade between Phil Collins and the Dylan track. She did not even like Bob Dylan, but playing a song that was off the playlist felt like a jail break. She had no idea what Dylan was going on about in the song, but Seth clearly did. He sang along in his best nasal folk singer voice as he took records off the shelf. Even Rad seemed to be enjoying the little act of musical rebellion.

"Can you move that box?" Clara said, demonstrating that it was blocking the large rack with the commercial carts so she could not spin it.

"Oh man, it's heavy," Seth said. "Which spots do you need?"

"Raider Hardware, Erickson Hardware, Jim's Hardware and Arlo's Pizza."

"One of these things is not like the others," Seth said. He handed her the carts and went back to his Dylan impression while moving some of the albums from the over-full box to a different box.

"There's a break after this; be ready," Clara said, putting the first commercial carts into their slots. Clara opened the mic and the on-air light came on, and the speakers cut off in the room. Seth and Rad stopped loading again.

"That was something special this morning on Saturn's Favorite Music, a solid gold oldie, and a classic, from Bob Dylan. It's 'Like a Rolling Stone.' Some mean harmonica on that one. On the way we have Janet Jackson, Whitney Houston and Go West. All that and more coming up after this break on your light rock, more music station, RTV." Clara turned off the mic and started running the commercials.

"It will be interesting to see how the new system works," Rad said. "I'm hoping it has options to program things like tempo and mood, not just chart positions and year. I could do a lot with something like that."

"Again, something human beings can do," Seth said.

Rad picked up one of the boxes with a groan and carried it out of the studio. He passed Leslie, who was on the way in. "Wow, it looks so weird in here," she said, then she sneezed.

197

"Bless you," Seth said. Leslie sneezed four more times. "Are you done?"

"I think so, um, nope." She sneezed again.

"Bless you."

She sneezed again,. "It's the dust." She put her left sleeve over her nose, and with her right hand she started to brush dust from the newly empty shelves. As she did that she noticed some papers sticking out from behind some of the remaining albums. "What's this?" She reached in and pulled out a collection of browning pages.

"What is it?" asked Seth.

Ed entered the studio, "Do you need help with the records?"

"Look at this," Leslie said, standing beside him so they could both read the papers. "It's a script from a radio drama."

"It must be from the 1940s or 50s," Ed said.

"Is the station that old?" Clara asked.

"Yeah," Ed said. "It used to be a full-service station. Live bands, news, radio auctions, dramas."

"That's so cool," Leslie said, flipping to the second page.

Rad returned to the studio and said to Ed, "These boxes are really heavy; can you help me with this one?" He and Ed lifted the box with a grunt and inched out of the studio.

Seth went over to Leslie to look at her pages. "It's a detective drama," he said to Clara. Then to Leslie, "Can't you just picture them here, back in the day?"

"Those 1940s hairstyles and the stockings with the seam in the back?" Leslie said.

"Hold on," Clara said, raising her hand. "Hot mic… It's 10:42 on Saturn's Favorite Music, RTV. That was Go West and 'Faithful.' We're doing a bit of moving here in the RTV studio, and we discovered a little treasure behind a shelf of records. Apparently, before RTV played the best mix of your light favorites and great oldies, we used to broadcast radio dramas, and we just found one of the old scripts."

Seth ducked behind the monitors and sat down at the guest mic. He put on the headphones and gestured to Clara to pot him up. "Seth Jones is with me now, and he has a copy of this discovery. What was the name of the play?"

"It's Saturn Theater of the Air, Murder in the Afternoon," Seth said.

"What a great name, 'Theater of the Air.'"

"It says 'sound effect of a door opening.'" Seth made a creaking door sound with his voice. He slid the script closer to Clara and pointed to a character named Birdie. Clara leaned in and read, "Hello, Boss."

Seth put on the voice of a boss, "Hello, Birdie."

"Hello Mr. Fletcher."

Seth put on another voice: "Hello, Miss Scott."

"They spend a lot of time saying hello to each other," Clara said.

"Well, Seth said, "they have to so you know who is in the room."

"Of course," Clara said, then returned to the voice of her character. "There was a call for you, Mr. Fletcher, a man called Broadway Jim, it sounded important."

Seth read in the voice of the boss, or possibly James Cagney, "What was the message?"

"He said that he had information on the dockside murders."

"Did he sound on the level?"

"Why, I don't know, boss."

When Clara glanced up, she saw Kirchner outside the window. He was standing with his hands on his hips, glaring through the glass. Seth, who could not see him, switched to the voice of Mr. Fletcher: "Broadway Jim? Why, that's the man who evaded the police on that smuggling charge two years ago."

"Well," Clara said, looking at Kirchner, "unfortunately, we don't have time to reenact this whole drama."

"It would be so much fun," Seth said.

"Maybe one day," Clara said. "In the meantime, here's Toad the Wet Sprocket with 'Walk on the Ocean.'" Clara pushed the button on the CD player, and closed the two mics.

"You're a swell dame, Birdie," Seth said. Clara laughed, "Thanks, Seth, you're the bee's knees." As Clara was putting the next disc in the CD player, the light on the phone started flashing.

"RTV Studio."

"Hi, yes, I was just calling to say thank you for reminding me of that old radio play."

"Did you used to listen to the radio dramas?"

"I didn't just listen, I was in them."

"You acted in this play?"

Leslie perked up, and came close to the phone, leaning on the bank with the turntables. Seth put down a box of LPs he was about to take into the next room and also came close to the phone.

"Yes, I was one of the Theater of the Air players."

"Were you Birdie?"

"I did all the female voices. One day I'd be a secretary, the next day maybe a little girl or an old woman." Seth started to gesture for Clara to put the call on speaker so he could hear it. Leslie nodded.

"What is your name?" Clara asked.

"Phyllis Case."

"Phyllis, would you mind if I put your call on the speakers? Seth would like to hear you too."

"Of course."

Clara put the line on hold, put down the receiver, and then depressed the line and the speakerphone button. "Are you there, Phyllis?"

"Yes.".

Seth said, "Phyllis, I'm Seth Jones. I'm very interested to hear more of your story."

"Hi Seth, I know who you are. I listen to you every morning."

"Thank you. How did you get involved in radio drama?"

"It was my brother; he was the director of the Saturn Theater of the Air. My brother was the first person to show me a radio when I was a little girl. This was a long time ago, mind you. My brother liked to tinker with things, and he asked me 'Hey kid, wanna see a magic box?' It was this little mechanical contraption, and voices came out of it. I couldn't figure out how the voices got in there. It was like magic. Theater runs in the family. I wanted to be an actress from the time I was this high. Oh you can't see that," she laughed. "I acted in school and then in the radio company." Clara walked away from the phone to cue up the next CD.

"Did you do the shows right here, in the same building that we broadcast from?" Seth asked.

"On the corner of Main and Maple, yes. I haven't been in there in a while. I don't think the inside is quite the same. I think they divided the old studio up. We had a big studio for actors and musicians, and then the control room was through a window. I think some of the equipment, the meters and so on, might be in the same place. I didn't know much about that."

Seth's face was animated. "I am so glad we found your script."

"I am, too. Everything was live back then, so I don't have many recordings."

"I'd be glad to send this script to you if you don't have it."

"Oh, would you? That would be wonderful. I didn't keep them at the time. You're not thinking about that sort of thing when you're young."

"It must have been fun. I had fun just reading a few lines, coming up with different voices."

"It was. I liked creating something in people's imaginations using only your voice. You could be anything. On radio, no one knows what you look like."

"In my case, that's probably a good thing."

"I'll tell you a secret," Phyllis said, "When they did publicity photos for the Theater of the Air, they would have a model put on a business suit and stand in for my part."

"That's terrible."

"Oh, I didn't mind. It was all about illusion. It was the imagination business. It wasn't really about me. I think people lost some of the ability to imagine when television came around and showed them everything."

"There's some truth to that."

"Of course, my parts weren't the most interesting. My lines were mostly 'Help me' and "There's a call for you, sir.' The men got the best parts-- the heroes, villains. A lot of them came and went, though. I acted longer than any of them. We had listeners all over the state. You must have them too. You still have that big tower."

"Yes, we do."

Clara, interrupted, "I have a break coming up."

"Listen, Phyllis, we have to get off the studio phone, let me put you on hold."

Seth put the call on hold, and Seth and Leslie dashed out to her desk. Clara could see Seth continuing the conversation with Leslie leaning in to listen. In truth, Clara did not understand why they were so interested in talking to the old woman. It was cool to find the script, like a hidden treasure, and Clara had fun reading it for its goofy melodrama. But it was hardly fine art, and she bristled at the idea that young people these days lack imagination.

Old people were always wanting to remind you of their time, and tell you how much better it was then. "Quality music died with Elvis." "It was better before those talking pictures ruined everything." "Flappers will be the downfall of society." Somehow the young always seem to have enough imagination to invent a culture that is different than the one they've been handed. Clara was much more interested in looking forward than back. Seth and Leslie talked to the woman for a good ten minutes before returning to the studio.

"It's a crazy day," Clara said.

"That was great," Leslie said. "I didn't know about any of that. I love talking to people whose time overlaps with yours. Know what I mean?"

"I'm not sure," Clara said.

"You know, people have an era," she said, "But you overlap with people who go back before you. So you get to know a little bit about the times just before you."

"It's not like reading a book," Seth said.

"Oh, no," Leslie said. "It's so much better when people tell you from their experience. When you know someone who did something, It's like you're connected to it."

Rad and Ed came back into the studio, picked up another box of records and lugged it out. "I bet the back room was the studio that they used, and our studio was the control room," Seth said.

"Can't you just picture them?" Leslie asked, "With one of those big old-fashioned microphones with scripts in their hands?"

"It was just their everyday life," Seth said. "Someone came in and unlocked that door, and maybe they took readings off this same old meter, and someone was fighting with his boss over something no one remembers anymore and someone was having a bad day because his wife didn't understand him. And they went on and did a show. Ordinary life. This was their boring background, just like us."

"And all those shows that just went out into the air, never recorded," Leslie said. "Poof, it was there and it was gone."

"And it mattered," Seth said.

"Yes it did," Leslie said. "It all mattered. "

Ed and Rad came back in the studio with a couple of empty boxes. "These were the last two boxes we could find," Ed said. "I think the rest of the records should fit in here."

"You know what?" Leslie said, "We should put something back behind this shelf where the CD players are going to be. Can I borrow this?" Leslie picked up the log and left the studio. A minute later she returned. She had made a photocopy of the title page of the log with the date and

Seth and Clara's signatures. She had Rad sign his time slot. Then she and Ed wrote their names at the bottom. Leslie took the signed page and an RTV bumper sticker and wedged them into a spot behind the shelf. She sneezed. "Excuse me," she said.

"Bless you," said Clara.

This is great, Seth said, "One day someone will find this, and for about two minutes maybe they'll stop and wonder who we were."

Clara smiled at Seth, but inside she was thinking that she planned to make more of an impression on the world than that.

Live Assist Mode

That Sunday, Clara returned to the studio for a training meeting for the new automation system. The shelf that had once held the records had been replaced with a bank of CD players. There were 24 in all, each fitted with a six-disc changer. On the top shelf was a monitor showing a programming log in a green terminal font. Next to it was a second monitor that showed the upcoming news, weather and satellite feeds that were slated to be recorded into the system. The spinning rack with commercial carts was gone, and in the corner next to the turntables was a dot matrix printer with a large spool of continuous paper in the feeder. Over the board, where there had once been an easel with clock hours and commercial copy, was another computer monitor. Its keyboard sat on the console over near the guest microphone. The scene reminded Clara a bit of the missile command center in the movie *War Games*.

Sitting in the driver's seat was a man in khaki slacks and a polo shirt with the name "Chad" embroidered over the automation company's logo. Clara, Seth and Rad stood behind looking over his shoulders as he demonstrated the features of the automation software. Kirchner stood further behind, near the bank of CDs, looking imperious. Chad had a bright smile that exuded excitement over the station's new toy. Rad, who was scribbling lots of notes into a spiral notebook, seemed to share

Chad's enthusiasm. Seth, on the other hand, alternately took a sip from his coffee cup and eyed the trainer with extreme skepticism.

"The computer handles everything," Chad said. He explained that the system had two programming modes, fully automated and "live assist." In automated mode, instead of having an operator on the board, the system would play pre-recorded voice tracks between the songs and commercials.

"So we don't have to be here on holidays anymore," Rad said, "We can record them in advance."

"Exactly," Chad said. "The computer does it all. You put your show in the system, and then you can walk away and let it do its thing."

"What is 'live assist?" Seth asked, "It sounds like the people are helping the computer instead of the other way around."

"Live assist is for the programs that run in real time with an operator on the board," Chad said. "Usually that's programs with a lot of live elements, traffic and weather updates and so on. Instead of running a voice track, when a break comes up, you pause the system," Chad demonstrated by pushing the enter key. "You see, now the system has stopped. It won't roll into the next element until you push enter again. So you pause, you speak live on the air, and then you start the system back up and it will keep playing until you pause it again."

"Your show will be live assist," Kirchner told Seth.

Clara's muscles tensed. It was the first moment that it occurred to her that her own show did not contain the time-sensitive traffic and weather updates that Chad had mentioned.

"What about my show?" she asked.

Kirchner explained that there would only be two live programs going forward, morning and afternoon drive. Rad stood a bit taller and grinned at Clara. The midday show, Kirchner said, would be "fully automated." For the next week, while the staff was getting used to the system, Clara would stay on the air, running in live assist mode. After that she would record all of the voice tracks for her show in the production room. Then she would have "other important tasks" to perform.

"What important tasks?" Clara asked.

"That is to be determined," Kirchner said.

"Of course there will be a few glitches in the beginning as we iron all the bugs out of the system, but in the end we will have a station we all can be proud of," Kirchner said. "It is an exciting time for RTV."

Chad stepped aside to let Seth sit down and practice with the system. Clara left the studio and sat down on the sofa beside Rad's desk. She felt dazed. Her voice would still be on the air. What would her body be doing? Chad came out of the studio, followed by Rad and Kirchner. "This is a really cool system," Rad said to Clara. "You should get in there and play with it."

Clara was wondering if she should quit on the spot. Chad pulled a second chair up to Rad's desk to instruct him on how to use the music programming computer that had been installed on his desk. "Each week you'll get an envelope like this with any new CDs and a floppy disc like this one," Chad took a 5 1/4" floppy disc and a sheet of paper out of the envelope. This sheet has the instructions for which discs to swap out from the machines in the studio, if there are any that week. Then you come back here." Chad took the floppy disc out of its sleeve and slid it into the drive until the large button popped out with a click. Chad showed Rad how to type in a command at the prompt to run a program that merged the data for the music with the programming log. "You put the date in here, and that's it," Chad said. "It's all good to go for another week."

Rad looked confused. "How do I adjust what songs it plays?"

"You don't have to," Chad said, still smiling. "The computer does all that. The music is all programmed by the service. You just have to change the discs from time to time."

Rad looked at the stack of books and magazines on his desk, the charts and notebooks full of his programming notes. His smile disappeared.

The first time Clara walked out of the studio as a song was ending it felt daring and thrilling, and also unsettling, like jumping out of an airplane and trusting the chute would open. Leslie, Seth and Clara stood in the lobby looking up at the speakers, and then through the window to the empty studio as the music changed itself-- and their futures along with it.

Desk Jockey

One week after the automation system was up and running, Clara came into the station to find Ed, Seth and Kirchner gathered around Leslie's desk. Leslie was putting her family pictures into her purse.

"This is a mistake," Seth was saying.

"This isn't personal," Kirchner said, "it's a business decision."

"Of course it's personal," Seth said, making an assertive gesture with an open palm in Leslie's direction. "It's her life."

"It's OK, Seth," Leslie said in a calm voice, "They're giving me a good payout."

Seth started pacing. "This is bullshit."

Ed turned to Seth, "Isn't your record ending?"

Seth looked at him. "Automation," he said, throwing up his hands.

Ed gave Seth a long stare, "I think you should go check anyway."

Seth went over and gave Leslie a hug. "If you need anything, call me," he said.

"I'm fine," she said. Then Seth went back into the studio muttering something under his breath.

"He can be a little high strung," Ed said to Kirchner, "But he's invaluable. He'll calm down."

"He'd better," Kirchner said.

"What's going on?" Clara asked.

"Can I see you in my office," Kirchner said. Clara shot Ed a pleading look. He nodded in a reassuring way, but it did nothing to dispel Clara's certainty that Kirchner was cleaning house and that she was about to be let go.

"Have a seat, Miss Jane." Clara thought of correcting him, telling him her last name was Andrzejewski, not Jane, but she decided it was not worth the bother.

"You are doing a great job here," Kirchner said.

"Thank you."

"The show sounds great. Of course, now that we have the new system, it is not a full day's work to do the shift. So we're adding some roles to your portfolio. You are being promoted to traffic director."

"Promoted?"

"Yes," Kirchner said. "This is a great opportunity for you. We expect you to be here from 8-5. You'll have an hour's lunch break. After you've finished recording your airshift, you will be responsible for the traffic logs, overseeing commercial production and the front desk."

"The front desk? You mean Leslie's job?"

"You do know how to type?"

"Yes, but I'm a radio announcer. I'm not a receptionist."

"This is what the position now entails," Kirchner said. "If you don't want to accept this opportunity, we will have to advertise for someone to fill the position as it stands. You're a Harrison School grad, aren't you? We get tapes from Harrison grads every day. I'm sure one of them would be happy to accept the position if you are not interested in it anymore."

"No," Clara said. "I'll do it. Thank you for the opportunity."

When Clara left Kirchner's office, she found Leslie still at her desk collecting her personal items. She handed Clara a copy of the latest *Weekly World News.* "Werewolf Battles Cops in Alabama!"

"Here," she said, "Souvenir."

"You know it's important because it has an exclamation point in the headline," Clara said in a mournful tone.

"Looks like it's up to you now to keep the staff informed of the UFO invasions."

"I'm sorry," Clara said. "I think they're making a mistake. I don't want your job. I want mine."

"I know," she said. Down the hall, the women could see Seth going into Ed's office. "Keep Seth out of trouble," Leslie said.

"You know we're not really a couple," Clara said.

"Well, maybe not," Leslie said, "but he listens to you. He's going to mouth off to Kirchner, and he's not going to be as flexible as Ed. Seth doesn't like people telling him what to do."

"I noticed."

"There's no point in all of us getting fired."

"What are you going to do?"

"I'm not sure," Leslie said, putting on her jacket. "The severance package will last a while. Maybe I'll go back to school or something. My cousin just became a dental technician. The money is really good."

"If you can stand spending all day scraping people's teeth."

"There's that," Leslie said. Then they both looked up as if they could see the sound in the air. There was something strange about the music playing over the speakers. Something not quite right. It took a moment to process.

"What is that?" Leslie said.

"I think it's... Billy Joel? Or is it Sting?"

"I thought it was Phil Collins," she said.

It dawned on both of them at the same time- it was Billy Joel and Sting and Phil Collins. The computer was playing three CDS at once. Clara ran towards the studio. As she rounded the corner she collided with Seth who was running from Ed's office. Clara hit her head when she fell to the floor. There was a loud "thump" as Seth fell against the door.

Ed had followed Seth out of his office. "Are you all right?" he asked, as Clara and Seth helped each other up. Then Kirchner came around the corner. When he saw Ed, Seth and Clara standing by the studio door he shouted, "Why are you just standing there? Do something about that noise!"

Professional Attire

A few days after she started working at the front desk, Ed called Clara into his office. "So Mr. Kirchner asked me to discuss this with you," Ed began. He rubbed his cheek and cleared his throat. "Now that you're at the front desk, he'd like you to, uh, dress in business attire."

Clara had to look down to see what she was wearing. She had put on what she thought were nice black slacks, a black tank top with an orange vest over it and a long necklace. She was doing a silent inventory of her wardrobe. She owned exactly one power suit, the one she had worn for her interview. It was dry-clean only. "What does he mean by business attire?"

"You don't have to wear a suit every day," Ed said. "Business casual. When clients come into the station, they want to see it as an office."

"Right," Clara said. "OK." The next day she dressed exactly as she had for her job interview. She felt out of place and was uncomfortable the entire day. She wore the same outfit again the next day. The third day she could tell that the jacket was becoming a little fragrant. She didn't have money to clean it, so she started exploring the recesses of her closet. She put on her black slacks and a long-sleeved shirt with red and black vertical stripes. She pinned her black hair up in a tight bun, which she thought made her look close enough to a librarian to pass the "business casual" test.

A couple of hours into her shift, Kirchner walked past her desk. In her new role as secretary/traffic director/voice track announcer, Clara always had either way too much or not enough work. When commercial affidavits needed to be filled out, there were not enough hours in the day. During the slow times, like this day, if Kirchner was around, he would cast glances at Clara as though she was not doing enough work to justify the $5.30 an hour he paid her. Clara reached into her desk and pulled out a random folder and started shuffling through the papers in order to appear busy. Then she glanced up and gave Kirchner a broad smile, the kind that does not cause wrinkles in the corners of the eyes. Kirchner's look did not soften. He went into Ed's office, and then left for the day without saying anything to her. A few minutes later Ed came out to Clara's desk. He spoke without making eye contact. "Mr. Kirchner wanted me to mention your clothes."

"I only have one suit," Clara said. "I can't afford to dry clean it every day."

"You don't have to wear a suit," Ed said. "Kirchner is just more traditional. You know, it's a conservative area here."

"I thought this was conservative," Clara said. "It's slacks and a blouse."

"Well," Ed said, he looked her up and down and shrugged. "Maybe you should try a dress."

The next day Clara wore a long-sleeved black trapeze dress cut just above the knee. She had paired it with some dainty dress shoes and a string of imitation black pearls that she used to wear at City Club. She wore her hair down and avoided the black eye pencil. Yet again, Kirchner gave her a look, and Ed called her into his office. After the confrontation, she took her RTV mug off her desk and headed to the kitchen, as though she was going to refill her coffee. In reality, she was looking for a more private place to cry.

A few minutes later, Seth came in. He said, "Hi," but barely looked in Clara's direction as he made a bee line for the coffee. As his back was turned, Clara quickly wiped the tears from her cheeks with the back of her hand and sat up straighter. When Seth turned, he started to smile, but then noticed Clara's expression.

"Hey, what's wrong?" he asked.

"It's nothing."

"Are you sure?" He pulled up a chair beside her. "What's going on?"

"It's stupid," she said.

"Don't worry about that," Seth said, resting a hand on her arm.

"It's just, they keep telling me I don't look 'professional' enough," she said with a sniffle.

"Who does?"

"Ed and Kirchner."

Seth moved his hand to her shoulder, "It's not stupid."

"I don't know what they want. They wanted me to wear a dress." She clutched the fabric of her skirt. "I'm wearing a dress. This is what I've got. I can't afford a whole new wardrobe."

"You look nice."

"Ed says Kirchner thinks my skirt is too short."

"It's a little short, but it's not…"

"Now you're looking," Clara tried to stretch the fabric and make it longer.

"No, I'm not. I mean, not that way. There's nothing wrong with how you're dressed."

"It's only me, you know. I'm the only one who has to look 'professional.' I mean look at what you're wearing." Seth was wearing black jeans and a faded long-sleeved Kinks t-shirt. "No offense."

Seth laughed. "None taken. I think I picked it up off the floor and gave it a sniff."

"It just feels so icky." Clara felt the tears welling up again. "It makes me so self-conscious, walking in and having this old man scrutinizing me all the time. I just put on clothes. I wasn't trying to be a sex object."

"It's his issue, not yours."

"I never wanted to be a fashion model. I don't know why I should have to be. I'm supposed to be a DJ."

"Hey," Seth said, giving her a hug, "Don't let them get to you."

Just then Ed walked into the kitchen, his face turned pink and he said, "Sorry, guys," turned around and walked out. This caused Clara and Seth to break into a cathartic fit of laughter. Clara wiped her nose with the back of her hand.

"I hope I didn't get snot on you," she said.

"Don't worry, it would probably be an improvement," he said.

"Oh man," Clara said, taking a deep breath.

"Listen, no matter what you wear you'll still be CJ the DJ," Seth said. "A little of that alternative girl will always shine through."

That evening Clara stood in front of her full-length mirror and thought about what Seth had said. Her dress was just a dress, a plain dress. The only thing that made it seem at all edgy was that an "alternative girl" was wearing it. That was when the solution dawned on her. She went to the store and bought a box of light blonde hair coloring. "Goodbye, Alternative Girl," she said as she squeezed the liquid onto her hair.

The next day Clara used a curling iron to sculpt her hair into mall-girl waves. She did her makeup with pastel colors. She wore her black slacks with a burgundy sweater and the imitation black pearls. She wasn't quite Barbie, but she wasn't Siouxie, and that was what mattered.

Clara walked into the studio and leaned against the door frame, "Hi."

Seth quickly glanced over his shoulder, "Hi." He turned back to the screen and then his head snapped back in her direction. "Wow."

"Do I look like DJ Barbie?" Clara asked, using her right hand to fluff up her hair.

"Um, do you want to?" Seth said, "I don't want to get in trouble."

Clara laughed. "No. I don't think of myself as the Barbie type."

"You can take the girl out of the alternative but you can't take the alternative out of the girl."

Clara furrowed her brow. "Does that actually mean anything?"

"Hmm," Seth said, his eyes rolled upwards. "No, I guess not. Sometimes I shoot for clever and miss."

Clara laughed again. "You look good," Seth said. "But then, you always look good."

"Nice."

"Right answer?"

"I swear it wasn't a trick question."

Clara returned to her desk. An hour later, Kirchner walked by. He glanced at her, and then kept walking. Ed did not call her into his office. Over the next few days Clara experimented with her clothes. Nothing she wore earned her a meeting with the boss. After a couple of weeks, she decided to try wearing jeans. She took a cup of coffee into Kirchner's office just to be sure he saw her. He said nothing. Finally, she came to work in the same trapeze dress that had earned her a reprimand.

"That's a nice dress," Ed said.

Although Kirchner had many ideas about the business of his station, he knew absolutely nothing about the day-to-day tasks of putting on a show. He once asked Clara what the transmitter was, as though he had never seen one before. As far as Kirchner was concerned, Clara's most important duty at the station was answering the phones. Kirchner emphasized again and again that she should reduce the time she spent in production and spend more time at her desk. Fortunately, he was not at the station every day and rarely came into the studio. Clara's strategy was to maintain a low profile. Kirchner probably even figured she liked him, although she suspected he didn't care much if she liked him or not. She was part of the equipment that he had bought, along with the music library, the building and the weird equipment he could not identify.

Demo Tapes

By the time Clara finished up at work and got back to her apartment the sun was starting to go down. She was anxious for spring to come so the days would be longer and she would not be going and returning from work in darkness. Clara stopped at the mailbox and took out her mail. She set it on the passenger seat next to her purse and a bag of Chinese takeout. As she pulled up to her door, she noticed there was a large package on the doorstep. Clara picked up the stack of mail and put it in the take out bag so she would have a free hand to pick up the package. From its weight and the sound it made when she shook it, Clara could tell that the box contained her order of blank 5-minute cassettes. She balanced the box on her hip as she fumbled in her purse for the keys. Once she was inside, she dropped the package just inside the door. She set the takeout bag on the coffee table, took off her coat, and hung it on the coat rack near the door. Clara sat down on the couch and used the remote control to turn on the TV. As a sitcom played in the background, Clara took the mail out of the bag. The envelope on the bottom had a bit of General Tsao's sauce on it. She licked her fingers and opened the letter.

"Thank you for your resume and interest in Star 99.3. I have reviewed your resume but unfortunately...." This was only one of two envelopes with radio station call letters. She opened the second. "I wanted to send you a quick note to let you know that we have filled our recent opening from within, however I appreciate your interest in Mix 101.7..."

Clara stacked the two rejections on top of one another on the corner of the table. She kept a file folder with all of her rejections. She wasn't sure why she did this. If anyone were to ask her, she would tell them that it was to help her keep track of her applications. It was more likely that it was so much work to apply for jobs that it was reassuring to get any response, even a rejection, instead of shouting into the void. Maybe she was just masochistic.

Even though Clara's voice was still on the air as many hours as it had been before, she no longer felt like an announcer. She saw herself the way the boss saw her, as an office worker who happened to record voice tracks. Often, on her lunch break, she'd go to a restaurant and hear her own voice in the background. There was something strange in knowing that the waitress had no idea she was serving the same person she was listening to on the radio. She'd sometimes try to prompt a reaction by saying something like, "So, you listen to RTV, Saturn's Favorite Music?" No one ever made the connection. How could they? The voice was coming from the radio station, and Clara was sitting right there.

Clara had to admit that her automated show was cleaner. Every break was well-thought-out and error- free. It had a perfection that it would have taken her years to achieve with a live show, if she could have achieved it at all. But she felt no pride in it. It represented no mastery, just editing and compression. To her mind, she had regressed. Every day her show was a version of her overworked Harrison School demo tape. It was a production, not a performance.

Had Clara known she would be looking for a new job so soon, she would have recorded more of her shows, especially some of the morning shows with Seth. When she listened back to the few airchecks she had recorded they mostly made her cringe. She kept listening until she managed to find a few breaks she didn't absolutely hate. Using her dual cassette deck, she transferred them all onto a single tape and wrote "Demo" on the label. Now her living room looked like a mailing center with stacks of resumes and demo tapes and boxes of padded envelopes.

Clara sorted through the rest of her mail. There were the usual catalogs and bills. Her copy of the "On Air Tip Sheet," a radio publication full of classified ads for on air positions, had arrived. Of most interest was a hand-written envelope. Its return address revealed that it was from her Harrison School friend Joe. Clara put Joe's letter aside, and started opening the cartons containing her dinner and unwrapped the chopsticks. Between bites Clara flipped through the pages of the "On Air Tip Sheet," circling ads for jobs that sounded interesting. It was only when she had finished her meal that she opened the personal letter.

Dear Clara,

I hope you're doing well. Things are going really well here. I thought maybe my marketing job would keep me at a desk all the time, but it hasn't been that way at all! We are always doing big promotions and events. So part of my job is going to concerts and shows at dance clubs. It is a lot of fun. I thought of you the other day. I remembered you liked Depeche Mode. They came and did a live interview at the station. I had to go pick them up at the airport and then take them back to their hotel.

They were really nice guys. So if you were worried about me not getting a job on the air, don't. I am really enjoying my job. I hope you're having a great time being a famous radio DJ.

Your friend,
Joe

Cherryland

On Clara's solitary day off she often drove an hour to Traverse City, a destination known for its beautiful bay and its annual cherry festival. For Clara it held something even more important. Thoreau had gone to the woods to live deliberately. Clara went to the Cherryland Mall. It was an environment that said, "human beings are here"-- human beings in large enough numbers to need food courts and Spencer's Gifts, enough to do big things and make life interesting, even if the mall itself, strictly speaking, was not. The fact that the mall had no sense of place or local color was the whole point. The mall had no windows but was always brightly illuminated, allowing no natural sense of the time of day or the weather. It had a familiar smell, which Clara imagined was created by chemicals sprayed on clothing by manufacturers to keep them from wrinkling in transit. It was no different from the malls in any of the cities where Clara imagined she belonged. On her first trips that was enough to make her feel at home, but the novelty of the mall and the long, solitary trek to get to it were wearing off quickly.

As Clara walked through the concourse, she noticed a new kiosk with large framed posters. Two people were standing staring at them. At first Clara thought they were supposed to be abstract art of some kind, but they were ugly. They all looked the same, like static on the TV. She would have walked right on by, but the others were staring so intently that it stopped her in her tracks.

"Oh, I see it now," said the man.

"I don't see it," said his companion.

"What is this?" Clara asked the clerk.

"They're Magic Eye posters," he said. "There's a 3D image hidden inside."

"You have to relax your eyes," the first man chimed in. "Don't look at the surface, focus like you're looking off in the distance."

"Oh," said the woman. "I see it now. That's cool. That's really cool."

Clara kept staring at the poster. All she could see were squiggly lines. She suspected that she was part of some elaborate set up, the emperor's new clothes. She did not believe there was anything in the poster, and could not understand why anyone would shell out $25 to put ugly noise on their wall.

She gave up, and continued on her mission. Clara's favorite shop was not a chain, but a boutique that played modern rock over its speaker. The smell of the incense, which it sold by the stick from large glass jars, wafted into the sterile hall. In the display window, the clothes were a combination of post-punk, grunge and retro 70s. Everything in the store excited her. She wanted her clothes to say what she couldn't quite yet feel about herself, "I know who I am. I'm self-defined." But she couldn't afford to buy clothes at boutique prices, particularly clothes she was no longer allowed to wear. Clara walked right on past and headed to JC Penney to buy "professional attire."

Clara wandered through the racks feeling uninspired. It was hard to know what to buy, as she was shopping for Mr. Kirchner's taste, not her own. She found her way to the clearance rack. If she was going to pretend to be someone else, she could at least do it on a budget. She picked out a couple of pastel blouses and a pair of grey slacks. She put them on her credit card and held her breath as she waited for the transaction to go through.

As she headed back to her car, she stopped again at the Magic Eye kiosk. She found herself once again staring at the static. "Don't try to see it," the clerk said, "Just gaze like you're looking through it."

Suddenly the poster revealed its image to Clara. The outline of a horse floated above the noise, and then it disappeared as quickly as it had manifest. Clara moved over and tested the technique on another poster. It still required some effort, but after a few moments she was able to see the form of a dolphin jumping out of the sea. She now understood why people would pay $25 for an ugly poster. The pleasure was that it took a bit of work and mastery. There was beauty in the ugliness, but you had to learn how to see it. If you got it, you were part of an exclusive club. People need to feel like insiders somewhere, even when they're wandering the mall all alone.

Her eyes hurt.

When Clara passed the record store, The Smiths' "How Soon is Now" was playing through the speakers. It drew Clara in, and in a back corner near the racks of posters and t-shirts, Clara closed her eyes and swayed to the sound, trying to evoke a memory of her old life. In a moment she was back at City Club, that dark cocoon of a place where being an outsider was in. "How Soon is Now" always got everyone on the dance floor, and in her mind's eye Clara could see the crowd swaying to the pulsating guitar.

How could anyone fail to recognize the beauty of that music, the way the guitar woke you up, vibrated right through you? It spoke of life, while Morrisey's mournful vocals crooned about loneliness and isolation. A band called Soho had sampled that guitar for a dance track a couple of years before. They had a hit with it, but to Clara that totally missed the point. "How Soon is Now" was not a collection of parts, it was a sonic story. It conjured the sense of being at the heart of the action, yet feeling all alone. You could picture Morrisey in a club, standing to the side, waiting for something to put him in sync with the rhythm. Morrisey sang about going to a club on his own, and standing on his own, and going home alone to cry. The song was about the kind of emptiness that you could only feel surrounded by other people. Ironically, in all of the times that Clara had heard it over the speakers at City Club, she had never felt that way. There she had been among friends, and among strangers who felt like they were on the same wavelength. It was only now that she fully felt the song's meaning deep in her gut.

Clara was in the mall on her own, standing on her own, and she was going to go home on her own. She had driven all of the way to the civilization of the mall because there were enough people there to have food courts and record stores and movie theaters. But did it matter if there were human beings there if none of them saw her? The brightly lit, sterile halls no longer filled Clara with the comfort of home. She just felt lonely.

Clara opened her eyes. The door to the staff room was mirrored, and she caught a glimpse of her blonde reflection. When would she get her break? When would she escape from her desk job? If it didn't happen soon, Clara thought, she might lose her true self forever. How soon *is* now, she wondered. How soon is now?

Valentine's Day

Clara was sitting at her desk in the lobby. Her head was tilted down and she was rubbing her temples, trying in vain to stop a pounding headache. Seth came around the corner with a bright smile and a bounce in his step. He stopped at Clara's desk, reached into his pocket and pulled out a Valentine, the kind kids give each other in school. "Be my Valentine?" he said. The card had a picture of Clifford the Dog on it, with a big heart and the words, "It's nice to have a friend like you." Clara gave a weak smile and took the card from him. "It was left over from the box for Ashley's class," Seth said.

"And I thought you'd gone out special and bought this for me," Clara said. "What grade is she in?"

"Third."

"It's sweet; thanks." Clara reached out and touched Seth's arm. Just then Kirchner walked through the door. "On your own time," he said. Seth's hand curled into a fist. Clara rested her hand gently on top of it, and he released his grip.

As Kirchner walked to his office, Clara's voice came across the speakers. "Happy Valentine's Day from RTV, Saturn's Favorite Music. I have all kinds of wonderful love songs coming up in the next hour from Phil

Collins, Mariah Carey, and The Beatles. Plus, tune in this afternoon to Rad Farr's show. He'll be giving away a dozen red roses from Morgan's Florists. Right now it's a lovely one from Gloria Estefan, 'If We Were Lovers'."

Ignoring Kirchner's edict, Seth asked, "So do you have a hot date for Valentine's Day?"

"Yeah, right."

"Well, since neither of us seems to have a hot date, why don't we go do something, see a movie or something."

"I couldn't stand being out on Valentine's Day, seeing all those lovers gazing into each other's eyes."

"We'll stay in then," Seth said. "I'll come over; we'll rent a movie, something where they blow things up, maybe. We can have a completely anti-romantic evening. Fill out tax forms or something. I'll fart and read the newspaper and ignore you. We can even have an argument if you want."

Clara laughed in spite of herself. "Thanks, Seth, I'm just not really in the mood. I have a really bad headache. I'd be rotten company."

Seth shrugged. "Just don't sit around tonight being miserable. If you get bored, call me, OK?" Seth passed the mailman on his way out the door.

"Thank you," Clara said, taking the mail. She started sorting it into piles- - bills, sales, letters from listeners. She looked back and forth to make sure no one was watching as she held an envelope addressed directly to her. Clara recognized the handwriting. The letters from the alien calling himself Zog had continued to come once or twice a month. Clara had hated the fuss over the first letter. She didn't like being treated as a vulnerable girl. So when the next letter arrived, she put it in her desk drawer and told no one. Each subsequent letter had a similar list of dates and times and the "signals" she had transmitted. As time went on, they became longer and more elaborate and made less and less sense. By now Zog had all but dispensed with text. After the catalog of her signals, this one had six pages of drawings, graphs and pictures cut from magazines. Having gone for months without telling anyone about the letters, she didn't know how to say anything now, so she filed it away with the others, but it made her uneasy.

That evening Clara walked into her apartment and dropped a stack of mail on the coffee table. On top was Seth's valentine. She reached around her back, and undid her bra. Then she slipped it out under her shirt and threw it on the couch. "Free at last," she said to herself. She flipped on the TV. It was on the E! Channel. "Talk Soup" was playing. The addition of snarky commentary by the host, Greg Kinnear, made its daily roundup of the most outrageous talk show moments seem more like comedy than pure rubbernecking.

With the disembodied voices to keep her company, Clara went to the kitchen and started making spaghetti. It was one of her go-to meals, but today, as she waited for the pasta to soften in the boiling water, she felt sorry for herself. She was tired of eating poor people's meals. She imagined herself at Chef Joseph's European Cafe at a candle-lit table enjoying the 2-for-one steak dinner with champagne they advertised on the station. She was trying to imagine what Seth would look like in a suit. She wondered if he owned one.

She poured the hot water and spaghetti into a colander, then dumped it onto a plate, and then dumped on room-temperature, store-bought sauce straight from the bottle, sprinkled some Parmesan from a green shaker and sat down to watch a clip from the Rikki Lake Show of a gay man who was in love with his straight friend and then Greg Kinnear's reaction to it. She got bored with "Talk Soup" and picked up the remote control. She flipped right past the evening news (she heard the news all day at her desk) through the reruns of "Three's Company" and "Roseanne." She thought about getting back in her car and driving to Hollywood Video to find something to watch that wouldn't melt her brain, but the idea of having to put her bra back on was enough of an excuse to stay in front of the TV.

Clara looked at Seth's valentine. She started to spin it with her fingers. She thought about Seth as a dad. This was much easier to picture than Seth in a suit and tie. She could see him crouching down so his eyes were level with Ashley's as he zipped up her coat. She imagined Seth in Saturn Drugs with Ashley, her little hand in his, as they picked out just the right box of Valentines for her friends. They would go back to his apartment, and Seth would listen to her talk about her friends as she filled out the envelopes in a child's block letters. She let the story play on in her mind to the end of the day when Seth would pack Ashley into his cheap car and take her back to the house her mother shared with her rich new husband and wave goodbye to her as she walked inside. Clara started to regret that she had not accepted Seth's invitation.

Clara poked at the spaghetti on her plate for a while, then spent another half hour clicking through channels and playing with the valentine before she finally decided to give Seth a call. She took her plate back to the kitchen, dumped the uneaten spaghetti in the trash, and took the receiver from the phone hanging on the wall. She stretched the cord over to the couch. She hesitated for a moment before dialing.

"Hello?" Seth answered.

"Hi, it's me."

"CJ the DJ. Did you get bored with being miserable?"

"Something like that. Did I get you at a bad time?"

"No, it's almost my bed time but I can talk for a while."

"I forgot about that."

"I'm out of sync with the world," Seth said.

"Maybe the world is out of sync with you."

"One or the other. Did you have an anti-romantic evening?"

"Hmm. Hard to say. What's the opposite of romance?"

"I hope it's not calling me."

"No, no." Clara laughed. "I like talking to you."

"Glad to hear it. I'd hate to think you dialed the wrong number."

"You caught me, I was trying to call Rad." Clara got up and started to pace, stretching the long telephone cord over a lamp on her end table as she walked.

"I knew it. So what's your beef with Valentine's Day?"

"I don't know. Don't you sort of resent the people who try to make money selling flowers and cards by telling you what day you're supposed to feel love?"

"Which day do you prefer?"

"The third Thursday of every month with an R in it."

"Hmm. February has an R in it."

"It does."

"Should I mark my calendar?"

"Maybe."

"Interesting."

Clara got tired of pacing, and stretched out on the couch, making herself comfortable for a long conversation, "How come you don't have a hot date tonight?"

"Oh, it's not so easy to meet people when you fall asleep by eight."

"I can see that."

"Anyway, I don't like dating. I never liked it."

"Yeah, me too. Like you're doing a job interview for someone to be part of your life."

"Exactly. I thought when I got married that I was done with all that."

"Do you miss being married?" As soon as she asked, Clara wondered if she was getting too personal.

"Oh, I'm sure you've heard all the gory details," Seth said.

"Some of them."

"It was hard to stay married after I walked in on them making out in our living room. Did you hear that part?"

"Uh, no. Leslie didn't mention that."

"Really? I'd have thought she'd led with that. That's the big dramatic part of the story."

"What did you do?"

"I turned around and walked out. I don't know. What are you supposed to do?"

"I don't know. I missed that section of Emily Post."

"Yeah. Me too." There was a pause in the conversation. Clara had no idea what she should say. After a moment, Seth continued, "That wasn't really what ended it though. We were already in trouble. That was just a big humiliating bow on the top."

"Well, I don't think you're the one who should feel ashamed about that."

"Maybe, but that's easier said than done. I mean, it's not exactly a badge of honor, is it?"

"I suppose not."

"I don't know. It was almost a relief, really. I think we would have ended up in the same place either way, but it gave us a quick out. Like pulling off the band aid." There was another brief pause. "So, was that anti-romantic enough for you?" Seth asked.

"Oh yeah, it was brilliant."

"Now you."

"Now me, what?"

"Your most humiliating love story."

"Oh god," Clara sat up.

"I told you mine," Seth said.

"Well, can I go back to high school?"

"Whatever you want."

In truth, Clara had not had many serious relationships. There was really only one, and it had been a nightmare, one she hadn't entirely shaken. "I can't believe I'm telling this to you."

"Go on."

Clara got up and started pacing again. "OK, his name was Robert. Not Bob. Robert."

"He's off to a bad start already."

Clara laughed. "Yeah. It was senior year. He was my first..."

"Sex?"

"I was going to say real boyfriend or something, but yeah, that too."

"OK"

"It was all new and exciting. I hadn't felt anything like that before."

"Sure."

"And then he dumped me for this girl who did teen modeling for catalogs."

"Ouch."

"But wait, there's more," she said in the tone of a Ronco television commercial. Seth laughed. "He decided that he didn't want to be committed to me, but still liked having sex with me. So he would show up and get back together long enough to do that, and then after we did it he'd dump me again. And it kept... I kept letting it happen. And I didn't know much, so I thought, maybe it's like the movies, you know?"

"What do you mean?"

"Like that passion where people start out hating each other, and they also can't resist each other. But he just wanted control. He would say things like, 'Why are you so obsessed with me?' And I blamed myself because if it was my fault, maybe I had some kind of control. I could at least figure out what was wrong with me...."

"I don't think you should be the one to feel ashamed of that."

"I've heard that somewhere before." Clara had paced over to the refrigerator. She opened it and took out a bottle of white wine.

"How good looking was this guy?"

"What makes you think he was good looking?"

"An educated guess."

With her free hand, Clara started rummaging in the kitchen drawer for a bottle opener. "You know the lead singer of INXS?" She asked. "He kind of looked like that. Same hair style."

"Figures."

"And then this other guy, Tom, asked me out, and I thought, 'See, someone else is interested,' you know? And I thought, 'I'll show Robert. I have other options. I'm not just some toy for him to play with when he wants. So I made a date with Tom, and I made sure we'd go somewhere I knew Robert would see us, right?" Clara cradled the phone on her shoulder so she could open the bottle.

"Of course."

"I had no interest in Tom," she said, yanking out the cork. "I just wanted to show Robert I wasn't 'obsessed' with him. So we go out, and Tom gets really pushy, wanting me to go home with him. I said no. And for a while I felt bad, like I led Tom on. Then Robert comes up to me and says, 'You know, the only reason Tom went out with you is because I told him you were a sure thing.'"

"That's disgusting."

Clara poured the wine into a glass and walked back to the couch. "Yeah, it played with my head for a while. You go from feeling attractive and desirable to... It's this weird thin line, sexy, slutty. He loved that I wanted him, but he was fine with using that against me. What is it with guys?"

"You're asking me?"

"Yes, I expect you to answer for your entire gender."

"Well, as a group, we could probably do better."

Clara took a sip of her wine. "You want to hear the humiliating part?"

"That wasn't it?"

"No, here's the punchline. I got back together with Robert. Three more times."

"OK, you win."

Clara hummed the jingle from the Erickson Hardware Commercial.

"Stop, stop. Fine. It's a tie."

"Ha! See, love sucks."

"Bah humbug. Are you still in touch with Robert?"

"No way. I can't stand him. You know, it's not even him. I can't stand that I was in love with him. It's so embarrassing. I never want to lose myself like that again."

Clara thought she could hear Seth rummaging in his own refrigerator and opening a bottle of a carbonated beverage. "When I met Helen I thought she was perfect," he said. "There were things that I didn't let myself see. I didn't want any contradictions to mess up that great love story. Of course, there were things about me that she overlooked, too. She was more than happy to let me know about all of them while we were in that process of coming apart. We're all idiots when it comes to love, don't you think?"

"I guess life would be boring if we got everything right." Clara sighed. She lay down on the couch with her feet on one armrest, her head propped up on a pillow and her free arm across her forehead. "I'm so sick of everything right now. I don't want to go to work tomorrow. I'm dreading it."

"I know. It's not as fun there anymore."

"I mean, why did I bother to go to broadcast school? If I was just going to answer phones for barely more than minimum wage, I could do that anywhere. I didn't need to upend my whole life and come to Saturn for that. The whole reason I went into radio was to avoid a boring 9-5 desk job."

"Just hold on a little longer. Keep sending out tapes. You're good. Something better is coming."

"Let me ask you something. Do you think if the midday person was a guy they would have turned him into a secretary?"

"I don't know. Probably not." There was a pause and then Seth said, "You know, I bet they would have just fired him and had a part timer do the voice tracks."

"A friend of mine from the Harrison School, he decided not to try to get a job on air. I guess I felt kind of superior, you know, because I was doing it. He went into sales and marketing and now he's hanging out with rock stars all the time, going to concerts, parties. It's some sort of cruel joke. God, did I just sound totally petty?"

"No, just human. So how can I cheer you up?"

"I don't know."

"Well, I've got some ideas for our next movie night."

"Hit me."

"OK, two choices. First we've got *Zombie Lake*. It's a French movie about zombie Nazis."

"Zombie Nazis. That has promise. It sounds terrible. And what's the other choice?"

"*Caveman.* Ringo Starr grunting like a caveman and inventing fire and stuff."

"Well, who doesn't love Ringo?"

"Ringo it is," Seth said. His words were distorted by a yawn. "I'm sorry. I think I have to go to bed now."

"Good night, Seth," Clara said. "I'm glad I called."

"Me too. Good night, Clara. See you in the morning."

Green Slips

The next day, after Clara had recorded her tracks for the day, she joined Seth in the studio. From her place at the guest mic, she could not see out the window and was, therefore, not aware that Kirchner was in the lobby looking in on them.

"Your light rock, more music station, RTV. Saturn's favorite music. It's 9:26. That was Sade in her inimitable mellow fashion," Seth said, "Kiss of Life."

"Inimitable," Clara said. "Impressive."

"I'm erudite."

"Indeed."

"Sade says the sky is the color of love, so it is now confirmed. Love is blue."

"I don't think that's what she meant."

"You don't think love is blue?"

"No."

"What color is the sky?"

"Right now? It's partly cloudy."

"Love is partly cloudy. You heard it here first on RTV. Since she's already started, let's let CJ give you the weather." Seth fired the music bed; Clara's eyes widened. As the singers intoned "RTV Weather!" Seth held the weather copy up away from her. Clara reached for it, and slapped his hand. The music continued to play for a moment.

"Thanks, Seth," Clara said, in her cheeriest voice, while shooting daggers at him with her eyes. Finally he gave her the paper. "Here is your RTV weather center forecast brought to you by," she quickly scanned the page, "....Saturn Powersports. Now with Saturn's best deals on new and used snowmobiles."

Clara did not know then that this would be the last time she would banter with Seth in his morning show. As soon as the break was finished and the computer was back to playing the music, Kirchner came into the studio. As Clara emerged from behind the board, Kirchner said, "You missed three phone calls while you were joking around in here."

Although Kirchner was looking at Clara, it was Seth who answered. "It's a morning show. Joking around is the product."

"Maybe so, but it doesn't take two people to do it. You," Kirchner said pointing to Seth, "do the morning show. You," pointing to Clara, "record the middays. And when you're done, you answer the phones. I don't want any more crosstalk."

"The listeners like it," Seth insisted.

"Have you market tested that?" Kirchner asked.

It looked as though it was taking all of Seth's will to keep from lunging at the boss. "I don't need to market test it," he said. "I've been doing this for 18 years. I know a little bit about what the audience wants."

"Eighteen years is a long time," Kirchner said. "Maybe you need to update your skills."

Clara physically placed herself between Kirchner and Seth. "It's fine, Seth. I'm going back to my desk, OK? Don't worry about it."

"I'm worried about it because I care about the quality of my show," Seth said.

"It's your show as long as I say it is," Kirchner said, leaning around Clara to make eye contact with Seth.

Clara turned to Seth, "OK, Seth." She gave him a look that she hoped conveyed the idea that he should stand down and live to fight another day. Seth turned his back to Kirchner and put his headphones on, even though he did not have another break coming up for several minutes. He scrolled down the text on the computer monitor as though he had important business. Kirchner turned his attention to Clara. "Crosstalk is not part of our new programming strategy," he said.

"I understand," Clara said, and left the studio. She sat down at her desk. She felt as if she'd been physically slapped when she caught a glimpse of the phone bill open in front of her. One of the first things that Kirchner had done when he came to the station was implement a new system for accounting for long distance calls. The system mostly applied to the sales people who called potential clients all over the region. Clara did not understand why a new system was warranted. The phone system already kept track of long-distance calls. Anyone who made a call had to key in a personal code number, and the phone bill came sorted under each of these codes. If someone made a call to Bora Bora, you would know who had done it.

Under the new owner, each sales person also had to fill out a little green slip for each call explaining its purpose. The job of processing those green slips fell to Clara. Each month she had to go through the phone bill, line by line, locate the corresponding green slip, and check it off. If there was a call on the phone bill that did not have a slip, Clara had to go back to the person whose code had been used and ask what the purpose of the call had been so she could retroactively create a green slip. If the sales person could not remember, Clara had to call the phone company and ask them who the number belonged to. She would then have to go back to the caller and find out if they had, in fact, called the "Bonanza Broadcasting Company" or whatever it was. If they had, Clara could then create a green slip and check the call off. If there were any calls that were still not documented, Clara was supposed to make a list for Mr. Kirchner.

The job was tedious, but that did not bother Clara as much as its utter pointlessness. The system didn't actually keep anyone from making calls to their uncle in Idaho. Callers just had to log any personal calls on a green slip and make up a purpose like "sales call" or "ordering supplies." Thus the calls that did *not* have a slip were overwhelmingly legitimate calls lasting 5 minutes or less. Clara had to spend days following up on them. After an hour of checking off slips, a day of tracking down sales people and asking them about numbers, another day calling the phone company and asking the sales people again, she usually had accounted for all of 70 cents.

248

As Clara organized the green slips by dialing code in neat piles next to the phone bill, Ed came in for the day. "Morning," he said as he headed to his office. A few minutes later, Clara noticed Seth walking to Ed's open door, "Can I talk to you a minute?" He disappeared inside. Clara started through the first stack of green slips, checking off the calls in that caller's section on the bill. After a few more minutes Seth left Ed's office and returned to the studio.

"Good morning, it's 20 degrees at 9:53 on Saturn's Favorite Music, RTV. Thanks for tuning in today, my favorite DJ is on the way next. It's Clara Jane and a Superstar Seven in a Row. Have a great day. I'll talk to you tomorrow."

When Clara was about half way through the green slips, she saw Ed come around the corner and head down the hall towards Kirchner's office. She looked back down at the phone bill. When Clara had finished checking off the calls with green slips, there were five still unaccounted for. She got up and headed back to the sales office to see if any of the sales staff were in. As usual, no one was there. Clara headed back towards her desk. As she passed Kirchner's office, she heard Kirchner say, "I'm not paying him to flirt with his girlfriend on the air."

Clara shook her head and continued back to her desk. She set the phone bill off to the side. She was typing up a production order with her back to the lobby when Ed returned to his office. A few minutes later, Kirchner left for the day. Out of her peripheral vision, Clara could see Seth and Ed having a conversation in the back room. They were both holding coffee mugs. As Clara finished typing, Ed and Seth starting walking towards her on their way to the kitchen. "Guys like that are why I left Chicago," Seth said as they passed the desk.

"Kirchner's just micromanaging because RTV is his new toy," Ed said. "In a month or two he'll be focused on his other stations and he'll hardly be here. Just try not to piss him off before that."

As Clara started sorting through the papers in her in box, she was treated to the sound of her own voice. "Good morning, you're listening to another Superstar Seven in a Row on Saturn's Favorite Music, RTV. I hope you had a great Valentine's Day yesterday. Just because the holiday's over doesn't mean the love songs stop. Stay tuned for some romantic hits from Janet Jackson, Jon Secada and Billy Joel. It's all on the way."

Ed and Seth, now with full mugs, walked back into the lobby. Ed continued to his office, but Seth stopped at Clara's desk. He gestured to the coffee. "I just put on a fresh pot."

"When you cut yourself shaving, what comes out, blood or coffee?" Clara asked.

"Coffee."

"Did I hear you say you worked in Chicago?"

"Three years," he said. He took a sip of his coffee.

"What happened?"

"Didn't like it," Seth said. "I quit. Came back here."

"Why?" To Clara, a successful radio career had only one trajectory, from small station to large. She had never heard of anyone purposefully going the other direction. As much as she admired Seth, in the back of her mind, she'd always assumed that he was in Saturn because he couldn't make it anywhere else, or because he'd been afraid to try. The idea that

250

he might prefer RTV to a major market station had never occurred to her.

"Everything was just more controlled and micromanaged in Chicago," Seth said. "'Talk fast and get to the commercials.' The big cities are all full of Kirchners, and now they're bringing that shit here."

Clara always believed she had approached Seth (and everyone else) as a blank slate, filling out his story the more she learned. For just a moment the secret was exposed. Her mind was not a neutral collector of facts. It could not tolerate ambiguity and filled in the blanks in people's stories the same way it corrected for the blind spots in vision. What else, she wondered, had she gotten wrong about Seth?

"You know, I heard Kirchner tell Ed..." Clara stopped in mid-sentence. Over the speakers, a few familiar notes started to play. "Oh shit," Clara stood up.

"What is it?"

"I think I forgot to load the...."

Clara heard her voice start to announce the Good News, but she had forgotten to load the feature itself into the system. For a moment everything seemed to move in slow motion. It was as if Clara was watching two trains heading towards one another on the same track, and there was nothing she could do to stop them. She knew that there was no recording in the system to play after her introduction and she also knew what programming element was scheduled to follow.

"And now the Good News for Saturn," Clara's voice said. After a brief hesitation the computer pressed on with the next thing on the log. Clara's voice continued, "Mrs. Edith R. Strict of Manistee passed away..."

Nessun Dorma

The telephone rang and woke Clara up with a jolt at 12:30 AM. When she picked it up, it beeped at her three times, then said in a computerized monotone: "This is the W-R-T-V remote control... system, please- enter- access- code." It was the Gentner. They'd told Clara they were going to put her on the Gentner's phone list, but she didn't know they'd put her on yet. She thought they had told her the access code, but she couldn't remember what it was... Something to do with the date, was it? Or the call letters? What time was it?

"Goodbye," the Gentner said and hung up. Clara went back to bed.

The Gentner was the part of the automation system that constantly monitored the outgoing signal and made sure it was operating within normal parameters, not coming in at low power or blasting all the other stations off the dial. If something caused the programming log to miscue, for example, if the machine tried to access a feed that had not been loaded into the system, or if a code was typed in wrong and the programming log stopped advancing, the Gentner system would go through a list of phone numbers until someone corrected the problem. The station itself was the first number on the Gentner call list, then Ed and then the full-time operators in order of seniority: Seth, then Rad and finally Clara.

Ten minutes later, the phone rang again. "This is the W-R-T-V remote control... system. Please-enter-access-code." Clara was a little more awake this time. She remembered the code-- it was the station's zip code-- and punched it in. "Alarms pending," the Gentner said. Clara pushed a button on the key pad, "Alarms pending," it repeated then said something about no signal.

There was nothing Clara could do about no signal from her bed. The most likely scenario was that it was a problem with a feed. Overnight RTV programmed a number of syndicated shows from satellite feeds. If a few local programming elements misfired in sequence, the system could advance to a syndicated feed before it had been aired and recorded. Usually the problem resolved itself in a few minutes when the feed started and the Gentner sensed sound again. Once Clara punched in the number to clear the alarm, everything should go back to normal.

But 10 minutes later the phone rang again. "This is the W-R-T-V remote control... system. Please-enter-access-code..." Clara hung up. Why wasn't Ed at the station making this stop? Seth had to get up at 4 in the morning, but what about Rad? They must have all taken their phones off the hook. The phone rang again. "Damn it," Clara muttered to herself as she got out of bed. She let the phone ring and put on her coat and boots on top of her pajamas, then got in her car and drove to the station.

She expected everything to be dark, but the lights were on when she arrived. Seth was in the studio, punching buttons on the computer. He was unshaven and his hair was a mess, but unlike Clara, he'd taken the time to get dressed. "Nice pajamas," he said. Clara pulled her coat more tightly around her. "CJ the DJ in P.J.s," Seth added, laughing to himself.

A code that was supposed to appear at the end of the previous day's log had been left off. It was what instructed the computer to load the log for the next day. Lacking common sense or free will, the computer stopped playing all together and awaited further instruction from the human beings. Seth had just finished loading the next day's log manually when Clara came in.

It was now well after 1 in the morning. "I have to get up in 2 ½ hours, and it's a 20 minute drive back to my house," Seth said. "I think I'll just stay here." He went and lay down on the couch. "For a list of ways that computers have improved our quality of life, Press one," he said with a yawn. "These pajama parties just aren't the way I remember them."

The next morning Clara put on her new RTV sweatshirt-- the purple brought out the color of the circles under her eyes. She stopped and got some bagels to share with Seth, who she was sure would not have had breakfast. She asked him if he slept well.

"It was hard to sleep," he said. "The radio was going in the background, I had the strangest dream. It was like a newscast about this man named Gentner who was standing on the roof of the radio station shooting people."

When Ed came in and saw how tired Seth looked, he said sheepishly, "My wife must have taken the phone off the hook; I didn't know she did that."

The expression "The Gentner is calling" soon morphed into "Gentner is calling." Gentner was the entire station's robotic nemesis. He was unrelenting, single-minded and always literal. One misplaced comma would throw him, and it was impossible to reason with him once he'd set his mind to something. Until he got his way, no one would sleep.

The Spec Spot

The Beatles' "Day Tripper" was playing. Seth was singing and dancing around the studio, doing his meanest air guitar. He was startled when Clara came in and shut the door behind her. He stopped dancing immediately. "Oh, hi." His cheeks were crimson.

"It's a good song," Clara said with a laugh.

The bank of CDS clicked as another set of trays was loaded and the light, ethereal opening of "Heartbeats Accelerating" by Linda Rondstadt started to play.

"I never realized how good our music mix was until they started programming it," Clara said. "Who would put these two back-to-back? It's like running full force into a brick wall."

"I don't think it matters anymore," Seth said. "I can't decide if I like this song or hate it. It's sitting right in that space."

"Kirchner's in," Clara said, glancing out the window to see if they were being watched. She handed Seth a stack of papers. "Pretend you're talking business."

"OK," Seth said. "I put all my dividends into blue chips because I'm worried volatility in the market will affect my return on investment."

Clara laughed. "Do you know what you just said?"

"If I did, I'd be richer than I am. What did you just hand me?"

"Four spots and a spec spot."

The "spec" in spec spot is short for "speculation." It is a commercial that an announcer goes to all the trouble of producing in the hopes that when the prospective client hears it, he will be so blown away that he will have to buy time on the station. When Mr. Norton owned the station they did not have to produce many of them, but now that Mr. Kirchner was in charge, they were producing spec spots on an almost daily basis. What Kirchner and the sales staff wanted when they asked for a spec spot was an all-out top-of-the-line spot with more production than the average bear, especially if the client was being courted by Kirchner himself.

"I don't do spec spots," Seth said. He handed the page with the words "spec spot" written on the top back to Clara.

"Yes, you do," she said, handing the paper back to him. "I have stacks of these and all the car dealership co-op spots. They're driving me crazy." She rubbed her left eye.

"Another headache?" Seth asked.

"I'm trying to fight it off." Seth turned the chair around and gestured for Clara to sit down. "I can't. I have too much to do. I'm waiting for Kirchner to shout at me about the phone bill. I missed the early bird deadline, and it's going to cost him an extra $5."

"Come here," Seth said, gesturing to the chair again. Clara sat down. Seth came up behind her and started massaging her shoulders with a firm motion. "Ouch," Clara said, tensing.

"I know, I know," he said. "Try to relax. Don't tense up. Give it a minute." He ran his thumbs along her shoulder and the side of her neck. "How is that?"

"Actually," Clara said, rotating her shoulder, "that's a lot better. How did you learn to do that?"

"I dated a massage therapist once."

"Really? That must have been nice."

"For a massage therapist she was surprisingly stress-inducing. But I learned this." He gestured for Clara to get up and then sat back down at the console. "This is a crazy idea," he said, "but why not wait until Kirchner actually yells at you to get upset?"

"It's more efficient this way," Clara said rolling her head around to stretch her neck. "Have you ever noticed that it's the stupid little things that suck all of your energy?"

"For me it's the pointless things. The bureaucratic things that you shouldn't have to do in the first place." Seth glanced at the computer monitor. He didn't have a break for another 10 minutes and he seemed not to know what to do with himself. "You should tell him you're not doing the phone bill any more. That's what I'd do."

"I know that's what you'd do. I'm not you."

"You've got to put your foot down," Seth said. "Get in touch with your inner bitch." Through the glass Clara and Seth saw Kirchner walking down the hall. He stopped to watch them through the window.

"Hand me some more papers," Seth said. Clara picked up a stack of papers from beside the turntable and handed them to Seth. He flipped through them and nodded. Without looking up he said, "Is he buying it?"

"I don't think so," Clara said. She left the studio and went back to her desk. Kirchner was holding the phone bill. "Why is this just on my desk now? It's very important that you get this to me by the deadline, or we have to pay a higher rate."

"I had a lot of work to do," Clara said.

"You have to get it to me before the deadline," he said in a stern voice.

Clara reached into her purse and pulled out a $5 bill. "Here," she said, handing it to Kirchner. She sat at her desk, turned to the computer and started typing random letters. Kirchner didn't say another word; he just went back into his office. He kept Clara's $5.

In Clara's inbox was another stack of orders for spec spots. She took the first and read the description. Sales needed a spot for Saturn Aviation, a flight instruction school at the local airport. The sheet had a list of facts about the business and instructions on how to write and record the spot. Clara sat and stared out the window as she tried to come up with aviation copy. After a few false starts, she composed the following:

[Effect: **traffic**]

Person in Car: Three hours on the road and that's not even counting delays for construction and traffic jams.

Traffic Announcer: Traffic is backed up for miles on the south bound due to a semi truck blocking the left lane.

Person in Car: You know, if I could fly there, it would probably only take me half an hour.

Announcer: Why waste your time wishing? You could wait until you sprout wings, or you could call Saturn Aviation at the Saturn Airport and learn about their professional flight instruction and ground school. They are open seven days a week and on evenings so you can learn at your convenience. [Effect: **traffic**] You could keep sitting there in traffic. [Effect: **airplane**] Or you could look down at the traffic as you fly by. Call Saturn Aviation at Saturn Airport today and learn how!

She typed it up with instructions for Rad to produce the first half, and Clara would voice the last section. Rad arrived at the station around 12:30 and produced the first half. He stopped by Clara's desk to tell her he'd finished his part and then went into the studio to begin his airshift.

"Fulfilling your manifest destiny for great music. This is Rad Farr on your light rock, more music station WRTV, Saturn. Expose, 'As Long as I Can Dream' kicks off our first Superstar Seven in a Row."

Clara went into the production studio to finish the spot. She listened to the opening that Rad had created. It featured a traffic effect as requested. Clara looked around the studio trying to figure out where Rad had gotten it. Kirchner had never re-subscribed to the sound effects library after he took over the station from Norton. There were a few old vinyl effects discs in the back room. Clara took them into the production studio and listened to all of the traffic effects she could find, but none of them seemed to match Rad's section. Clara went into the main studio.

"Where did you get the traffic effect that you used on the Saturn Aviation spot?" she asked Rad.

"It's on my personal CD," he said.

"Oh, OK, where is it?"

"It's on my personal CD."

"Well, can I use it?"

"No."

Clara laughed. "Where is it?"

"I'm serious, you can't use it."

"What do you mean?"

"See, I paid my own money for these, and they don't belong to the station."

"You use them on your production."

"Yes, on my production."

"Your production goes on the station."

"It is only for my production."

"This is your spot. If I don't use the same traffic effect, the two halves of the spot won't match."

"I'm sorry," he said. "That's just my policy. I paid my own money for them and I can't let anyone use them."

Had Clara not been so incredulous, she might have come up with a pithy comment. But she was too distracted by a scene playing in her head. She was transported back to kindergarten, to the home of her next door neighbor, Lori. When Clara visited, Lori wouldn't let her play with anything.

"They're just my toys," she would say.

Clara went back into the production studio and finished the spot without a traffic effect in the second half. That evening Clara called to complain to Seth. "I'm sure all the people who hear the spec spot are going to say, 'Oh that Rad, he's such the production whiz. It's too bad they had to let Clara do the second half. She didn't even bother with effects. That Rad has such talent.'"

The next morning, when Clara arrived at the studio, Seth came to her desk and said, "I hope you don't mind, but I touched up your spec spot, tell me what you think." He gestured for her to follow him into the production studio. Seth sat down at the computer and toggled to the Saturn Aviation spec spot in the computer system.

Instead of the traffic effect, the commercial started with Rad's line: "Three hours on the road and that's not even counting delays for construction and traffic jams." Then Seth's voice cut in. He was making car sounds. "Vrooom Vrooom. Beep Beep," he said. Clara started laughing so hard that she became light headed and tears streamed down her cheeks.

"I have an idea," Seth said, "I'm going to have this run in Rad's show." He started punching keys on the keyboard.

"No, Seth, don't. Seth. Don't do that. Seth!" Clara shoved Seth, but he was on a mission. He assigned the spec spot a number and then manually edited the log for Rad's show, punching in the number so the ad would run only once.

When Clara came in the next day she could hear Ed yelling at Seth through the closed door of his office. "Not funny..." he was saying. "Pay a lot of money to advertise their products... What do you think pays your salary?" Then Seth said something that Clara couldn't hear through the door, but she gathered it was not complementary.

"Get out of here, you're fired," Ed shouted.

"Thank God!" Seth shouted. Ed's door flew open and Seth came charging out. He slammed the door behind him. He grabbed his green denim jacket off the back of a chair and stormed out without saying anything to Clara. Clara put her jacket and purse down at her desk and then walked over to Ed's door. She hesitated for a moment before knocking on Ed's door. "What?!"

Clara opened the door and peeked in, "Can I come in?"

"What is it?"

Clara sat down at Ed's desk. "I saw Seth leave."

Ed rearranged some papers on his desk. "I need you to fill in on the morning show tomorrow," he said.

"Was this about the spec spot with the vroom vroom and all that?"

"Did you hear it too?"

"No, I mean, not on the air."

"It's not the first time he's pulled something like this," Ed said. "It was completely unprofessional. Seth has a problem with authority."

"I, I know he does," Clara said. "But this is all my fault." Clara made her eyes as wide and ingenuous as she could without actually batting her eyelashes. "He never meant to put that on the air. It was a joke between us, and I must have made a mistake and typed in a wrong number and that was why the spot ran. He was just protecting me."

Ed contemplated Clara. Had he given it more than a moment of real reflection, he would have realized that a spec spot should not have had a number in the system to begin with. In fact, Clara suspected that Ed knew she was not telling the truth, but that he didn't really want to fire Seth and might be willing to accept Clara's excuse to avoid it.

"He knows the business," Ed said. "He knows better than risking a client like that. It's not a harmless joke when you sound like you're making fun of a potential buyer on the air."

"No, you're right."

"He thinks there are no rules for him. It's not different here than anywhere else. There are standards."

"It's the good and bad of him, right?" Clara said. "He plays around and takes risks. It makes his show interesting."

"No one wants Seth to stop being Seth, but when you do something stupid you can't just act like it's no problem."

"You're right," Clara said. "But this one really was my fault."

Ed tapped his fingers on the desk. Finally he said, "If that's true, if he comes back and apologizes, he can have his job back, but he'd better be back on the air by tomorrow. And he has to apologize."

"Great," Clara said, standing, "Thanks, Ed."

As she left the room, Ed called after her. "He has to apologize. If he isn't willing to apologize, be prepared to do the morning show tomorrow."

After Clara was done recording her voice tracks for the day, she went to her desk and dialed Seth's number. The answering machine picked up. "Hi Seth, it's Clara. Can you give me a call at the station?" A half hour passed. She tried again, and again got the machine. She tried again a few minutes later.

She concluded that Seth must be screening his calls. Clara popped her head back into Ed's office, "Hey, I'm having trouble getting Seth on the phone. I think I'm going to try to stop by his place after work. Do you know where I can find his address?"

"What do you mean?" Ed said, "You've never been there?"

Creative Freedom

Clara pulled up to a nondescript, beige block of apartments. She looked down at the slip of paper on the passenger seat. Building 4, apartment 20. She found a parking space next to a car port. For a moment she wondered if she had made a mistake driving there. Maybe she should go home and try to call Seth again. But she had no reason to think her next call would have any more success than the last. She took a deep breath and walked up to the building. There was an intercom panel on the door. The name panel next to buzzer 20 said "Butkiss." She pushed the button and stood, shuffling from one foot to the other.

Finally a tinny version of Seth's voice answered, "Hello?"

Clara leaned into the intercom, "Seth, it's me."

"What are you doing here?"

"You didn't answer my calls," Clara said.

"I know."

"Well," Clara said, "I'm here now." There was a loud buzz and Clara grabbed the door handle. She walked down a dim hall. Seth was standing in his doorway. "Come in, then," he said. Inside the door, Clara was immediately greeted by an enthusiastic basset hound. The expression about people looking like their dogs came to mind, but Clara decided against saying anything to Seth about it.

"I didn't know you had a dog," Clara said, patting its head.

"His name's Fido," Seth said.

"Stop it."

"No, really. His name's Fido. Come here Fido." The dog jumped up towards his master's face.

"You really named your dog Fido?" Clara took off her jacket and folded it over her arm.

"He didn't look like a Spot," he said, and gestured for Clara to enter the space. His tiny apartment was decorated in the style known as early single-guy. Seth had been sitting on a futon that Clara suspected doubled as his bed, drinking a beer and watching a video tape of Star Trek, which was now paused. An end table next to the futon was stacked with empty cans and dirty glasses. Somewhere in there must have been a phone with a flashing answering machine light.

"Not too big on housekeeping, huh?" Clara asked as she hung her jacket over the back of the futon.

"What are you talking about? This place is immaculate." He gestured for Clara to sit beside him on the futon.

"I don't know, it looks pretty 'maculate' to me," she said, as she took a seat.

Clara noticed some framed pictures of Seth and his daughter on the end table. She picked up an image of Seth with a massive grin, with a laughing toddler sitting on his shoulders. "Is this your daughter?"

"Ashley, yeah."

"She's adorable. You're adorable together." Clara put the photo back on the end table.

Seth looked at the photo. His expression grew warm. "She's doing the heavy lifting there, in the adorable department," he said. "She's lucky. You never know how that's going to go. If Einstein and Marilyn Monroe had kid, she could get Einstein's brains and Marilyn's looks or the other way around. I think she got the best mix of the genes. She got her mother's looks, not mine."

"Why do you put yourself down?" Clara asked. "I like the way you look."

"You do?"

"Mm-hmm."

"You're weird."

"Well, I can't argue with that, but I don't think that means I'm wrong."

"There's an expression about tastes and colors, you can't discuss them."

"What did Ashley get from you, then?"

"Humor maybe," Seth said. "Knock, knock."

"Who's there?"

"Wooden shoe."

"Wooden shoe who?"

"Wooden shoe like to know."

Clara chuckled. "Yeah, that's probably your side of the family."

"So did you come here to make fun of my domestic skills?" He took the last swig from his beer can and then threw it across the room. It landed in the kitchen sink.

"Only partly. Ed wants you to come back."

"He sent you?"

"Sort of. Guess he figured I could smooth things over because we're sleeping together."

"Oh yeah, I keep forgetting that," he said, and looked away.

"Well?"

"Well, what?"

"Will you come back?"

"Ed can screw himself. Want a beer?" He headed to the kitchen area. Clara followed him. Inside his refrigerator were a six-pack and a single can of beer, a bottle of ketchup, some bacon and some kind of fast food bag. Seth took the six pack and gestured for her to follow him back to the futon. "Who is he putting on tomorrow morning?"

"Well, me," Clara said, sitting down. "I mean, if I can't get you to come back."

"I thought so," Seth said, cracking open a beer. "They're going to give mornings to you. You should take it."

"Me?"

"They're not going to give it to Rad."

"No. They'd do a job search, find a wacky morning guy. They don't put the girl on hosting the mornings."

"They'll give it to you," he said, opening a second beer and handing it to Clara. Clara felt pride welling inside. Was she really the heir apparent to the station's top show? But she held fast to her mission. "I wouldn't want to be promoted at your expense," she said.

"It's not my expense if I don't want it."

"Don't you?"

"I don't know," Seth said. "You know, I think the happiest I ever was in radio was the first station where I worked. I didn't make enough money to live on, but it was just a bunch of guys who loved music trying to hold this station together with duct tape. There were managers, but I don't think they were making much, either. We were just motivated by different things. We were trying to do something together. I'm glad I started then, not now."

"I'm starting now," Clara said.

"I'm sorry," Seth said.

"Thanks."

"No." Seth said, "You're lucky. It's good to be young. When you get older, you start to feel like maybe you're running out of time to make good. Maybe I should have just sold my soul in Chicago and been done with it. Everyone else would call that success."

"Not you?"

"The more they pay you, the more they own you."

"Hmm. I'd be willing to risk it, I think."

"I always thought in a big market I'd have enough status that I wouldn't have people looking over my shoulder, but it was worse. There's too much at stake. Too much money. Everyone is afraid of losing, so they don't take risks. They're constantly giving you notes. It's like there's someone standing between you and the audience. It feels like selling. There's more creative freedom here, or there used to be."

"It's hard to pay rent with creative freedom."

"Yeah, well, there's that. You need to eat. You need to make a good life for your kids. I just want the good life for Ashley to be about more than material stuff. I don't want it to be harder for her to have the real kind of good life. If you don't have the courage to stand up to money, you'll eventually compromise on everything. That's what I want her to know. Am I making any sense?"

"Yeah, that makes sense."

Seth took a big swig that emptied his can of beer. "Anyway, she's got the rich step dad now. He's the rich dad; I'm the poor loser dad. He's probably going to buy her a car when she turns 16."

"OK," Clara said, picking up one of the photos from the end table, an image of Seth pushing Ashley on a swing. "Ashley is beautiful, and I can tell she adores you. You're wallowing in something right now." She handed Seth the photo and he sat looking at it for a moment. Fido barked and wagged his tail.

"You are actually aware that this was your mistake, right?" Clara said. "You put that spot on the air."

"Rad deserved it," Seth said, handing the photo back to Clara to put on the table. "I'm just sick of people like Rad, always keeping score. 'It's mine, I paid for it. Get your own.'"

"Yeah, but you have to admit playing that commercial on the air wasn't exactly the smartest thing to do."

"It was worth it. Don't tell me you didn't enjoy it."

"Just a little." Clara smiled.

"Helen always said I was too impulsive," Seth said. "That was after she stopped liking me. When we were first together she thought I was 'spontaneous.'"

"Two sides of the same coin, I guess."

"Which do you think I am?"

"Context is everything."

"This situation."

"Let's see. Making the spot-- spontaneous. Putting it on the air-- impulsive."

"And quitting?"

"Pig headed."

"Aw, come on," Seth said.

"I guess it depends on whether you meant it to be a big final 'fuck you' or if you were just blowing off steam."

"I'm not sure."

"Are you really going to let Rad get you thrown off the air? Are you going to leave me all alone in that madhouse? Do you want that hanging over your head?"

"So what you're saying is you want me to come back because you'll miss me."

"Well, yeah. I look forward to seeing you every day. It's the only thing I look forward to." Seth gazed into Clara's eyes. His face relaxed into a gentle smile. Clara looked down, afraid of what she had revealed.

Seth let out a deep sigh, then finally said, "OK, I'll come back, but only because I'd feel guilty leaving you alone with those idiots."

"Good, I feel better now."

Seth turned around and lay down so his feet were on the arm rest and his head was in Clara's lap. As he looked up at her, Clara instinctively ran her hand through his hair. Seth closed his eyes. "So furniture's not a big thing with you?" she asked.

"Helen got the furniture," he said, without opening his eyes. "I got Fido." The dog wagged his tail.

"Have you eaten anything," Clara asked, "or just the beer?"

"Just beer."

"Are you drunk?"

"No," Seth said in a tone of half sleep. "Just a little drunk."

"You should eat. What have you got?"

"I have bacon," Seth said and after a pause added, "And saltines."

"Were you going to have bacon and saltines for dinner?"

"I don't know."

"I could go to the store and get some lettuce and tomato. Make BLTs."

"Hmm."

"Seth?" Seth had fallen into rhythmic breathing. As Clara watched him sleep she was filled with affection for his funny face, his insecurity and arrogance, his sadness and his humor, the fact that he was imaginative about everything except naming pets, and that he rebelled by moving *away* from the city to the small town. Most of all she felt affection for who they were when they were together. And then her leg started to go numb. She tried to shift without waking Seth. After a bit of wiggling she managed to restore the circulation but began to wonder how long she would have to sit on the couch. Would she have to sleep sitting up? She experimented with stretching out her arm and laying her head down, but she got a crick in her neck. She tried to slide out from under him, but there was not enough room. Finally she shook him, "Seth."

He opened his eyes with a start. "Huh?"

"You have to let me out."

"Did I fall asleep? I'm sorry." He sat up and rubbed his eyes.

"It's OK," Clara said. She patted Seth's thigh and then stood up. "I'm going to get going. You get some sleep. Will I see you tomorrow?"

"Bright and early."

Clara had never told Seth the part about apologizing to Ed. Seth showed up to work as usual the next day. Ed never brought the commercial up again.

Low Power Alert

"This is the W-R-T-V remote control...system. Please–enter–access–code."

Clara was at the front desk, punching in the access code for the 20ᵗʰ time that day. Her jaw was clenched, and she could feel the warning signs of a migraine behind her left eye. The town of Saturn was having problems with its power grid. The entire town was operating at low power. Since WRTV was *in* the town, it, too, had low power, and Gentner was very concerned about it. In the good old human-operated days, a person would make a note on the logs, then go on with life. Gentner was not content with that. He wanted the problem fixed. He rolled through his phone list again and again trying to alert the humans. As the station itself was the first number on the list, Clara was stuck at her desk. Every 10 minutes without fail the phone rang.

"This is the W-R-T-V remote control...system. Please–enter–access–code."

"Make it stop!" Clara shouted to Ed, who was in a huddle with the station's engineer, Max.

"There's nothing we can do!" He shouted back.

The phone rang again. Clara picked up and started punching in the code before she realized there was a person on the line.

"Hello?"

"Oh, sorry, this is RTV, can I help you?"

"It's Seth. What the hell is going on? Gentner is calling." Clara had missed a couple of Gentner's calls, and they had rolled through to Seth.

Clara told Seth about the low power and Gentner's childlike faith that human beings could fix anything if he could just get their attention.

"Oh no!" Seth said. "I'm not having that thing calling me all night. Put Ed on."

"Seth wants to talk to you," Clara shouted to Ed.

"I'm a little bit busy here," Ed called back.

"Ed says he's busy."

"When is this going to be fixed?" Seth asked.

"We can't fix it. The city has to fix it."

"There's no way to shut Gentner up?"

"Hold on, there's another line ringing."

"This is the W-R-T-V remote control...system. Please–enter–access–code." Clara cleared the alarm, then opened her desk drawer and took out a bottle of aspirin. Her left temple was throbbing. She put two aspirin in her mouth and swallowed them without water. With her left eye closed, she picked up Seth's line again.

"I have a terrible headache," she said. "Hold on, another line is ringing." She put Seth back on hold and picked up the flashing line. It was Ed's wife.

"Ed, it's Janice," Clara called out. Ed went into his office, and she saw the line go off hold. She clicked back to Seth's line. Rubbing her temple she said, "Are you still there?"

"I'm still here."

"I'm ready to scream."

"Go ahead. Do it."

Clara was in too much pain to laugh, "I'm at work," she said.

"Should I scream for you?" Clara was about to say no when Seth, thankfully far from the phone receiver, let out a scream.

"Thanks," Clara said. "That... That totally didn't add to the chaos. Oh shit, hold on."

"This is the W-R-T-V remote control...system. Please—enter—access—code."

The light on Ed's line went off, and he came out of his office. The engineer followed. "Janice is getting Gentner calls," Ed said.

"Sorry," Clara said. "I'm trying to catch them all."

"It's not your fault," Ed said.

Rad had just finished announcing the Superstar Seven in a Row. The computer was now running the tracks, which meant that he had about twenty minutes before he had to be back in the studio. He came out to the lobby and sat down. "What's the deal with the Gentner? Can't we shoot it or something?"

The line with Seth's call had now been on hold long enough that it was beeping. "Is that Seth?" Ed asked.

"Yeah," Clara said.

"Put him on speaker."

"You're on speaker Seth."

"Seth, this is Ed. I talked to the electric company and they don't think this is going to be resolved until tomorrow afternoon."

"So this is going to go on all night?"

"No," Ed said. "I am making an executive decision. We're going to sign off the air after Rad's shift. That's the only way I can think of to put Gentner to bed."

For a moment no one spoke. "What did Kirchner say?" Seth asked.

"I'm not asking," Ed said. "It's easier to get forgiveness. Rad, go through the steps with Max to make sure you know how to shut down. End your show, do an announcement, and in the morning, Seth, come in a little early because you'll have to put us back on the air."

"He's not going to like it," Seth said.

"I'll take responsibility," Ed said. "I'm not going to have this robot keep the entire staff awake all night."

Changes

Clara could only watch helplessly from her desk as Kirchner stood outside Ed's office and watched him gather his things. Seth had wrapped up the morning show, leaving things in the computer's control. He was in the lobby, pacing back and forth, shaking his head.

"It's not right," he muttered.

"Don't say anything," Clara cautioned.

"Standing there while he cleans out his office, like he's a criminal or something."

"Don't say anything."

"I'm not going to say anything."

Ed had been so certain he was going to be fired that he had brought a canvas bag with him to the station for his personal effects. He emerged from his office with the bag slung over his shoulder.

"I'll take your keys," Kirchner said. Ed reached into his pocket and took out his key ring. It took him a moment to get the station key off the ring. He handed it to Kirchner, who stayed back by the office as Ed walked into the lobby. Clara just stared at him, not knowing what to say.

"It's not right," Seth said.

"It's OK," Ed said.

"You should be proud of what you did here," Seth said.

"Seth, you're a pain in the ass, and I'm going to miss working with you."

"I love you man," Seth said, and gave Ed one of those hugs that men do, where they slap each other on the back.

Ed turned to Clara. He waved and said "Good luck," then he walked out the door.

"That sucks," Seth said.

"Don't say anything," Clara said, as Kirchner started walking towards them.

"I'm not going to say..."

"The show is over," Kirchner said, looking at Seth. "If you don't have a reason to be standing in the lobby, I suggest you get to work or go home."

"With pleasure," Seth said. He went to the back room to get his jacket. On the way out the door he turned to Clara, "I'll call you later."

"Bye, Seth," she said.

"Miss Jane," Kirchner said, "Let's talk in my office."

Clara sighed and headed down the hall. Once she was seated in a plush leather chair, Kirchner began without any of the normal social niceties. "I want you to know that letting Ed go was not a spur of the moment decision," he said. "The incident with the computer moved up the timeline, but I was already planning to make a change."

"Oh," Clara said. She did not know how she should react because she could not figure out why he was telling her this.

"Under Ed's leadership, our sound has not been cohesive. We're playing popular music, but the rest of our programming elements are provincial and backward. I had a lot of discussions with him, and Ed was very committed to this hyper-local idea. That is not where radio is going, and it doesn't attract sponsors. Sponsors don't want to put their money into something that sounds small. So that's why we're making this change. Do you have any questions so far?"

Clara's only real question was, "What has this got to do with me?" Instead she replied, "No, no questions."

"I want a new program director who is younger and more forward thinking." He paused, as though he was expecting Clara to say something. When she did not, he continued. "I want you to go through our programming with a fresh eye. We're going to cut everything that screams small town and replace it with something more universal. No obituaries and anniversary announcements. I want you to coordinate with sales and find new elements for those sponsored slots. And no more contests where we give away a pizza coupon. We need to have prizes that are worth winning."

Clara's eyes were wide. Kirchner had skipped right over the part where he asked her if she wanted the job. "Are you saying... Are you offering me Ed's job?"

"There is a small increase in pay," he said. "You'll be responsible for coordinating everything that goes out on air and making sure we have that cohesive brand."

"A cohesive brand," Clara nodded. She was excited by the idea of such a promotion, but inside she was screaming, "Why me? A year ago I was still in broadcast school." She could not believe that all of those self-help books about faking it until you make it had been right.

"I do have one concern," Kirchner said, "As the program director, you have to manage the airstaff."

"Yes."

"I'm just going to put my cards on the table here," he rapped twice on the top of his desk. "I don't like Seth. I'm sure it's mutual. We don't need to like one another. He's got the major market resume, and that's the sound we're going for. The listeners and the sponsors seem to like him. As long as that's true, there's no reason to make a change there. But he's not a team player. I realize this might put you in a difficult situation. If you are the PD you need to represent the station. Do you see what I am saying?"

"I think so."

"You can sympathize with him personally, but professionally, if there's a conflict involving Seth, would you be able to take the side of management?"

Clara was not sure. "Yes," she said. "Of course."

"I don't want to belabor this point," Kirchner said. "But I do want you to really think about it. I don't have any plans to change the morning show now, but I can foresee a situation where I have to let him go, and if that happened, as the PD it would be your job to fire him. Could you do that?"

Kirchner was operating under an incorrect assumption. Seth was not her boyfriend. But being asked to imagine siding against Seth, even firing him, made her realize just how connected they were. It was her and Seth against the world. She didn't ever want to be on the other side. Clara wanted the promotion, and there was only one right answer to the question, but she couldn't bring herself to say it. "I-I don't know," she said.

"Well, that's an honest answer," Kirchner said. "I appreciate that. Hopefully it won't come to that. You might actually be the best person to run interference with him. So, are you our new PD?"

"Well, I mean, yes. Thank you."

"Do you have any questions for me?"

"So will I be moving into Ed's old office? Will we be hiring a new receptionist?"

"Ah," Kirchner said, "No. We'll still need you on the front desk. Just keep doing what you've been doing. You can do the programming job from there. I wouldn't be offering this to you if I didn't think you could do it," he said. "You have a bright future here." The flattery worked. For the moment at least, Clara felt proud that she had been trusted with a new responsibility instead of annoyed that she was being asked to do what had previously been three people's jobs.

"So do I just start?"

"We'll officially give you the title at the end of the week, and that's when the new pay rate will kick in," Kirchner said. "In the meantime, I want you to work on making our voice more cohesive."

"OK"

"That afternoon guy..."

"Rad."

"He's doing something with a big intro," he imitated the voice, "Far out."

"Yeah."

"It's ridiculous. Talk to him and get him to tone that stuff down."

That was a conversation Clara knew would not go well.

"I like what you're doing with your show. His show should sound more like that. Have him listen to a few of your airchecks so he can get the idea of what we're going for."

Clara laughed.

"Is that funny?" Kirchner asked.

"No," Clara said, thinking it was hilarious. "I'll get right on that."

Program Director

"Good morning, Boss." Seth gave Clara a salute.

"At ease," Clara said, putting her stuff down at her desk.

Seth sat down on the lobby's new stylish leather couch. Over the speakers, the track automatically advanced from one song to the next. "I still can't get used to being able to just sit out here like this," he said.

"I can't get used to, you know, being," she shrugged, "the boss."

"You can do it. I have faith in you."

"I was afraid maybe you'd think it was disloyal to Ed or something."

"No, I think it's great. They could have brought in some hard ass from outside."

"You didn't want it?"

"Me working directly for Kirchner? Yeah, that would go well."

"Yeah," Clara said. She decided against telling him what Kirchner had said about firing him. "Kirchner wants me to keep you in line," she said.

"You think you can?"

"No."

"You don't have to worry about me," Seth said with a warm grin. "I'm always on your side."

"OK I'm making Rad your co-host in the mornings."

"Almost always." They both laughed.

"Where is Kirchner anyway?" Seth asked.

"He's in a sales meeting."

"Great," Seth said. He put his feet up on the coffee table.

Clara shook her head. "You are so going to get me fired."

Clara looked at all of the papers on her desk, a bit overwhelmed. In addition to her previous duties, she had two new tasks, scheduling the part timers, and merging the programming and commercial logs (each of which was stored on its own 5 ¼" floppy) on the computer each week. "I don't actually know what I'm supposed to be doing," she said.

"Easy. You get to take the blame anytime something goes wrong," Seth said.

"Thanks, Seth."

"Come on," Seth said, standing up. "I want some more coffee. Come take a break with me."

Seth put his arm over Clara's shoulder as they walked down the hall, "You've got this," he said. "You're going to be great."

They had made it almost to the kitchen when Rad stormed through the front door. He had a piece of paper in his hand and a determined look on his face. He marched towards the kitchen but turned and opened the sales office door without knocking. From their vantage point, Clara and Seth could see inside the room. Kirchner and the sales people were sitting at a table. Everyone stopped talking and looked at Rad. Clara and Seth looked at each other and then stood to watch as Rad announced, "I need the fax machine. I need to fax my resume."

Rad punched a number into the fax and fed his resume through. "Where is the green slip?" He picked up one of the phone slips and announced out loud what he was writing on it, "Purpose of call, faxing resume to competing radio station."

Seth leaned into Clara and whispered, "Don't tell anyone, but I think I'm starting to like Rad."

Rad stood for a moment with his hands on his hips as he waited for the fax to go through and print its transmission receipt. Kirchner did not say a word to Rad. He looked back to the sales team and said, "So we were talking about the fourth quarter..."

Rad seemed disappointed that he had not gotten the reaction he wanted, and he stormed off down the hall.

"Miss Jane, can you close the door?" Kirchner called out.

Clara closed the salesroom door. She turned to Seth, "I guess he heard I'm the new PD."

Lovable Shrapnel

Kirchner had decided that WRTV needed more visibility in the community, and, with the sales and marketing staff, he set out to do more remotes, tie-ins and event sponsorships. One of the biggest was a 4th of July celebration put on by the city. It was a fair with carnival rides, a concert stage and fireworks. RTV had cut a deal to be the official radio station of the festival. There would be ticket giveaways, a remote broadcast with Seth Jones, and Clara would introduce the headlining act on stage.

The organizers had booked a British band called Lovable Shrapnel, who had a couple of high energy MTV hits a decade before. The station had received a promo copy of the new album they were promoting. It was an exuberant confection with nonsense lyrics, power chords and plenty of hooks. Clara thought it was as good as anything they released in their heyday, but the public had tied them firmly to a moment and moved on. The new single had not even cracked the Billboard 100. Their sound was guitar heavy for adult contemporary but not heavy enough to alienate the audience. Since they were sponsoring the show, Clara thought RTV should give it some airplay. She approached Rad, but he refused. "They don't fit the format," he said.

"Don't *we* decide that?" Clara asked.

"There are some standards," Rad said. "I don't know why we're sponsoring a concert for a band we don't even play."

"Right," Clara said, "Well, there's an easy solution to that." She held the CD out to him. Rad did not take it.

"I don't control the music mix anymore," he said. "Talk to the computer."

"OK," Clara said, "why don't you get a little creative and put it in the system as a programming element like news or something, give it a number."

"Too much work," Rad said.

For some reason, Clara could not bring herself to say, "I am the program director. I am your boss and I'm telling you to do this." Instead she pleaded, "It's just a matter of recording it into the system and giving it a number."

"Why don't you do it?"

Clara raised her voice, "Because you're the music director!"

"Whatever," Rad said.

Through the studio window Clara saw that Jason Briggs had walked into the lobby, presumably to claim his prize of the month. "We're not done here," Clara said, and ran out to the front desk to take care of her receptionist duties. After dealing with the contest winner and answering a series of phone calls, her work day had nearly ended and she had not returned to her conversation with Rad. She watched him through the window as he stood at the microphone."

"It's 4:37 on your light rock more music station, RTV," Rad said. "We'll be kicking off the RTV Car Tunes at 5 O'clock, and you'll have a chance to win tickets to Saturn's 4th of July Fest featuring Lovable Shrapnel. Our own Seth Jones will be broadcasting live from the festival, and Clara Jane will be on stage to introduce the band. You won't want to miss that. After the break, a song that Elvis Presley wanted to record, but Dolly Parton turned him down. It became one of the biggest hits of last year. It's all on the way on Saturn's Favorite Music. Stay tuned."

It occurred to Clara that Rad's show was run in live assist mode. He didn't need to program the song into the system at all. If he wanted to, he could just pause the computer and plop the song in the CD player. She sat for a moment trying to psych herself up to go into the studio and assert her authority. "I'm the program director, and I am programming this song. Pause the system and put it in after Whitney Houston."

Clara hated confrontation, and she resented Rad for forcing her into it. Part of her knew that if she did not stand up to Rad in this moment she would never have any authority, but an even bigger part of her just wanted to avoid the stress. She didn't care enough about getting the song on the air to develop an ulcer over it. She went home for the day without saying anything to Rad.

When Clara arrived at the station the next day, Seth was sitting on the stylish new sofa in the lobby drinking what Clara assumed was his 8th cup of coffee. "Hi boss," he said.

"Are you ready for the big day?" Clara asked.

"As ready as I'll ever be. I'm going to have to go home and take a nap before this remote. I have a mean program director who expects the morning guy to be able to stay up for fireworks."

"She sounds terrible," Clara said. "At least you can sleep in on Saturday."

"I'll try," he said, standing up to return to the studio for his break. "I usually wake up before God no matter what."

"Hey," Clara said, grabbing the Lovable Shrapnel CD off her desk. "After you plug the concert, can you play this?" Clara handed the disc to Seth.

"Sure," he said, reading the cover. "Which track?"

"The single is 'Cannon Indeed.'"

"Clever," Seth said. Clara followed him to the studio and watched as he put the disc in the player and cued up the track. "I tried to get Rad to play it on his show yesterday. He wouldn't do it."

"What do you mean he wouldn't do it?"

Clara imitated Rad's voice, "'We shouldn't be sponsoring a band we don't play. It's not our format.' I mean, I don't know why we're sponsoring a concert by a band we don't program either, but that's not the point. We are."

"Also you're the boss."

"Yeah, that's the point."

"He wants you to fail," Seth said, sitting in the driver's seat.

"You think?"

"You're going to have to slap him down. He'll walk all over you if you let him."

"Yeah, I just don't know if I can. It's just not my personality. I hate confrontation."

"The break's coming up." Seth hit a key to pause the computer program. As the music faded out, Seth potted the microphone up. "Happy Fourth of July. I hope you're feeling independent. That was Rod Stewart on Saturn's Favorite Music, RTV. I hope you'll come out this evening to the Saturn Fourth of July Festival. Clara Jane and I will both be there with the Incredible Broadcast Machine. We'll be broadcasting live, giving away t-shirts and other prizes. Hope to see you there. Of course there will be fireworks and a performance by this band, all the way from England. It's Lovable Shrapnel with Cannon Indeed."

Seth pressed play on the CD player. The song opened with a barrage of percussion followed by a cannon blast and a robust guitar slide.

"Well, that will wake them up," Seth said.

"You're hot," Clara said.

"Huh?"

"The needle." She pointed to the VU meter, which was well into the red.

"Thanks," Seth said, dialing the pot down.

"I think it's pretty good," Clara said, referring to the song. "It's kind of fun and goofy. It hasn't cracked the top 100. I don't know why."

"People are fickle when it comes to pop stars," Seth said. "They put them on and take them off like fashion. These guys are bell bottoms."

"Bell bottoms are back."

"Really? What about the big collars and wide ties?"

"Yeah, those are never coming back."

"Then those guys are wide ties."

"I had a picture of them in my locker in junior high. I could do that whole dance from the video." Clara waved her arms over her head, imitating the motion.

"Were they your favorites?"

"Not, like, camp out overnight for tickets kind of thing, but I liked them."

"Who did you camp out for?"

"U2."

"Respectable."

"I'm glad you approve."

When the song ended, Seth pushed a button on the keyboard, and the computer took over again. He stood up and started flipping through a stack of papers describing the sequence of events for the night. "So the remote starts at 5:30. We go for two hours leading up to the concert, which starts at 7:30. You'll be emceeing."

"Right."

"The show and then, boom, fireworks."

"Cannon indeed."

"Cannon indeed. So I think after my shift I'll go take a nap, for real, then be back here, say 2:30 or 3." He put down the papers. "Do you think the bus needs gas?"

"Probably."

"So maybe 2:30."

"If you want to voice track your last breaks so you can take off early, that would be fine."

"Nah," Seth said. He reached out and rubbed Clara's upper arm. "I'll hang out here. I like the company." Clara smiled. "Are you coming in the bus?" Seth asked.

"No," Clara said. "I'll come later. The band is coming around 4 to do a couple of live interview segments. I want to be here for that."

"You're having Rad do the interview?"

"That's when they could come in."

"OK," Seth said, sounding skeptical.

"It'll be fine," Clara said. "Rad is too vain about his show to do anything obnoxious on the air."

Live Interview

That afternoon, Clara sat tapping a pen on the surface of her desk. As the hour of Lovable Shrapnel's arrival approached, something happened that Clara had not expected. She was getting nervous. She'd met a number of famous people when she was an intern and had always been cool about it. But this particular band had looked out at her from a poster of her locker door. The idea of meeting them awakened some 13-year-old version of herself. Clara had discovered them at just the right time, when she was starting to imagine what it was to be a woman, to be hungry for it and to fear it too. She didn't know what sex was back then, but based on everything she had seen in pop culture, she believed it must be glorious, and these painted men with their rousing music had appealed to all the senses. They had put themselves on display as a model of what the world of eroticism and autonomy would be. They were one of only a handful of bands who had imprinted themselves on her at just that moment and who could therefore summon something from deep inside her imagination. She wanted to make a good impression.

At 3:45, a red tour bus pulled into the lot and parked in the spot where the Incredible Broadcast Machine had been an hour before. Clara stood up. She was wearing the special RTV event t-shirt that Kirchner had ordered, and which the station would be selling on site. She ran her hands over it to straighten out any wrinkles. Then she ran her fingers through her Barbie hair, hoping it was not too messy.

The first person through the door was a young man in a suit. He introduced himself as the record label's publicist. "We spoke on the phone," Clara said. "It's good to finally meet you."

Clara shook his hand, but she was glancing over his shoulder to the men who were filing in behind him. On stage Lovable Shrapnel were known for their flamboyant costumes. In their street clothes, mostly t-shirts and jeans, they appeared very ordinary. Yet in the context of a radio station, all of them, the lead singer John in particular, possessed the mythological glow of the rock star, especially to someone who had seen them between classes every time she reached for her Trapper Keeper. Clara reassured herself that the musicians could not know what was happening inside of her. Nor did they realize that only a month before she was only nominally a DJ. She was the girl who recorded voice tracks and answered the phones. In spite of her own casual attire, she believed they would view her as someone important: a radio personality and the manager of the station where they had come to promote their show. Clara's hand trembled as she reached out to shake theirs.

"This is Mike"

"Hello, Mike."

"This is Simon"

"Nice to meet you."

"This is Graham."

"Graham."

"And this is John."

In their videos, the lead singer had a powerful, energetic persona. Yet here, what was most striking was how short he was. When Clara went to shake his hand, it seemed almost disrespectful to be as tall as she was.

"Hello, Clara Jane," John said, in a soft-spoken English accent that Clara took to be cockney. He did not hold eye contact long. She found herself musing that the kids in study hall would be jealous, and this made her proud. If only she had the phone numbers of the girls who bullied her. She would love to rub this in their faces. Her sense of accomplishment came crashing down, however, when Rad came around the corner.

"I see you met our receptionist," he said. Clara felt her face flush. She wished she'd had a mug in her hand so she could lob it at Rad's head.

"I'm the afternoon announcer," Rad said. "I'll be doing the interview." He led the band to the studio. Once they were inside, he stood at the door, still in earshot of the band, and asked Clara, "Why are we promoting these guys? They had a couple of hits ten years ago. We don't even play them. I'm only doing one break. Then I'm dumping them."

"You're doing two breaks," Clara said, "That's what it says on the log. That's what we agreed to."

"I'm only doing one."

Clara took a deep breath. If Rad wanted a confrontation, he would get one. "If you want to keep your job, you are doing two breaks."

"You can't fire me."

"Try me." For a moment Clara and Rad stood eye to eye. Rad finally looked away. "Fine," he said, and retreated into the studio.

Clara went back to her desk. Her nerves were on edge. She was furious, and embarrassed that she'd lost her cool in front of the rock stars, but she was also proud that she'd finally stood up to Rad. The rush of adrenaline gave her a brief sense of euphoria, a euphoria that Rad, once again, quickly undermined.

He began his interview with, "Our listeners may not know who you are..." And it went downhill from there. Clara felt tears welling in her eyes. She went to the bathroom and allowed herself a moment to cry in frustration. Then she threw some water on her face to try to make her eyes less red and puffy. When she returned to her desk, Don Henley was playing over the speakers. Simon and John came out of the studio. Simon wanted directions to the restroom. John sat down on the new sofa. He smiled at her. Clara couldn't think of anything to say to make the situation better.

"I'm so sorry about Rad," she said.

"He doesn't seem to be a fan," John said.

"I'm just mortified," Clara said. "It's actually not about you guys. He wanted my job. It's actually me he's trying to undermine."

"You don't need to apologize," John said, "You've been quite nice."

"For what it's worth, I really like the new CD."

"So you're the one," John said with a smile.

"Anyway, I am sorry about all this."

"You're apologizing again."

"Yeah, sorry. I mean…"

"You're sure you're not English?" He asked, with that wonderful down tone on the end of his question.

"I'm from Michigan." God, what a stupid thing to say, Clara thought.

"We're going to Michigan, I think." He pronounced "Michigan" as though there were a "t" in it. "Detroit, that's in Michigan, right?"

"Yeah. You're actually in Michigan now"

"Are we? Right." There was an awkward silence.

"What is it like being on tour?"

"It's like living in a very small town that happens to move around. You see the same people every day, and do the same things over and over. But the scenery changes."

"That wasn't the answer I was expecting."

"What is it like being a radio manager?"

"It's the same, except it's actually a small town and the scenery doesn't change."

John gave a genuine smile, and this time he held eye contact. If Clara didn't know better, she would have sworn they were having a moment.

John broke the silence. "Do you ski?"

"Huh? Do I ski?" John gestured towards the mug on her desk. "Oh, the mug. No, it was a joke. The morning guy has a weird sense of humor." Simon had finished in the restroom by now and was coming up the hall.

"Come on, John," he said. "Quit flirting with the DJ."

"Gotta go," John said.

Flirting? As John and Simon disappeared around the corner, Clara sat up straighter, buoyed by a sense of blissful lightness she had not experienced for some time. Not even Rad could puncture her sense of confidence and delight.

"We're back with Lovable Shrapnel live in the studio on your light rock, more music station. The band is going to be headlining at the RTV Saturn Fourth of July Festival tonight. So, John, I understand your new single hasn't cracked the Billboard top 100...."

The Event

Clara went home for a quick bite to eat before the event. Clara brushed her hair and then went to look at herself in the full-length mirror. She had a strange relationship with her reflection. There were times, usually when she was feeling low, that she looked at herself and was surprised by her own beauty. There were others, like today, when she was shocked by how plain she looked. With her blonde hair and generic promotional t-shirt, she hardly recognized herself. She threw on her RTV lanyard. No one really knew what DJs looked like, and the pass would get her back stage, although she knew from experience that the real way you got backstage was not the possession of a lanyard, but by acting like you belonged there.

When Clara entered the fairgrounds, she spotted the Incredible Broadcast Machine near the stage. Behind it she could see the red Lovable Shrapnel bus. Clara had arrived too late to drive over to the van, so she parked with the rest of the crowd and walked to the stage. On one side of the stage, in front of the Incredible Broadcast Machine, was a long table with the equipment for the remote. Beyond that was another table covered in RTV merch being run by the sales staff. The band's own merch table was just beyond that.

Seth was handing a stout woman an RTV bumper sticker as Clara approached the table. "Look who's here," Seth said. "I heard the interview."

"Oh my God," Clara said. She joined Seth behind the table. "I can't wait to tell you about it."

"Are you Clara Jane?" asked the woman with the bumper sticker.

"That's me."

"I love your show."

"Thank you."

"How come you two never talk together on the air anymore? I used to love that."

"Thanks," Seth said, "We enjoyed that too."

"Could I have your autograph," the woman asked. At first Clara thought she was being teased, but the woman handed her a bumper sticker and a Sharpie, so she signed. Then Seth leaned in and signed beside her.

For the next hour, Clara kept trying to find a moment to tell Seth about her confrontation with Rad, but there were breaks, and contests, and a constant stream of listeners. They did their last break at 7:15. "You'd better get back there," Seth said, pointing to the stage. He started packing away the bumper stickers and logs.

The members of the band were just starting to gather behind the curtain when Clara got there. Simon was dressed in a zippered leather jacket that had to be too warm for the stage lights and the July weather. "Hey John," Seth called out, "your DJ is here."

In his stage makeup and his admiral's jacket, John looked taller than Clara had remembered. "Clara, hi," he said.

"You guys ready?" Clara asked. "Let me know when I should go out and announce you."

"Ready as we'll ever be," John said.

Clara walked out onto the stage and looked out over an entire field of spectators. She spoke on the air every day, but she had never stood in front of a crowd that size. "How is everyone doing?" The crowd cheered, and Clara was startled by the rush she felt. "My name is Clara Jane from RTV." Another cheer. "Happy Independence Day! Thanks to my friend Seth Jones, who's been broadcasting here live all evening. Give him a hand." Seth looked up from his packing and waved from his spot at the table. "If you haven't got one yet, we have RTV shirts available for another hour, and the band has merchandise over here too. So about the band. Are you ready for the main event?" Clara held the microphone out in front of her to capture the loud cheer. "OK. We're going to have fireworks later on, but right now, fireworks of a different kind. Let's hear it for Lovable Shrapnel."

The musicians, except for John, entered from the wings and waved at the crowd. Clara left the stage and stood in the wings. Behind the drums Graham raised his arms and struck his sticks together. Then the guitars played the riff from one of their minor hits. The multi-colored stage lights flashed and the intensity built until John finally took the stage. The crowd roared. The stage lights created a dazzling halo around John. He was transformed. Clara could not take her eyes off him.

When Seth had finished packing the equipment into the Incredible Broadcast Machine, he joined Clara back stage. He stood close to her. "They're good," he mouthed over the music. Clara smiled and nodded.

"Here's one from our first album," John said. He turned and faced the side of the stage where Clara was standing, "It's called 'Spend the Night.'"

Clara was sure she was imagining things. She had often felt as though a musician on stage was singing directly to her. That had to be what this was. As the band seemed to be wrapping up the main part of its show, Seth headed back down to help the sales staff with the t-shirts.

The band came off the stage. John leaned over, breathing heavily. The crowd was cheering, calling the band back for the obligatory encore. John stood up and grabbed a towel and wiped his face. The members of the band stood for a moment, listening to the cheers. As he was heading back to the stage John turned to Clara and said, "you'll stick around a bit after, won't you?" He didn't wait for an answer.

The encore had the entire crowd on its feet, miming the dance movements of the band's most famous video. As the band filed off the stage, John walked past Clara. "I'm going to change," he said. "I'll be back."

Clara walked out onto the stage. "Lovable Shrapnel," she shouted. "Have you all been having a good day so far? The fireworks are starting soon. In the meantime, it's your last chance to pick up some of our RTV t-shirts or some of the merchandise from Lovable Shrapnel right over here. Have fun, and happy Independence Day."

Clara walked down to the RTV t-shirt table. Between the salespeople and Seth they seemed to have everything under control, so Clara sat on the stairs leading up to the stage where she would have a good view of the sky. As the first fireworks began to explode, John returned. He was in the same clothes he had worn at the station, but his cheeks were more flushed. He sat on the step beside her and looked up.

"You're celebrating being free of us," he said.

"I suppose there is a certain irony having an English band for Independence Day, now that you mention it."

There were very few moments in Clara's life when she felt like a success. This was one of them. No longer was she the younger sister whose lack of serious direction worried her parents, or the secretary in frumpy business clothes, or the manager who could not control her staff. For the first time in her radio career, Clara was experiencing a little bit of the glamour that had drawn her to the profession. She was living what she had dreamed in junior high, casually chatting with the lead singer of Lovable Shrapnel. It was intoxicating.

"We're staying at the conference center," John said, still looking up at the sky.

"Oh," Clara said. She looked at John. Was he saying what she thought he was?

John looked over at Clara, "Would you like to come by?"

The rock star was inviting her to have a one-night stand. Clara looked at him for what felt like five minutes. In reality, it could only have been a few seconds. Could she really go back to this man's hotel after speaking to him basically twice? If John were not a rock star, he would not be attractive to Clara, but he *was* a rock star, and this gave him a special magnetism. She had the chance to do something other people could only dream of. The teenage version of herself would never believe this was happening.

Out of the corner of her eye, Clara could see Seth loading boxes of t-shirts into the Incredible Broadcast Machine. They hadn't come to the concert together, as a couple. There had been no promises between them. Yet, that was not the full story and Clara knew it. She was torn. She didn't know exactly what she and Seth were to each other, and it was not something that would be resolved in the split second she had to make her decision. In that moment, she longed for a chance to be a pure, uncomplicated object of desire to someone the whole world found desirable. She had been given a call to action, one that would not come again, and if she said no, she was sure she would always regret it. John was leaving the next day. It could only be one night. She told herself she could go with him and Seth never had to know. Nothing had to change.

"Yeah," she said.

"Great," John said. "Do you want to come in the bus?"

"I have my car."

"You can meet me there. I'm in room... room. Was it 147, or was that yesterday? Wait here." John went off to his tour bus. As Clara waited Seth returned. "The van's all packed up." He was relaxed and smiling. Clara tensed. She had to figure out a way to get him to leave quickly.

"Hey, I'm sorry we didn't get the chance to finish our conversation about Rad," Seth said, putting a hand on her forearm.

"You must be pretty tired," Clara said, looking over her shoulder. "It's really late for you."

"I've got a little energy left in me," he said. "This was fun. Do you want to stop by for a beer before I conk out?"

"Oh gosh," Clara said, "You know, I think I'm pretty tired."

"Oh, sure," Seth said. In her peripheral vision Clara could see John coming out of his tour bus and heading her direction. She spoke quickly, "You should probably get the bus back to the station, right?"

By then John had arrived. He put his hand on Clara's shoulder. "It's room 217," he said. Clara stiffened. "I'll see you there?" he asked. Clara nodded, glancing at her feet.

"Great," John said. "Just come up to 217. Knock on the door. I'll be there." He ran off back to the bus.

Clara pressed her lips together and turned to Seth. For a moment his eyes, sad looking on the best of days, appeared absolutely stricken, but it was only a flash. He quickly composed himself. "It looks like you have other plans," he said.

"I-I don't have to go," she said.

"If you want to go with him, go. It's not like we're a couple or anything."

"I feel bad."

"Don't be silly," he said with an unconvincing smile. "Go, have fun."

Clara felt a twinge of regret. Seth knew, and whether she went with John or not, at this point the damage had been done.

"Seth..."

Seth waved and turned away. He walked quickly, with his head slumped. Clara watched him until he got into the Incredible Broadcast Machine and drove away.

Room 217

Clara did not know what she would find on the other side of the door marked 217. She was on the precipice of something, and she had no idea what. Today she would not neutralize the life force within her. She would live fully and taste what Anais Nin called a "descent into sensuality... dark... magnificent... wild." At least that is what she hoped a casual adventure would be like. She had never had one herself, but they seemed exciting in the movies.

Her ideas of what rock stars' hotel rooms looked like were formed by the movies as well. There they were usually expensive suites with guitars lying around, and maybe a grand piano. There would be bikini clad models bingeing coke off of gold records and underwear hanging from an empty bottle in a champagne bucket.

For a moment she considered walking away. But she took a deep breath and knocked. A moment later, John opened the door. He had bare feet. He was not at all like the man on stage, in control and powerful. He seemed a little awkward and utterly plain, "I'm glad you came," he said, then stood aside to let her enter.

Clara looked around to get her bearings. It was an ordinary three-star hotel room with a king bed dominating its center. There was a TV, a small round table with two chairs, and a dresser. John was not using it. His suitcase was on the floor near the closet. Suddenly, Clara wondered what she was doing in this stranger's hotel room. She couldn't stop picturing Seth's pained expression, and how he slumped as he walked away. She wanted to hold him and tell him that he was more special to her than this man would ever be. But a kind of inertia kept her from apologizing to John and going home. She had set something in motion, and she didn't know how not to see it through.

John sat down on the edge of the bed. "Sit down," he said in a gentle voice, patting a space beside him. She sat down. For a moment they sat smiling at one another. They both knew why she had come, but starting was awkward.

"I'm glad you came," John said again. He reached over to her and ran his hand along her arm. He leaned in and started kissing her. It was not long before his hand found its way to Clara's breast, and she shuddered. He sighed, and the foreplay portion of the evening was finished. Her jeans and underwear were down, her shirt was pushed up, and John was unzipping his jeans. He reached into his pocket and pulled out a condom. He had trouble getting the packaging open. As he fumbled, Clara had an opportunity to say she'd like to stop, but things were so far along she felt it would be unfair to disappoint him.

John finally got the condom sorted, and he crawled on top of her. Clara closed her eyes. She hoped he would not try to impress her with a lengthy performance. After what seemed a reasonable number of thrusts, Clara gave a few soft moans and then accelerated them, signaling that it was time to wrap things up. John made a deep grunt, then collapsed on top of her, breathing heavily. When he had caught his breath, he rolled off her, and turned away.

"Drive safely," he said.

Clara let out a small laugh. She dressed quickly, and sped out of the room. "What was that?" she wondered as she drove home. "What on earth was that?"

Clara slept in late on Saturday. When she woke up, she stayed in bed, looking at the ceiling. She felt empty. Not only had her adventure not given her what she wanted, it had taken something from her. For many years, Clara had been driven by the notion that there was a more glamorous and exciting world somewhere out there, and that all she had to do was go and find it. She had craved a life full of wonder and the unexpected, but was that even possible in a world where even rock stars were banal?

Clara got up and put on some coffee. The smell of the coffee reminded her of Seth. She wished that she had just gone with Seth and laughed with him over a beer. This was her punishment; she had wounded her friend for something absolutely pointless.

Clara wanted to call Seth, but she didn't know what to say. She paced for a while, holding her mug in two hands. "About last night..." Is that how she would start the conversation? She sat down on the couch and picked up the phone. Then she set it down again. She paced some more. She picked up the phone again. This time she took a deep breath and dialed. She got Seth's answering machine.

"Hello, Seth. It's me. I wanted to... Can you call me back when you get this? OK, bye."

Clara waited, but Seth did not call.

The Morning Show

On Monday, Clara dreaded going to work. She knew she would have to give Seth an explanation, but she didn't understand what had happened herself. She thought about calling in sick, but that would only delay the inevitable. As she drove to the station, she rehearsed the conversation. "I'm sorry about the concert..." When she walked in, she could see Seth through the window of the studio. He did not look up. She took a deep breath, steeled herself for the talk, but before she could head to the studio, Kirchner came down the hall.

"Miss Jane, can I see you in my office?" This was generally not how Clara liked to start her day.

"Sit down," Kirchner said, directing her to one of the plush leather chairs. "You've been doing a good job here. You're a team player. We've decided that it will be good for the audience in the morning to have a familiar voice, so we'd like you to take over the morning show when Seth leaves."

"When Seth leaves?"

"It's the most important day part, and it's a big responsibility, but I think you can handle it."

"Seth is leaving?"

Kirchner was surprised by the question. "I assumed you knew," he said. He shuffled in his chair. "Yes, Seth put in his two-weeks' notice today."

"No, he- he didn't tell me."

"Well," Kirchner said, clearing his throat. "Since you worked closely with him, I think you're the logical choice to take over that time slot."

"He can't be leaving," Clara said. "It makes no sense. What did he say?"

"I can't share that type of thing for HR reasons," Kirchner said. "I can tell you there was no conflict. He just wants to move on to other things."

"What if he changes his mind?"

"I didn't get the impression that he would," Kirchner said, looking down. He seemed uncomfortable. He cleared his throat again. "Give it some thought. I'd like your answer by the end of the week."

When the meeting was finished, Clara marched directly to the studio. "Kirchner just offered me your job."

Seth was unshaven and his hair was tousled. "I told him he should pick you," Seth said without looking away from the computer screen.

"You told him? Why didn't you tell me?"

"You know now."

"You quit?"

"I've had enough," he said, still not making eye contact.

"Did you get a new job?"

"No."

Clara walked up beside Seth, placing herself in his line of vision. "You weren't talking about leaving on Friday."

Seth threw his arms up in a gesture of surrender. "Impulsive," he said.

"But, why?"

"Why are you surprised?" He turned to face her. "I wanted to leave after Rad's spec spot, you remember? You talked me into staying." He imitated her voice, "I'll go crazy here if you leave."

"I will."

"That's not my responsibility." Then gesturing towards the screen he said, "Everything's pretty easy with the computers. You don't have to do anything until your break comes up. You know how all this works. They call up with traffic reports every 15 minutes until 9 O'clock. You record from the phone here. Don't forget to update the weather phone."

Clara leaned against the console. "What are you going to do?"

"I don't know. Head up the National Bureau of Useless Skills." He picked up his mug and brushed past Clara heading to the door. "I need some more coffee, do you want some?"

"I'm fine," Clara said, shaking her head. Seth left the studio. When he came back, he had a full cup of coffee and the newspaper.

"*The Free Press* is good for finding little things to talk about," he said, dropping the newspaper on one of the motionless turntables. "It's good to be topical."

"Seth..."

"Eye opener trivia is at 8:30."

"You're mad at me."

"I'm not mad at you."

Clara folded her arms across her chest. "I feel bad about the other night."

Seth finally made full and sustained eye contact. "I felt bad about it too."

"Yeah," Clara sighed. "I'm sorry. Really. I wish..."

"I have a break coming up." Seth sat down in the driver's seat.

Clara glanced at the computer screen. "You've got a few minutes. Are you leaving because..."

"Not everything is about you." Seth picked up the headphones.

"No, I know. It's just the timing..."

Seth pressed a key on the computer keyboard to make the system pause after the next song. "There's really not much to do with the computer," he said. "Just make sure you're ready for the breaks."

"Can we talk about the other thing?"

"Nothing to talk about."

"I think there is."

"You're an adult," Seth said, turning back to Clara. "You can sleep with whoever you want. You don't owe me an explanation."

"I think I do." Clara continued to stand with her arms folded across her chest. She bit her lower lip.

Seth shook his head, "Look, obviously, I misread some signals with you. It's fine. It happens."

Clara sighed. "No, you didn't."

"OK," he said. Clara could not read the emotion in his face. There was confusion tinged with anger and hurt, but there was also something else, maybe curiosity. Seth turned back to the computer and scrolled ahead and back on the log. Finally he turned around and said, "I don't know what to do with that."

"We just... I know we... We never really talked about what we..." Clara finished her sentence with a gesture, waving her hand back and forth between them.

Seth shook his head again. "I didn't think we had to."

"I know, but..."

"I don't want to talk about this."

"You *are* mad at me."

"OK, yes, I'm a little bit mad at you. Are you happy?" He slammed the counter with an open palm. In the old vinyl days, the records would have skipped. Now, he just made his own coffee splash in his mug.

"No." There was a long pause. Clara continued, "We always joked about it, but we weren't-- I just didn't know if..."

"You did know," Seth said in a voice barely more than a whisper. "Stand by," he said at full voice, putting on his headphones. As the music faded out, Seth opened the mic, "Jimmy Cliff with 'I Can See Clearly Now,' on your light rock, more music station RTV. It's 9:26, Congratulations to Jason Briggs winner of a chance to grab cash and prizes in the Magic Cash Booth in today's Eye Opener Trivia contest. Listen this afternoon during Rad Farr's Car Tunes for another chance to win. It's going to be a great day today, lots of sun in the forecast. How much? We'll tell you, but not yet. Psych! Stay tuned for your RTV Weather Center forecast and music by Fleetwood Mac after the break."

Seth turned off the mic and hit a key on the computer. As the log advanced to the first commercial, a line printed out with a high-pitched grind of the dot matrix printer. Clara's voice played through the speakers.

"The friendly folks at Erickson Hardware would like to remind you that summer is here." Seth took off his headphones. His eyes rolled upward and he shook his head. His jaw was set. "Erickson has everything you need to make your summer more fun, and right now they're selling all gas grills, gardening supplies and patio furniture at 10 percent off. That's right, 10 percent! Trees and shrubs, outdoor lighting, propane tank refills. Everything you need for summer is 10 percent off. Hurry in now to Erickson Hardware, two miles north of the airport in beautiful downtown Saturn."

Seth sat for a moment, looking at Clara, saying nothing. He seemed to be contemplating her, summing her up. Clara looked down and kicked at a ball of dust on the carpet beside the turn tables.

"You know, I'm 37 years old," Seth finally said. "I'm not like you. I don't have the luxury of imagining that my life is going to be perfect. The ship's sailed on that one."

Clara looked up at Seth. "I, I don't know what you mean."

"No, obviously," he sighed. "Life is messy. Whatever you try to do, half of it won't turn out like you planned. More than half. You're in this town, but you're too good for it. You're holding your nose and waiting for some real life to start, some far off life that will be full of, I don't know, rock stars and bullshit. You're here now. This is where you are. You have to live where you actually are or you're not going to live at all."

"I know that."

"Do you?"

"I'm not like that."

"Just go home and think about it before you brush it off."

"I don't want to fight with you. You have a right to be mad."

"Thanks for the permission."

"Seth, you're my best friend, my only real friend here. I do..." Clara wanted to say "love you," but she was afraid that the words meant more than she wanted to say, or maybe less. "What I mean is, I think about it. Maybe I've been afraid of what would happen if things changed. But that's not so strange is it? I don't want to lose what we have. What if we got together and then it didn't work out?"

"What if it did?" he shouted. He looked down and shook his head then glanced up at Clara. "Or maybe that's your problem." As he held her gaze, Clara felt like he could see straight through her. What she feared was not having it go wrong, she was afraid of what would happen if it went right. Seth chose to be in Saturn. Clara could not imagine spending the rest of her life trapped in a small town. How could she let herself love someone who might derail all of her plans? There had been no risk that a one-night stand was going to change her life. Loving Seth could, and it terrified her.

Seth took a deep breath. "Did you hear me say I didn't want to talk about it? Because I'm pretty sure I said that out loud. I can open the mic and broadcast it if that would help."

Clara shook her head. "That won't be necessary."

"I'm only here for two weeks. Do you want to learn this or not?"

"Yes, I want to learn it." They did not bring that night up again.

Only a Woman's Heart

Clara never adjusted to rising at 4:00 in the morning. When she was given the morning show, none of her other duties had been taken off her plate. She was still the program director, still the traffic director. The only thing that she had given up was recording voice tracks for middays. These days they were voiced by a part-timer, a high school student with a deep voice, who came in on Sundays and recorded in advance for the entire week. Between all of her tasks, Clara was often still at the station until 4 or 5 PM. She had time to come home, eat, and try to be in bed by 8. She was naturally a night person, and her body rebelled against the schedule. She would toss and turn and never captured a full eight hours of sleep. If her alarm did not go off, Clara knew she would never wake up naturally in time for work. She set two alarms, her clock radio and, in case the power went out, a battery powered travel alarm as backup. She no longer woke up to the morning show but to a syndicated talk show that RTV broadcast overnight. It was designed more to lull people to sleep than to wake them up.

In her half-sleep, Clara hallucinated as she drove into work. She imagined herself driving in the phantom path of Seth's car as if time were folded in on itself and everything that had ever happened on the road was happening at once. As she drove, Seth drove too. She saw him when he was new to RTV's morning show and still enthusiastic. She could see him listening to the news and making mental notes of what to say during his shift.

Each morning she pulled into the gas station, the only store open at that hour, and bought a breakfast consisting of a pack of cherry Pop Tarts. The store was an early risers' club made up of truckers and folks with long commutes. The conversations were brief. They asked each other what they were doing up at that hour and talked about the weather. Clara pictured Bill Katz there saying, "It will be a little bit warmer today, but not a whoop dee doo warm up. Expect partly cloudy skies."

Seth and Clara had not spoken since he left the station. And in that time he had become, in Clara's mind, a current hit with a 10-minute rotation on a station playing only one song. She knew that going with John and leaving Seth behind had been wrong, yet she had done it anyway. It challenged her notion of who she was. She wanted someone to talk to, but she could not think of anyone. To talk to Seth would be painful, and to talk to anyone else truthfully enough to make a difference would be to reveal her shame, and she couldn't stand the idea of doing that.

Seth had seen something in her that she thought was well hidden, so well hidden that she had not wanted to admit it to herself-- her desire to be welcomed into places that excluded others, in the company of people who others wanted to know but could not get access to. He had seen both that, and her corresponding fear that she would live her life in mediocrity. It was ugly, and she wanted to erase her previous self and any record that she had ever existed.

Yet those ugly impulses came from something that had a kind of beauty, her desire for life to be more than it was. She wanted to discover what she really felt, not what she was taught to feel, to choose her life, not accept the path of least resistance. Her ambition, her desire, that was part of what was good in her. It was what made her try to be better. Her shame and her pride were two sides of the same coin. She was stuck with herself. All she knew how to do now was to shut down inside.

Clara arrived at the station, picked up the newspaper from the transom, unlocked the door and turned on the light. The station was still and dark, but not quiet. Even with no one there, the outgoing signal played through the speakers. There was also a mechanical hum of all the equipment, Gentner's way of saying "good morning."

Clara thought about the time that she and Seth discussed the end of the world. If they had dropped the bomb back then, when the people died, the station would have died with them. There would be no one to spin the records, record the news feeds, open the mic. It was different now. If she, and everyone in Saturn, were vaporized, the computer would play on. The music would continue, the cheery ads hawking phantom businesses would run and be logged, and pre-recorded human voices would talk about "Saturn's Favorite Music" until the power went out. Human voices speaking, but no humans to hear them.

Clara headed for the kitchen where she started brewing in the industrial-sized coffee pot. She could see Seth there pouring the first of his 10 cups of the day. She could see the future, too. She saw herself years down the line drinking her own 10 cups a day. She put the newspaper on the photocopier and made a copy of the travel weather map to read on the air. She imagined Al there impatient to get the paper because he was very, very busy.

She continued her sleep walk through the morning routine. As she walked past the lobby desk, she could picture Leslie there, handing Clara a newspaper with Bigfoot on the cover. Clara continued to the studio, where she wrote down temperatures and forecasts and looked ahead at the upcoming contests and announcements. When 5:30 AM rolled around, she opened the mike and gave a cheery, "Good morning! It's 5:30 on Saturn's Favorite Music, WRTV. I'm Clara Jane and we have a great selection of music lined up for you to start your morning. Phil Collins, Michael Bolton and Mariah Carey are all on the way! But first here's a new one, Eleanor McAvoy with 'Only a Woman's Heart.'"

Then Clara hit the enter key on the computer keyboard, closed the mike and put her head down on the console for a mini-nap until she had to talk again.

Glowing Screens

The next day Clara walked up to the studio door and picked the newspaper up from the step. She shook the raindrops off of its plastic bag and tucked it under her arm so she could get to her key and unlock the door. Once she was inside, she flipped on the light in the lobby and set her purse down behind the reception desk. She yawned and headed to the kitchen to put on her morning coffee. As the coffee was brewing, she stood at the photo copier and flipped through the paper until she had located the weather page. She photocopied the travel weather. The overnight talk show was playing over the speakers. Clara yawned again, and set the newspaper and photocopy down on the table.

She took her "I'd rather be skiing" mug down off the shelf. In her sleep-deprived state, her brain displayed small films of the previous Christmas. They appeared to her as something between a memory and a dream. By then the coffee was brewed enough for her to pour a cup. She filled the mug, blew on it, and took a sip. She rubbed her eyes, then picked the papers up from table and headed back to the studio.

Clara made it almost to the driver's seat before it dawned on her that something was unusual. The entire bank of computer screens, including the one over the audio board, was glowing purple. Instead of displaying logs or feeds, they were etched with spider-like lines. The bank of CD players clicked and churned as it switched from one disc to another at random, playing multiple discs at a time. Only the fact that the overnight feed was playing prevented an absolute cacophony from going out over the airwaves.

Clara set her mug and papers down on the counter. She had no idea how to reset the computer system. She picked up the phone to call the engineer and found the line dead. It was now 5:20 and the feed was slated to end at 5:30 AM.

Clara put the microphone in cue and got a level. The board itself seemed to be functioning. She then went into the news studio, and then the production studio. The computers in each of the rooms were in the same state. Clara tried rebooting the computer in the main broadcast studio. The tapped her foot as the seconds passed by. When the computer screen finally came back on, it had the same purple glow. Clara went to the bank of CD players and pressed the off buttons on each to prevent them from playing at random.

Clara then ran back to the reception desk and picked up the phone there. Finally, a dial tone. Whatever happened had only affected the equipment in the studios. She dialed the engineer. He did not pick up. Clara hung up and dialed again, "Come on Max, pick up."

"Hello?" Max's voice was hoarse. She had woken him up. Clara described the studio to him as quickly as she could.

"Sounds like there must have been a power surge in the storm," Max said. "Maybe lightning hit the antenna that sends the signal to the big tower."

"What do we do?"

It was now 5:25.

"Try rebooting the computers, see if that does anything."

"I tried that."

"Okay. I'm on my way in."

Clara's next call was to Mr. Kirchner.

"The entire studio is fried," she said. "I don't see how we can go on air."

"Is anything working?"

"The board is working, the transmitter is working, but the computers and the phone lines to the studio are gone."

"Just go back to the old way then," he said.

"It's not that simple. Everything is in the computer now, the music cues, the ads, the feeds."

Clara looked up at the clock. 5:28.

"You'll figure it out," he said. "I want to get up and running and make sure the ads and sponsorships air. I don't want a lot of make goods."

Clara ran back into the studio. The CDs and records had long ago been moved to storage. Out of habit she turned to the shelf where the carts with the legal IDs used to be. They were also gone. 5:59. Clara did not have time to go digging in the back room. She glanced around the room and then went over to the shelf with the bank of CD players. She turned on one of the machines, ejected the CD changer, pulled out one of the discs and looked at it. The CD itself was designed to be played by the machine, but Clara was glad to see that the front of the disc was printed with a track list, although there was no cover that she could place in front of her and no notation of the song lengths.

Clara put the disc into the old CD player, which was fortunately still connected to the board, although she could not be sure if it was functional. As the overnight program came to an end, Clara potted it down, opened the mic and said, "WRTV Saturn, Michigan." She did not remember the song she had cued up on the disc, so she could not announce it. She pushed play and said a small prayer of thanks when music came through the board. She took another CD from the ejected changer, grabbed a piece of paper and a pen, and quickly jotted down the track numbers and titles before putting it into the second CD deck and cuing up track 1.

Max arrived 10 minutes later. He went from one studio to another, looking at the computers. He returned with the verdict: "They're fried. We're going to need to replace them."

"Can you tell Kirchner that?"

"What did I ever do to you?"

"I'm a little busy here, and the studio phone isn't working."

As Max went to the lobby to call the boss, Clara tried to reinvent the morning show. There was no more clock hour in the studio, and no log. From memory, Clara knew that the first sponsored traffic and weather reports were supposed to come up at 6:10. But who was the sponsor? She looked around the studio in the vain hope that maybe the three-ring binder with the old sponsorship copy was still around, but it was not.

Clara had a thought. If the telephone on her desk had been spared, maybe the computer there worked, too. She let the tracks on the CD play one after the other with small gaps and no cross fades as she fired up the traffic computer on her desk and waited for it to load.

"Come on. Come on," she shouted at the machine. It was now 6:06. Her hands shook as she clicked through files. She managed to find the version of the logs that included the commercial schedule and print it out. Then she printed out the sponsorship lines associated with the avails. 6:09.

On the way back into the studio, Clara picked up the newspaper; in the upper corner was a weather forecast. She set it on the console in front of her, then she faded out the end of the song and opened the mic.

"Good morning. This is WRTV, Saturn's Favorite Music. This will be an unusual morning show, folks. Last night, our system was struck by lightning and our computer systems all went down, so you will probably hear a few technical difficulties as we work to get everything back on line. I'm afraid we don't have a traffic report at the moment-- hopefully your commute is not too bad-- and if you are stuck somewhere, we'll keep you company. It's now time for the RTV weather center forecast brought to you by Erickson Hardware." Then Clara did her best singing imitation of the opening to the jingle. "RTV Weather!" before reading the forecast from the paper. Then glancing up to look at the bank clock she said, "Currently 62 degrees at your light rock, more music station RTV."

She hit the CD, and a song she had never heard before started to play. She now faced a new problem. The first commercial break was coming up at 6:20, but there were no recorded ads. She ran back to her desk. Why hadn't she ever thought to make a single folder for all current ad copy? Instead, the copy for each client was stored in its own account folder, along with invoices, drafts and old versions of their ads. Working from the log she had printed, she managed to locate each sponsor's ad for the next break and print out the copy. It was 6:18.

Clara gathered the papers and ran into the studio. She tried to sort them into some reasonable order. Clara potted down the song and said, "Your light rock, more music station RTV, that was..." before realizing she did not know what the song had been and she had lost the paper on which she'd written down the tracks. "...Another great song this morning. Well, folks, if you're just tuning in, first of all, welcome. In last night's storms, RTV lost some of its equipment, so we are having to improvise a bit. We're going to take you back to the thrilling days of yesteryear, when announcers used to read their commercial copy live on air."

She then cleared her throat and read the copy for each ad, in turn. "Now back to the music."

Clara finally got to take the first sip of her coffee, now lukewarm. Max returned to the studio, "They're going to have to replace the system," he said, "but the company isn't in until 9, so there's no way to know how quickly they can get it done."

"I need some help here," Clara said. "Can you call Rad? Wake him up. See if he can get here early."

"Do you want me to call the part timers?"

"It's a school day," Clara said. "They'll both be in school."

That was when it occurred to her that there was no longer enough staff to cover the whole day with live air shifts. If Rad did not show up early Clara would have to stay on the air until school let out.

Rad arrived at the studio around 7:30, and Clara said some words she had never thought she would utter. "Rad, thank god you're here."

"What do you need me to do?"

"These are the ads that are coming up," she said, handing him a stack of paper. "I tried to put them in order, so the first ones in the schedule are on top. Can you really quickly record some of these so we don't have to keep reading everything live? Oh, also, can you look around and see if you can find any of the old liners, and the weather bed?"

After a few minutes Rad came back from the production studio. "There are no cart machines in the production studio. They took them out when they put the computer in."

"Try the news studio."

As Rad rummaged around the news studio, Clara pulled more CDs from the bank of players and started jotting down the track lists. Rad returned and reported that he had found a working cart machine in the news studio, but he had only been able to locate 10 carts. The next commercial break was coming up in five minutes. Rad would not have time to record five spots before the break, even if he had all the equipment he needed. Rad still had the copy in his hand. He sat down at the guest mic. "Look," he said, "Why don't we alternate reading them so it's not one voice."

"Good idea," Clara said. That was how they got through the next break.

Clara was starting to get overwhelmed by the papers on her console. "Let's... OK, let's... There are some manila folders in my desk. If we're going to have to read these live, we need to get them organized to find them quickly. I think we should put them in alphabetical order."

"I'm on it," Rad said, heading out to the lobby. On his way he passed Max, who was heading into the studio with a phone message. "Kirchner called to complain about missing the sponsorships on the traffic reports," he said.

"We can't do traffic reports," Clara said.

"He said, and I quote, 'figure it out.'"

"Of course he did," Clara said.

Rad came back from Clara's desk with a stack of copy in one hand, and the envelopes in the other. "I have an idea," he said. "We don't have enough carts to record everything, but if I record the spots onto a reel tape, we can have them all, and then we can put them on the ten carts and then erase and redub the carts when we need to."

"Do we have a working reel-to-reel?"

"We've got a couple of them."

"OK," Clara said. "Do that." Rad went into the production studio to start recording copy. Clara potted down the music and opened the mic: "The Beatles on Saturn's Favorite Music, RTV. It's 7:41. If you're just tuning in, and you think the station sounds a little different today, you're probably right. We were struck by lightning last night. We're still here, but our computer system isn't. So today you might be hearing some different music and you might hear us reading commercials live on the air. Normally, our traffic report comes on a regional feed that we do not have access to at the moment. So, if you have a good view of a road and you have something to report about traffic conditions, go ahead and give us a call, and we'll pass the information along. Our traffic reports are brought to you by Saturn Tire and Auto." Clara checked off the sponsorship message on the log she had printed.

Max found a long cord and managed to stretch the telephone from reception closer to the studio. Throughout the morning people called to share reports on the traffic they could see through their office and living room windows. It became a running game with the audience playing along, calling in to report delivery trucks in front of stores and people parking badly.

"This is an eye witness traffic report sponsored by Saturn Tire and Auto. Traffic Reporter Shane Hunter of Reed City called to say that while he was on his way to work a rude jerk just cut him off at the intersection of US-10 and US-131. Shame on you, whoever was in the black Buick Century."

By 8 AM Rad had recorded the most frequent spots, music beds and all, and put them on the 10 carts. Clara stacked them on the console in alphabetical order. Rad then went to explore the storage room in search of more carts. Around 8:10 there was a loud crash from the back room. Clara ran out of the studio. "Are you OK?"

"Yeah," Rad called. He came out of the back room holding a cardboard box that was nearly falling apart. "I found more carts."

"What happened?"

"The shelf fell down."

Clara returned to the studio to read a traffic report from someone who said she arrived late to work because she had gotten stuck behind some slow-moving farm equipment. Now Rad was dragging boxes of LPs out of the back room and putting them close to the studio door. The boxes of LPs were in no particular order. Some contained the records that they used to play, others were older. There were a lot of odd things in there, going back to the beginning of the station, like the John Wayne spoken word LP "America, Why I Love Her." Pat Boone. Zamfir.

"Did anyone ever play this on the radio?" Clara asked, flipping through the collection: "Astro Sounds," "Yankee Doodle Songs."

"I just took a call from an angry caller," Max said.

"What are they upset about?" Clara asked.

"They heard your traffic report and want to know what you have against farmers."

Radio Improvisation

When the offices for the manufacturer of the automation system finally opened at 9AM, Max was able to report that the new system would not be installed until the weekend. He started disconnecting the damaged monitors and setting them on the floor in the back room. Rad tripped over one as he raced from the production studio with a new commercial cart.

By mid-morning Rad had uncovered a couple of boxes of the old CDs, which he put on the table in front of the guest mic, while Clara continued to remove CDs from the changers. She started listing the tracks on post-it notes. She could then keep the list with the CD until she put it in the machine and have it on the console in front of her as it played. She was now comfortably cuing and cross fading between vinyl albums and CDs with a music mix that bore a reasonable resemblance to the old clock hours.

Clara stayed on the air until 2 PM, when Rad took the board and Clara started running back and forth to the production studio. The two part-timers arrived a little before 4 PM. Clara put one in the production studio and the other in the news studio, where they could record ads and liners. "Don't make them beautiful; they just have to be passable."

By now they had developed a system. The most frequent ads were recorded onto carts and kept in the studio. The less frequent ones were recorded first onto reel and then onto carts marked with pink highlighter. These would be run, then immediately erased and re-recorded from the reel with the commercials for the next break.

At 6 PM, Clara ordered pizza for the team, which she paid for out of petty cash. Rad's regular airshift was from 2-7, and the 7-10 slot was usually voice tracked by one of the teenagers. They decided to maintain the regular transition of voices. But at 6:30 it became clear that the part-timer had only recorded on the computer and had never been trained on the board. Clara gave him a quick tutorial and stayed in the room for his first hour to provide backup. He did not know how to cue a vinyl record, so they stuck to the CDs for his airshift. Clara told him to not to worry about the music mix and to put on whatever he wanted, as long as it fit the format. At 7:30, when Rad had been at the station 12 hours, Clara sent him home. She thanked him for all his help, told him to get a good night's sleep, and not to come in the next day before noon. She left the studio in the hands of the part-timer, and started printing out logs and copy for the next broadcast day.

When it was finally time to turn the nights over to the satellite at 10 PM, Clara fell on the couch, exhausted. It was more energy than she could muster to go home, so she decided to sleep at the station. She got up one more time to search for an alarm clock and something she could use for a pillow. She found it in the form of an old RTV promotional banner, which she bunched up and placed on the arm of the sofa. She was lulled to dreams by the voice of the overnight feed.

Clara's alarm went off at 5:00 AM. She walked to the kitchen with her eyes half closed, put on a pot of coffee and munched down a slice of cold pizza for breakfast. She rubbed her eyes. Her head felt heavy, and she had a crick in her neck. On the way back to the studio, she tripped over a box of LPs. The back room was strewn with boxes, monitors and mechanical equipment. The area in front of the guest mic was a mix of CDs from the boxes and the machines. To her right, where the box of music cards once sat, was a stack of labeled carts, a few of the pink carts and the folder with the text of the ads. Boxes of LPs sat along the base of the shelf with the bank of unplugged CD players.

Clara started flipping through the albums. She stopped when she found Gordon Lightfoot. "The Wreck of the Edmund Fitzgerald" was both long and fitting. She cued it up and put one of the new liner carts, with a legal ID, in the board. As the overnight feed came to an end, she fired the cart. There was a stinger, and then Rad's deepest radio voice: "WRTV Saturn, Michigan." Clara then fired the turntable and started slotting CDs into the two working players.

"Good morning, Saturn," Clara said when the song came to its end. "This is your light rock, more music station RTV in our second day of special lightning programming. We're still working on getting our whole system up and running after a lightning strike yesterday. Hopefully, things will sound a bit smoother overall today. Your RTV weather center forecast for today, brought to you by Arlo's Pizza, calls for..." Clara realized she had not picked up the newspaper, and had no forecast to refer to. "No lighting. We'll give you more details on that later. Right now it's 6:09 and 61 degrees. How about a little Billy Joel? It's Saturn's Favorite Music, RTV."

Clara started the music, closed the mic, and put her head down on the console. It was all she could do to keep from drifting to sleep. She jumped when she heard motion behind her.

"Sorry, I didn't mean to scare you," Seth said. "They never took my key back. I heard about the lightning. You sound exhausted. I don't think anyone else can tell, but... I can help if you need me."

Clara stood up and hugged Seth. She was so exhausted, she started to cry. He let her collapse on his shoulder for a long moment, saying nothing. "How long were you here yesterday?" he finally asked.

Clara separated from Seth. "I never left," she said, rubbing her nose with the back of her hand.

"Why don't you go home for a while, get some rest, I can do this."

"You don't work here," Clara said, "I can't leave you here on your own. Anyway, I need to be here if the computer people call, and the commercial break is coming up...." She started to speak rapidly, describing the situation with the carts and the CDs.

"Stop. Stop," Seth said. "If you don't rest you're going to break. That won't help anything."

"I don't know what else to do."

"Stay, but sit here." Seth led her to the couch and with his hands on her shoulders, pushed her down. "Just let me handle things for a while." He walked into the studio, then came back out, "Um, I just need you to explain what's going on in here...."

340

8:28

After she explained the chaotic system in the studio to Seth, Clara went back to the couch. "More than a Feeling" by Boston was playing through the speakers. Clara planned to just close her eyes for a few minutes. When she opened them, she heard a light hit by Madonna transitioning into the crackle and hiss of the cue burnt opening to American Pie. For a moment she wondered if she had dreamed that Seth had come back to the station, but then he appeared in the studio door. Clara sat up.

"What time is it?" she asked.

"It's a little after 8:30," Seth said sitting next to her on the couch.

"I just closed my eyes and I fell asleep." She stretched. "I can't believe I slept two hours."

"You needed it. Do you feel better?"

"Yeah," Clara said, rubbing her eyes."I don't know what I would have done if you hadn't shown up. I think I was about to have a nervous breakdown."

"If you're not careful you still could."

"Do you remember my first week here? The EBS test where the board wasn't patched?"

"A little."

"You had me cue up the pie song."

"8:28."

"8:28."

"We talked about the end of the world. Sometimes I think it's here." Seth looked at Clara with a gentle expression but said nothing. As much as Clara had thought about Seth over the past few weeks, she had forgotten this feeling, the sense of comfort and calm that she had in his presence.

She sighed, "You know, I think I had radio all wrong. I always thought that it was all about music, or the news and entertainment. You had to have commercials so you could pay for all of that, but it turns out I had it backwards. The on air stuff is just a vehicle for the commercials. The money isn't to support what we do; we're tools to make the money. Robots do it better. Human beings are so expensive and inefficient. Replaceable."

Seth shook his head, "You're not replaceable. Don't ever let them make you feel replaceable. What are you holding on to? You replace them."

"You mean quit? Like you?"

"I got out just in time."

"Do you miss it?"

"Days like this?"

"No, normal ones."

"Sometimes." Something occurred to Clara at that moment, something that in the rush of the morning's events she had not had time to notice. Seth had been listening to her show.

"You know, I've been arguing with you in my head since you left," she said.

"OK"

"You acted like I was shallow for wanting a career."

"I didn't mean to. If I said something like that, I didn't mean it." He looked down at his lap. "We were both a little upset the last time we talked." Then, looking back at Clara he said, "I'd never shit on your dreams. You've kept this place on the air with string and duct tape. You're a superhero." He gave her a friendly pat on the leg.

"I have to admit, it has been kind of fun in a perverse way. It was sort of like the good old days when you had to think on your feet and you were always working without a net."

"You've got a couple of metaphors jangled up together there."

"Yeah, well, I'm tired. Cut me some slack."

"Slack for when you're on the ropes, on your feet, and working without a net."

"Oh my god," Clara said with a laugh. "That was such a Seth thing to say."

"Thank you?"

"It's a good thing," she said. "Yeah, Seth things are good things." Seth smiled at her. It was a gentle smile that revealed itself more in the eyes than the lips.

"The morning show always was controlled chaos," he said.

"Of course, the balance between the control and the chaos right now..."

"Context is everything."

"Right." There was a lull in the conversation, but it was not uncomfortable. Finally, Clara said, "I had an interview, a phone interview, with a station in Delaware. It was an alternative station, on the ocean."

"Sounds like your dream."

Clara shook her head. "I blew it. I really wanted it. I mean, I needed it, you know? It felt like my whole life depended on it. I think I just sounded too desperate."

"It's their loss. There will be another one."

"I don't know. I feel like I'm failing at everything. It's all so hard. But I don't want to just give up. Lots of people do student radio, and a few work in radio for a year or two and then they give up and take a 'normal' job; get the station wagon, the suburban house. Then one time at a dinner party maybe they drop in how they did radio for a year or so when they were younger. I don't want to be that."

"Well," Seth said, glancing upwards, "eventually everything turns out to be something you did for a while when you were younger, when you think about it."

344

"I had a goal," Clara said. "I got into radio. I did what I set out to do. How can I just give up and admit failure now?"

"Deciding you don't like something any more isn't failure. You know what's failure? Doing something that's killing you because you don't have the imagination to come up with anything better. Look, all I have to say is, if radio is really what you want, great. If you love it, keep going, even if it's hard. But your life doesn't depend on it, you know? When you stop loving it, stop. You'll find something else to love."

Clara gazed at Seth. She was taking in his dark, tilted eyebrows and his beautiful, goofy, elongated face. She smiled and put her hand on his cheek. A stray hair was standing up on his right eyebrow and she smoothed it down with her index finger. She leaned in to kiss him, but he backed away. For a moment he sat looking startled, then he stood up and turned away from her.

"It looks like you have things under control here," he said.

"Seth, I..."

"If you need help tomorrow, give me a call." He darted out of the studio, leaving Clara alone with Don McLean, and his hymn to the day the music died.

Noise and Silence

It took about two weeks to get the entire system working again. It would have been sorted out sooner, but Kirchner had looked for bids on a new telephone system, a process that took a few days. He chose the cheapest option, of course. While the new system was being installed no calls could go in our out, and the DJs had to work around a team of the repair men. The new phones had a complicated voicemail system and an even more complex system for logging calls. The training session on the new phones took about an hour. When it was wrapping up, Clara asked the trainer, "So how do we put calls through the board?"

"What board?"

"In the studio," Clara asked, "How do I put a caller on the air?"

"Well, you can't do that," he said.

Kirchner had forgotten to mention to the company that the phones needed to be wired into the audio board. It took two more days to find another company and install an entire new system.

The next day Clara sat at her desk appreciating the novelty of managing a radio station with equipment that worked. But it wasn't long before the energy that had come with the challenge faded and her ennui took over again. The extraordinary exhaustion of the lightning strike was replaced with the mundane, unending, daily exhaustion of sleep deprivation, overwork and loneliness.

The mornings were the hardest. Clara generally woke up feeling sorry for herself that she had to endure another day at RTV. Once she was at the station, things were a little bit better. There were tasks that she had to do, and she could force her body, if not her spirit, to move through them. On the air, she was professionally cheery. The audience probably had no idea that anything was wrong. Did Seth? Was he still listening? "You sound exhausted. I don't think anyone else can tell, but..."

When the annual remote at Bob James Chevrolet rolled around, Clara was stunned both that it had been an entire year and that it had been only a year. The time had flown by since the day that she ran the board for Seth and the speakers blew down. It also seemed like it had been another lifetime. There had not been a remote broadcast since the July 4th Festival, and when Clara went to load the van, she found it exactly as Seth had left it that night, with boxes of event shirts and posters advertising the concert by Lovable Shrapnel. Clara gathered up the remnants of that night and put them in a dark corner of the back room with the old record albums. She hoped she would not see them again.

It took all of the energy Clara had to put on a smile as she gushed about the low prices of cars she could never afford. The fans who came to the event did not see past her mask as they walked up with free helium balloons and wide grins and signed up for a sweepstakes.

"I listen to you every day," said a bubbly young woman. "You're the first voice I hear every morning. I can't believe I'm talking to you."

"Thank you," Clara said, her face stretched into a convincing facsimile of a smile. The woman looked at her, expecting more to the conversation, but "Thank You" was pretty much all Clara had. After an uncomfortable silence the woman went over to a friend of hers. "Do you know who this is? It's Clara Jane from WRTV!"

"Oh, uh-huh," said the friend.

"I listen to her every day." the woman repeated.

"Thank you for listening." The woman kept staring and smiling. "Have a bumper sticker," Clara said.

"Thank you so much," the woman said, tucking the sticker into her purse. "What is Seth Jones doing these days?"

"I'm not sure," Clara said.

"I used to love to listen to you two in the morning when you'd talk together," she said. "You sounded like an old married couple."

"Thank you," Clara said again. Clara kept smiling until, thankfully, the song on the radio started to fade and Clara had to put on her headphones for a break. The woman stayed and watched the broadcast for a moment and finally wandered off to look at a car.

When the remote had wrapped up, Clara drove the Incredible Broadcast Machine back to the station. Occasionally people honked and waved as she drove past. She parked the bus in its normal spot and decided to unload the equipment another day.

The first thing she did when she got into her own car was to turn off the radio. She couldn't stand the sound of it: Rad's voice tracks, left-over commercials of Seth's, the same old liners, music without proper cross fades, music that didn't even sound like music. It was product, constant ever-present product, product that numbed with its sameness and banality, product that made her forget music as love, music as escape from problems, music as anything but the background against which she did her job. It was always there, part of the building, like the constant whirring of factory machinery, or office typewriters clacking. If anything was worse than the noise, though, it was the silence, the silence of her apartment, the silence of the phone not ringing. Meeting some of the listeners at the remote and being told she was heard and appreciated was surreal when set against the silence.

Clara checked her answering machine. The light was steady. She ached to call Seth. She missed the way he made her laugh about the stresses at RTV. Only he really knew what it was like there. But she couldn't stand the thought of reaching his machine, having him screen her call, and never return it. She turned on the TV just to kill the silence. Her dinner didn't have any flavor. She watched the sun going down.

Clara told herself that she just had to hold on tight to her goal to move up to a larger market. She would not be in Saturn long. But would another station be any different? It was like she was on a path with all these little voices surround her saying "Follow the Yellow Brick Road," but she wasn't sure she wanted to go where it would lead her. She hummed a bit of the song "Goodbye Yellow Brick Road" by Elton John. She was sure it must have some wisdom for her situation, but she never had understood the words Elton sang in that song. "Fa da la di di den yow. Back to the mortified cow..."

She looked at the phone. Her faraway friends didn't call often. They had whole lives and just didn't think of Clara any more. She was jealous of their ability not to call. Clara flipped through the channels with her remote control. She kept flipping until it all blended into one strange program-- a kind of a talk-show/drama about a chef who gets involved in a police chase while showing Matlock how to make a Cajun casserole with help from Barney. Television off.

It was only 6 PM, but Clara decided to go to bed. Soon it would be morning, and she could get up, go to work, and start over again. She didn't feel like making the bed, so she threw the spread on the mattress and used another blanket to cover her. She lay staring at the wall, too drained to get up, yet her mind was too chaotic for sleep.

The phone rang and Clara's heart jumped. Could it be Seth? She raced over and picked up the receiver with a breathless "Hello?"

"Hello, this is the W-R-T-V remote control... system. Please-enter-access-code..."

Yellow Sky

The next day Clara was sitting at her desk, working on weekend staff schedules, when the door opened and a man entered. He was a small man with thinning hair, in color it was midway between blonde and brown. He wore half-frame horn rimmed glasses, a tweed jacket and a yellow bow tie. He looked like he had been blown about in the wind. He was holding a small suitcase. He stood in front of Clara's desk, stared and said nothing.

"Can I help you?" Clara asked.

"I got the message," he said. His voice was soft and high pitched.

"OK," Clara said, picking up the folder with the list of winners. "Did you win a contest?"

"No," he said. "I got the message. It's time to go back."

"Go back?"

"To Delphani." The man looked at her with anticipation.

Clara sat frozen, "You're..."

"I'm Zog," he said.

"You sent the letters."

"Yes. I got the message," he said. "Is it time to go now? I packed my case."

Clara stood up. "Um, You know, I just have to check something in the-- Would you mind waiting right here for just a minute Mr...."

"Zog."

"Mr. Zog."

"Just Zog."

"Right, if you could just wait for just..." Clara dashed into the studio. Rad was standing at the mic, shuffling through some papers.

"The alien is in the lobby," Clara said.

Rad turned and stared at her with a blank expression. "Is that code?"

"The alien," Clara repeated. She pointed through the studio window to the lobby. "He's in the lobby."

"I think you read too many of Leslie's tabloids," Rad said.

"Do you remember that guy who was sending me letters saying he was an alien?"

"No," he said.

"Well, there was a guy who was sending me letters saying he was an alien. OK, you're caught up. The point is, he's out there. He wants to take me back to his planet."

"That guy?"

"I don't want to be alone with him. Do you think I should call the police?"

Rad looked at the computer and saw he had some time before his break. "I'll go out there, "he said, "you call them."

As she made the call, Clara could see Rad and the man through the studio window. As Rad spoke, the smaller man backed away from him. The more she watched, the less Clara feared Zog. He looked more like someone who was hurting than someone who could hurt anyone. She left the studio and stood on the precipice of the lobby, where Zog could see, but not reach her.

"We have to go back," Zog called to her. "They keep giving me drugs to make me forget, but I know you remember. Do you remember how warm the breeze was and the yellow sky? You remember, don't you? Our collective mind, how we could think each other's thoughts? You must know how to go back."

"I'm sorry. I don't."

"I packed my toothbrush," he said.

Clara felt nervous and uncomfortable, not because she was afraid of Zog, but because she had never been taught how to have a conversation with someone who did not share the same rules of human interaction, the same general reality. When someone says, "How are you?" you don't expect the response to be "a tomato." There are any number of things like that that should be beyond question.

"I heard your messages," Zog said, "I know you remember." Just then, a liner with Clara's voice started to play. Zog looked startled. "How are you doing that?"

"No, Zog," Clara said. "It's not magic it's..."

"Memorex," Rad said.

"You're not helping," Clara said under her breath. Holding up her hands in a calming "stop" motion she said, "It's something I recorded earlier."

Because the police station was right across the street, two police officers arrived almost immediately. The first looked at Zog, and it was clear that he already knew him. He spoke in a gentle voice, "How are we doing today, Andy?"

"No, no, no. You aren't real."

"Your sister has been worried about you," the officer said.

"Delphani is real," Andy said, pointing to Clara, "She can tell you. She knows. She is one of us. Tell them."

"Have you been taking your medication?"

"I'm Zog, from Delphani."

"He's harmless," the officer said to Clara. "He just gets confused when he's off his meds. Come on, Andy. Why don't we take you home." The second officer started to guide Andy towards the door.

"I need to go to Delphani," he protested weakly as the officers shuffled him out of the station and into their car. "I got the signal."

"Well, that was fun," Rad said, returning to the studio.

Clara looked out the window and watched the police car drive away. A vague sense of regret grew inside her. In his madness, Andy had heard a voice on the radio and chosen her as a partner in his illusion. He had so much faith that he'd packed a suitcase to travel to the stars. He would still need a toothbrush on Delphani. Clara wished she could somehow have delivered what he wanted from her.

Can You Hear Me?

When she got home, Clara opened a bottle of white wine and poured a large glass. She stacked five of her David Bowie albums on the record changer, making sure the sides that featured songs about aliens and alienation were facing up: "Loving the Alien," "All the Madmen," "Space Oddity." As the first track started to play, Clara took a sip of the wine and then lay on the couch with her elbow covering her eyes. As Bowie's otherworldly voice filled the room, she thought about Andy, the alien, nostalgic for a place that only existed in his mind. Andy was an exotic version of something perfectly ordinary. How many of us feel like we're a good fit with the world, Clara wondered. She certainly didn't. She could hardly get out of bed these days.

"You remember don't you? Our collective mind, how we could read each other's thoughts?"

All Andy wanted was deep human connection. He wanted someone to share his reality. There was a part of Clara that envied Zog. His mind had created a warm breeze and a yellow sky. Hers could only summon blackness. When everything seems impossible, there is a logic to shutting down, feeling nothing. "If you love it keep going," Seth had said. But in her depression, how could she know if she loved radio or not?

She uncovered her eyes to find the way to her wine glass and sat up just enough to take another sip and lie back down. She looked up at the ceiling and remembered Seth sitting on the couch beside her.

"Thirty years from now, someone from Alpha Centauri will be listening to yesterday's show and trying to dial in to win a pizza coupon."

"Can you hear me? Can you hear me, Major Tom?" The music from the turntable, "Starman," "Life on Mars," created a collage with her thoughts. The soundtrack made her thoughts seem more meaningful, even though she did not really know what they meant. It was insubstantial, it was nothing, the vision Clara had of herself as a success at a major market station. She always believed she would be one of the lucky ones, and she wasn't. She was as thwarted by circumstance as anyone, compromising in big and small ways. What do you even call the grief over something you never had to begin with? It would be simpler if there were a collective mind. On this planet, even if you have a microphone, you have no control over who listens and what the messages will mean to their alien minds. There are only so many people who are really your people, the ones who hear your subtext, who can finish your sentences.

"You're not replaceable. Don't ever let them make you feel replaceable."

Most of what she loved about RTV was gone, and it was not coming back. If she couldn't will it into existence, the only options were to die or stop wanting it; surrender to death, or surrender to life.

The last album finished, the needle clicked for a moment in the inner groove, then the stylus lifted and went back to its rest. The room was quiet except for the hum of the refrigerator. Clara knew what she had to give up. For the first time in months she felt a sense of peace and a sliver of hope. Maybe not everything she had loved was gone.

Movie Night

A week later, Clara paced her living room. She was contemplating making a phone call, but she felt like she was standing on the edge of an Olympic diving board. Clara knew she would never forgive herself if she did not at least try, so she sat down on the couch, dialed the number and then took a deep breath in preparation of the rejection she was sure she would receive.

"Hello?"

For an instant Clara thought about hanging up. "Hi, Seth. It's Clara."

"Hi."

"Did I catch you at a bad time?"

"No. How are you?"

"I quit RTV."

"Really? Congratulations. What made you finally do it?"

"Well, I thought a lot about what you said. I think I've been holding on to something that I don't love any more, and it was killing me, like you said."

"I'm glad you're getting out of there."

"Me, too."

"I'm glad you called. I've been thinking about calling you."

"You have?"

"Yeah, I felt bad about how I rushed out at the station."

"No. You shouldn't. I deserved it. I think I treated you badly. No, I mean, I know I treated you badly. I took your friendship for granted. I'm sorry. Sometimes I wish I could go back in time, be less stupid, and selfish."

There was a long pause. Finally, Seth said, "It happens."

"Things just got a little..."

"Waped?"

Clara laughed, "Waped. Yeah, that's the word."

"I knew you were trouble the minute you showed up in that Nine Inch Nails shirt."

"I miss those mornings when we did the crossovers. That was the best time."

"It was."

"It was never the same after you left. Do you think... I was wondering if maybe you would want to get together for a movie night?" When Seth did not immediately respond, Clara pressed on speaking more quickly. "I mean, feel free to say no. I completely get it. It's just an idea."

"I'd like that," he said.

When she got off the phone with Seth, the adrenaline of her anxiety was transformed into an energetic euphoria. Clara went over to the stereo and put on Nirvana's "Nevermind" CD at the highest volume she thought she could get away with without getting a knock on the wall from the neighbors. She danced around the living room to "Smells Like Teen Spirit." She was thrashing and whipping her hair back and forth when she caught a glimpse of herself in the bedroom mirror. She was still dressed in her "professional" receptionist garb. She did not have to be that person any more. She went in the bedroom and dug through her dresser until she found the Nine Inch Nails shirt and plaid skirt she had worn when she first met Seth. She put them on and stood before her full length mirror. With her blonde hair she did not look like the person she had been, and she wasn't sure that she was. She decided it was time for a trip to the store. Her color needed a revision.

The next evening, Clara paced as she waited for Seth to arrive. She was wearing the Nine Inch Nails shirt, but she'd paired it with some basic black jeans. On the table was a large bowl of popcorn and a gift bag, with a present for Seth. Clara lit some candles, then worried that it might seem like she was trying to create a romantic mood and she snuffed them out by licking her fingers and pinching the wicks. The little bit of heat helped calm her nerves. Clara looked at the gift bag. Was it too much? She was about to take it off the table and hide it in the back of the closet when there was a knock on the door. She took a deep breath before she opened it. There was Seth with a six pack bottle carrier in one hand and a Hollywood Video bag in the other. He was wearing an RTV t-shirt.

"You changed your hair," he said. "It's red."

"It's called 'auburn burgundy.' Do you like it?" Clara said, scrunching her hair on one side. "I'm not sure yet."

"No," Seth said. "It looks good. It's more you."

Clara gestured for Seth to come in. "Yeah, I thought it was time to say goodbye to Barbie, but, the black, maybe that's an old version of me."

"Yeah," Seth said, handing Clara the bag and kicking off his shoes. "It's got that little bit of funkiness. I like it."

Seth walked over to the couch and set the beer down on the table next to the popcorn.

"What is that?" he asked, pointing at the gift bag.

"I got you something," Clara said. She sat down and inched the bag towards him, "I saw it and thought of you."

"You got me a present?"

"Clearly." She picked it up and handed it to him. He took it and looked at it for a moment before pulling out the tissue paper. As she watched, she peeled bits of the label from her bottle of beer. He lifted out a mug with two lacrosse sticks and the words "LACROSSE COACH" in capital letters. He laughed. "You thought of me."

"I did."

"It's perfect." He wiped it out with a napkin, opened a beer and poured it into the mug. Then, lifting it up as if for a toast, "Thank you for the lacrosse mug. I'll cherish it."

"You'd better. It cost me $2.98. It's, I don't know, a peace offering."

"Not necessary."

"What movie did you get?"

"It's called *Samurai Cop*. The kid at the video store told me it might be the worst movie ever made."

"Excellent."

Samurai Cop lived up to the clerk's billing and more. It began with a scene in which a Japanese gang made up, apparently, of people who got Fs in high school drama class battled a second Japanese gang in comical, staged fighting. The main character was a muscular surfer dude with a strange creepy vibe. He was wearing a terrible, long, dark wig so oversized that a tiny baseball hat appeared to be perched on top of his head like a beanie. This caused Clara to laugh so hard that tears fell from her eyes, and she had trouble catching her breath. It was a masterpiece, scene after scene of incompetent acting, incomprehensible plot, pointless sex scenes, cartoon violence, lighting that changed hues between long shots and close ups and bad guys who fell down first and got shot second. Clara was almost helpless. At one point Seth laughed so hard at a fight scene that he spit out his beer. As they laughed, Clara forgot that there had ever been a conflict between them.

"That was amazing," Clara said, still trying to catch her breath, as the credits rolled. "You really outdid yourself."

Seth could also not stop laughing, "That part where he was holding the sword and his eyes were popping out of his red face!"

"Or where the bad guy pulled off his wig."

"That was amazing."

"Do you think they thought they were making art?"

"They did," Seth said. "They took incompetence to a genius level."

"Do you ever worry that our shows were like that, and we just didn't know it?"

"Oh," Seth said, his breathing finally back to normal. "We're probably all ridiculous and just hoping no one will notice."

"I haven't laughed that hard in ages." She leaned back against Seth and rested her hand on his thigh.

"I haven't either," he said, putting his own hand on top of hers. "The last two," he said, pointing at the beers. He sat up and opened each of the bottles then handed one to Clara. "We should have a toast."

"To what?" Clara asked, sitting up straight.

"To Kirchner," Seth said, raising his bottle.

"Kirchner?"

"Yeah. He's making money with a radio station in Saturn. More power to him."

"To Kirchner," Clara said, and they clicked bottles.

Seth took a swig of his beer and then said, "I think Kirchner taught us a lot about what we want, and what we don't want in life."

"Plus he gave us that whole fraternization carve out," Clara said. "We were the only ones who had permission."

"It's not like I was going to sleep with Rad," Seth said.

Clara shuddered, "That's an image I didn't need." For a moment Clara and Seth sat looking into each other's eyes. "It's a shame we never used it," Clara finally said. Seth raised his eyebrows, but said nothing. Clara scanned his face, trying to read his expression. "We should have," she said.

Seth gave a half smile. "You think so?" Clara nodded. Seth took another sip of his beer. Then set the bottle on the table. "Well," he said, "I had to be in bed by 8 back then."

"Not anymore."

"No, not anymore."

"Me neither." They sat for a moment, facing each other. Finally, Clara asked, "If I tried to kiss you now, would you push me away?"

Seth smiled. "Why don't you try and find out."

As Clara leaned in to kiss Seth, he leaned towards her and then, just as their lips were about to meet, he shoved her away and laughed.

"Oh my god. I can't believe you did that. You jerk."

"Come here," he said. He put his hand on her shoulder and pulled her back to him. As she grew close enough for his face to become a blur, she closed her eyes. Seth's kiss was slow and gentle, and Clara felt a warmth course through her body. Everything but the present moment faded away and she felt like she was home.

Clara leaned back, resting her palm on Seth's cheek. His face was flush and he looked at her with warmth and anticipation. She kissed him again. Their hands began to explore each other's bodies. Then Clara stood up and took off the Nine Inch Nails shirt. Seth stood up and removed his own shirt. He took Clara in his arms. As they kissed, Clara felt Seth's hands behind her back tugging at the fabric of her bra strap.

"It's in the front," she said.

"Huh?"

"It fastens in the front." She backed away from Seth and undid the front clasp. "Like this."

Seth gave a small laugh, then leaned in and kissed Clara's breast. She sighed. "Come on," she said, and led Seth to the bedroom. Soon they were making love.

"Ow, ow, Seth, you're on my hair."

Seth shifted, and in the process, he whacked his head on the headboard with a loud thunk.

"Are you OK?"

Seth fell over on his back. He reached up to his forehead. "Ah. Just, give me a second."

Clara leaned over Seth and ran her fingers over the spot where he hit his head. "I think you're going to get a lump," She said. "I'll go get some ice." She got out of bed and went to the kitchen, flipping on the light. She opened the freezer and took out a plastic ice tray, and then reached into a cabinet to get a plastic bag. She tried to dump out the ice cubes but they were stuck in the tray. She started banging the tray on the counter. By now Seth was standing in the bedroom door watching her. "It's fine. Forget the ice."

Clara turned, and they both laughed. They were standing fully naked across from each other in the brightly lit kitchen. Seth opened his arms wide, inviting Clara to look at him.

"Come here," Clara said, holding her arms out to him. Seth put his arms around her waist. She put a hand on his neck and he tensed. "Your hands are cold."

"Oh, sorry," Clara said.

Seth took her icy fingers into his hands, and warmed them for a moment, then kissed them. Then he kissed her lips. When they parted, Clara shook her head and whispered, "I am so in love with you."

"Come on," Seth said, gesturing to the bed, "Let's try not to kill each other."

Plan B

Clara woke up shivering. She was vaguely aware that her arm and half her leg were hanging off the side of the bed and that she was naked. This was not how she normally slept. As her consciousness engaged with her memory she rolled to her other side to look at Seth, who was in the center of the bed wrapped up in all of the covers. She inched closer to him trying to get a bit more room for herself and to free a bit of blanket without waking him up. He had somehow created a complete cocoon. She ran her hand down his back trying to find an edge. He started to move and stretch.

"Hey," Clara said, patting his back. "Blanket thief."

Seth turned to her. He smiled. "Sorry," he said. He lifted the covers, and Clara cuddled up to him.

"That's better," she said.

Seth kissed her forehead. "Good morning," he said.

"I've missed waking up to your voice."

"It's 6:23 on Saturn's Favorite Music..."

"Oh god," she said, burying her head in his shoulder, "don't do that."

"What time is it anyway?" Seth glanced around for a clock.

"Who cares? We don't have to know any more."

"Not today," he said. He stretched his arms above his head. His brow was furrowed.

"What is it?" Clara asked. She reached over and ran a finger through his hair.

He turned to her. "I'm moving," he said.

"Moving?"

"Yeah."

"You're leaving? Why? I thought you loved Saturn."

"It was time for a change. Someone convinced me I've been wallowing in things here."

"Yeah, but, I mean, you can probably wallow in things anywhere."

"It's easier to wallow where everything reminds you. The hardware fliers in my mailbox. RTV playing in the shops everywhere I go. Your voice."

"That would be annoying." Clara absentmindedly ran the tips of her fingers back and forth across Seth's chest.

"And I was thinking that maybe I'm the kind of person who should be self-employed. No bosses telling me how to do things."

"Yeah. That seems like a good call."

"I always thought if I wasn't doing radio it would be fun to run a record store. I found a great location near a burrito place and a coffee shop. Lots of foot traffic. So I took out a loan, and I signed a lease."

"Where?"

"Grand Rapids."

"Grand Rapids?"

"It's close enough to see Ashley whenever I want, but far enough...."

"That you don't have to listen to my radio voice." Clara rolled onto her back and looked up at the ceiling.

"Suddenly it doesn't seem as appealing now to run away," Seth said.

Clara shook her head, "It's not running away. It's a good plan. I definitely think you should have a job without a boss. It sounds perfect for you."

Seth rolled over to Clara and put his arm around her waist. "What are you going to do?"

Clara shook her head. "I don't know. I just figured out what I don't want to do. Isn't that enough?" She sighed. "I wish you weren't leaving."

There was a pause and then Seth sat up and said, "You could..." he looked down and shook his head. "It's a crazy idea."

"What?"

"Well, if you don't have another plan, Grand Rapids, it's not New York, but I could see you there. Concert tours come there. There are a lot of radio stations if you wanted to try again."

"No, I don't want to do that."

Seth turned away, "No, it was just a thought."

"Hey," Clara sat up. "No, I just meant I think I'm done with radio. But..."

"What?"

"Well, I mean, if someone had a brand new record store, maybe they would need to do a lot of promotion, like tie-ins with those concerts and maybe live music events, music trivia nights. Take all of that radio promotion stuff but apply it to a record store. That, I mean, hypothetically, that could be a fun job for someone who used to work in radio."

Seth's face became animated. "You would be great at that, hypothetically," he said. "And you could dress however you want. Wear all black. Wear nothing if you want."

"In the store?"

"In the back room." He raised his eyebrows. Clara leaned in and kissed him. She looked pensive. "But, hypothetically," she said, "I don't know if someone with a brand new record shop and a brand new loan would have the budget for someone to do that job."

"Well, probably not what she's worth," Seth said, running his fingers through her red hair. "But hypothetically, I think someone with a brand new record shop..."

"And a brand new loan."

"And a brand new loan, someone like that would be very motivated to find a way to make it work. We could build something together."

Clara shook her head. "It wouldn't be easy."

"When has anything worth doing been easy?" Seth continued with a bit of hesitation. "You know, I think, hypothetically..."

"Hypothetically."

"It might be cheaper for two people to live in Grand Rapids if they didn't have to pay for two separate addresses."

"Wow."

"Yeah."

"That's a big hypothetical."

"It is."

"You're not talking about, like, a roommate thing?"

"No."

"But we just, I mean just last night..."

"I know."

"It's so fast."

"I know."

"This is that impulsive thing you were talking about."

"Spontaneous."

"But, are you going to, like, spontaneous yourself out of the idea in a few days?"

"No. I mean, the record store is a done deal. I signed the lease."

"I was thinking more about the other thing."

"I know."

Clara scratched the side of her neck. "I'm not doing all the housewife shit."

"No. I'll clean up after myself."

"There is nothing in your history that says that's true. I've been to your apartment."

"That's only when I'm wallowing. In this hypothetical, I think I'd be very happy." He kissed her, then added, "I promise to put the toilet seat down every time."

"Oh, I can flip a seat down. That's not a deal breaker. But no hogging the remote control. And I get veto power if you play terrible music."

"I'm not going to play terrible-- You're the one with the weird taste in music."

"I can't believe we're actually talking about this."

"It's not so fast, is it? We know each other, don't we?"

"Yeah, we do."

"Say yes."

"Fuck."

Seth laughed. "No, say yes."

Clara looked up and screamed. Seth screamed back.

"OK," Clara said. "Yes."

"Yes?"

"Let's do it."

"Wow! We're doing it."

As Clara and Seth kissed, Clara could not remember a time that Seth had not been a part of her life, and she did not want to imagine a time when he would not be. "This was so not on my radar when I got up yesterday," Clara said.

"Mine either."

"What if everything goes wrong?"

"It won't," Seth said. "We're a great team. We have a great plan. Radio may be dying, but people are always going to need record stores."

About the Author

Laura Lee is the author of more than 20 books in a variety of genres. She is best known for humorous reference titles like *The Pocket Encyclopedia of Aggravation* and *The Elvis Impersonation Kit*. She has also written a well-received biography of the Oscar Wilde circle called *Oscar's Ghost;* a children's book, *A Child's Introduction to Ballet;* and the novels *Angel,* and *Identity Theft.*

For the past 20 years, when not writing, she has been producing and traveling on a national ballet master class tour with her partner Valery Lantratov. They have worked with studios in 47 states.

After earning a bachelor's degree in theater, Lee attended the Specs Howard School of Broadcast Arts and worked as an intern at alternative rock station 89X in Windsor, Canada. She went on to work at three radio stations with formats including Adult Contemporary, AC Gold and Country. None of the stations where she worked still exist. (She is fairly certain this is not her fault.)

Her on and off air roles included morning drive, middays, afternoon drive, commercial copywriter and program director. This was the period in which radio was going from analog to automation and she worked at two different stations that transitioned to two separate early automation systems before she left the industry to pursue her writing career.

Made in United States
Cleveland, OH
13 May 2025

16863564R10210